SATELLITE

DOWN

Also by Rob Thomas

SATELLITE

ROB THOMAS

DOWN

SIMON & SCHUSTER BFYR

New York London Toronto Sydney New Delhi

To my daughter, Greta, and my son, Hank. It's coming into sharp focus that you're not going to be jocks. Time to get reading. Oh, and I love you like crazy.

SIMON & SCHUSTER BFYR

An imprint of Simon & Schuster Children's Publishing Division
1230 Avenue of the Americas, New York, New York 10020
For information about special discounts for bulk purchases, please contact Simon &
Schuster Special Sales at 1-866-506-1949 or business@simonandschuster.com.
The Simon & Schuster Speakers Bureau can bring authors to your live event. For more
information or to book an event, contact the Simon & Schuster Speakers Bureau at
1-866-248-3049 or visit our website at www.simonspeakers.com.
Book design by Tom Daly.
The text of this book is set in Adobe Garamond
This SIMON & SCHUSTER BFYR paperback edition September 2018
2 4 6 8 10 9 7 5 3 1
The Library of Congress has cataloged the hardcover edition as follows:
Thomas, Rob.
Satellite down / by Rob Thomas.
p. cm.
Summary: Selected to be an anchor on "Classroom Direct," seventeen-year-old
Patrick Sheridan finds his journalistic idealism and his own self-image challenged when
he leaves high school in Doggett, Texas, for the glamorous life in Los Angeles.
ISBN 978-0-689-80957-6 (hc)
ISBN 978-1-5344-3010-5 (pbk)
ISBN 978-1-4424-6808-5 (ebook)
[1. Television broadcasting of news—Fiction. 2. Self—perception—Fiction.] I. Title.
PZ7.T36935Sat 1998
[Fic]-dc21
97-20950

Acknowledgments

Thanks to Jenny Ziegler, Jeff DeMouy, Michael Conathan, Jennifer Stephenson, Elena Blanco, Kim Bouchard, Peter Miller, Bob and Diana Thomas, Olivier Bourgoin, Greg McCormack, Robert Young, Loyd Blankenship, and Bob Patton. Special thanks to Russell Smith; my agent, Jennifer Robinson, of Peter Miller Associates Literary and Film Management; and my editor, David Gale.

I traveled throughout Ireland in the fall of 1995 in order to research *Satellite Down*. The following people lodged me, fed me, bought me pints, or shared priceless stories. In many cases they did all the above. This book would not have been the same without any of them.

In the Republic—

Chris Sauer, Yvonne Moher, Denis Ryan, Something Happens, the Fitzpatrick family (Patrick, Johanna, Mark, Ciarán, Maeve, and Áine), Ossi Schmidt and Deirdre Martin, Angela Tunney, Maria's Schoolhouse (Maria, Jim, and Francine), Mike Geraghty, Áine Ni Mhearáin, Noelle Angeley, and Norrie Goggin. I'd especially like to thank Noel and Cormac Sheridan for reading the first draft of the manuscript and helping me with the Irish details. (You cannot take a train directly from Belfast to Limerick. It's nearly impossible to withdraw more than 200 pounds from a cash machine. This is how one pours a Guinness, etc.)

In Belfast—

Kathleen Burke and Jennifer Lancaster.

Finally, thanks to Sandy Bell and Sherri Brown, who kept me laughing during my tenure at Channel One.

Prologue
DOGGETT, TEXAS

THE GOOFY WAY MR. LINDER IS STUTTERING—I have to look down at the floor to keep from just busting out laughing. His lame "Well, I didn't think it was necessary" and "Had I known I was violating policy"—I mean, who does he think he's fooling? Definitely not the school board members, who all seem to be clenching their jaws. I could've actually felt sorry for him, if he hadn't been such a slime when I interviewed him for my story.

The story didn't start out as a means of getting the old goat fired. It was just some dumb feature idea I had about the high cost of extracurricular activities. You've seen them before—stories about the killer costs of cheerleading uniforms, band instruments, and so on. When I was investigating it, though, everyone in band talked about how, when they went out of town for games, they had to buy their own meals. Normally they'd stop at a Grandy's or Luby's or something like that, which would only run five or six dollars, but after you include the play-off games and a few basketball games, it could end up as much as an extra hundred bucks a year. Then it occurred to me. No one else has to pay for their meals. The football players don't. The dance team doesn't. So why the band? That's what

2 • ROB THOMAS

I asked Mr. Linder. Which is when he made his fatal mistake. He made me mad.

"Why don't you just print the scores of the games and drop the *Hard Copy* act?" he said without looking up from the Jaguar brochure he had unfolded on his desk.

So this is what I printed.

BAND FUNDS UNACCOUNTED FOR

by Patrick Sheridan
Editor in chief

For the past two years the school board has budgeted five dollars meal money per student for out-of-town school functions. According to band members and their parents, none of that money has been used to provide meals for band students.

Band director Ned Linder initially denied such a fund existed. Later, when presented with a copy of the official school board policy, Linder claimed to have set up an emergency fund for instrument and uniform repair with the money.

"Our group has special needs," Linder said. "I've set aside the money in order to make sure we have functioning instruments and nice-looking uniforms. We don't get new uniforms every other year like the football team."

But Mrs. Terry Billingham, mother of

drum major Stanton Billingham, doubts such a fund exists.

"Stanton's had to get his trumpet fixed twice with his own money. Where is this money Mr. Linder claims he has set aside?" Billingham said.

Principal Charles Gruter promised to look into the matter.

"I'm confident everything's aboveboard," he said.

But apparently it wasn't, which is why I'm at the school board meeting watching Linder fry. My best friend Zeb leans across my other best friend Anderson and whispers, "Do we still tar and feather people here?"

"Just Yankees," says Anderson.

"He'll get off easy. They'll let him resign or something like that," I say. "It's almost impossible to fire teachers."

I'm only repeating what I heard my lawyer father saying earlier this afternoon, but he should know what he's talking about. He's on the school board. It's pretty obvious the direction he's leaning in when he asks the final question.

"Mr. Linder," says Papa, using the same tone of voice he used with me in seventh grade when he caught me copying Anderson's math homework, "have you enjoyed your stay here in Doggett?"

That question pretty much marks the end of the inquisition, and I'm able to stop taking notes. I glance at my watch. The school board is going into closed session—that means they leave the cafeteria and go hole up in the janitorial supply closet, smoke a couple cigarettes, compare the price of gas at Doggett's three gas stations, then come out and announce the decision they made ten minutes into the meeting. It'll be interesting to note in the newspaper how long it took them (officially) to come to reach it. I look for every angle I can get that I think Myron Tullow, the owner/editor/reporter of the *Doggett Daily Register*, will miss. Usually it's not tough to scoop him, even if the school paper, *The Ashes*, does only come out once a month. And by the way, you don't have to tell me that *The Ashes* is a stupid name for a newspaper. I already know that. Calling a newspaper *The Ashes* is just begging your readership to use it to start a fire. Maybe metaphorically it's a good idea—newspapers should spark a few civic fires—but folks here in Doggett don't think that deep. To them it's not much different from calling your newspaper *The Fishwrap*.

The reason for the stupid name is our stupid mascot. We're the Doggett High School Phoenix. Yeah, *the* Phoenix. It's not even plural. We're all *collectively* the Phoenix. A phoenix is a bird from mythology that consumed itself by fire and rose renewed from its ashes. Hence the name. I actually wrote an editorial calling for a change of the school mascot. I thought we should be some kind of canine. Doesn't that make more sense? The Doggett Dogs . . . or Greyhounds . . . or Bulldogs. No one got behind it though. So we're stuck as the self-immolating Phoenix—obviously a bird with self-esteem issues.

There's an unusually large crowd here for the school board meeting, mostly band parents calling for blood. Anderson's in band, but he's one of the few people who doesn't want to see Linder fired. He doesn't like Linder much. Really no one does, but Anderson's sentiment doesn't surprise me. He can see good in just about anyone and forgive just about anything. Zeb's just here because Anderson and I are. Like I said, the three of us are best friends. I know that technically you can't have two *best* friends, but I do.

The first thing that's important to know about us is that we don't play football. In Doggett, when you're born, if you're male, they weigh you, hand you to your mother, then order shoulder pads for you. It's probably this way of thinking that's led to Doggett's four state AA football titles in the past twenty years, but it's also cost all three of us to some degree. Zeb's probably gotten it the worst. You see, he's a specimen. He's six four, two hundred pounds, muscles popping out everywhere. Anderson says Coach Woodacre shakes his head in disgust every time he sees Zeb walking down the hallway, and says, "There goes number five," meaning a fifth state championship. To top it off, Zeb is, unlike Anderson and me, athletic. He's a nationally ranked junior tennis player, but it doesn't do Doggett High a lick of good. There's no tennis team here. Zeb's parents own the farm equipment dealership, so they . . . well, the way Mama puts it is, "They live comfortably." Zeb's dad, a Phoenix running back in the sixties, calls building the tennis court in their backyard the "most asinine" move he's ever made in his life, but he says it jokingly. At least that's what I think. It bothers Zeb sometimes when his father talks like that.

Coach Woodacre doesn't lose quite so much sleep over Anderson. There might be a couple girls at our school who Anderson could tackle, but they'd be freshmen.

Small, slow freshmen.

I'm not trying to sound mean, but I promise, Anderson wouldn't care. He'd agree. You know how you sometimes see those tiny guys who try to play sports, but they're not good enough, so they end up being a manager or statistician or something like that. And you just know they have all this hero worship for the star players. That's not Anderson. Sports genuinely bore him. Most things bore him, come to think of it. He's the only guy I know who won't even turn his head when a fire truck or an ambulance speeds by with its siren blaring.

The one thing Anderson gets excited about is food. Anything having to do with food. The history of food, preparation of food, but most of all, the consumption of food. Even though Anderson didn't weigh a hundred pounds until he was a sophomore, the boy can eat more than anyone I know. Zeb calls him The Disposal. In the Paul Newman movie *Cool Hand Luke*, there's this scene where someone bets Paul he can't eat one hundred hard-boiled eggs in an hour. Zeb and I watched it with Anderson, and afterward that's all he could talk about. He used to go around chanting, "One hundred and one! One hundred and one!" But when his mom caught us with eight dozen eggs out on the counter and her large pot full of boiling water, she "put an end to this foolishness" right there and then. One day, though, I know Anderson's going to do it. Zeb thinks we should take him on the road some summer like a pool hustler, stop just long enough in each town to sucker the town's big eater into a consumption duel, place every side bet we can manage, and hightail it out of town with our winnings before our disgruntled marks decide to kick our butts.

Very few people remember this, but I was a football player. For three of the most miserable weeks of my life, I got out there with all the other seventh graders and traded licks. The hitting I didn't mind, but they put me at receiver because of my body type—prepubescent lanky—and I could never get used to that ball coming in at me so fast. I would either close my hands too early or too late and, depending on the decision I made, either get my fingers jammed or end up with a fat lip or bloody nose. It took stitches in my lower lip before Papa would let me quit.

Suddenly the doors to the janitorial supply closet open, and the five members of the school board emerge from a cloud of cigarette smoke. They take their seats, and Mr. Edmonds, the board president, taps on the microphone.

"It's the decision of the school board that Mr. Linder be suspended indefinitely with pay contingent on the return of all funds earmarked for student meals. Thank y'all for coming out tonight. Don't forget the PTA sign-up sheet at the door. Drive safely, now, ya hear?"

There's enough grumbling in the audience that it's plain some folks were hoping Mr. Linder might be publicly drawn and quartered tonight.

"Pretty anticlimactic, don't you think?" Zeb says as we stand.

"I told you so," I say. "It actually costs the town less to pay the man than hire lawyers to battle it out in court. Now, at the end of the year, they can just not renew his contract."

"And you want to report on this for a living? These meetings make a science trip to Amarillo look fun."

"Yeah," I say, "but today I'm covering the Doggett school board meeting, tomorrow the Senate ethics hearings."

"Whoopee," says Zeb, spinning his finger around in little circles.

"DQ?" suggests Anderson as we begin filing out with the rest of the crowd.

"Yeah, I promised Kate a ride home," I say. Kate's my girl-friend and the only teenager in Doggett without a car. She works at the Dairy Queen, and she'll usually let us—Anderson, mainly—eat whatever's left over in the soft-serve ice-cream machine after they close.

As we push our way through the cafeteria doors, I run right into the back of Mr. Linder. He turns around, recognizes me, and glares. "Happy now?" he asks.

I think about it. Mr. Daugherty, my journalism teacher, has a motto that he's always repeating to the class. "The duty of a jour-nalist," he says, "is to comfort the afflicted and afflict the com-fortable."

"Yes, sir," I say to Mr. Linder. "I'm happy."

I restock all the napkin holders on the tables at the Dairy Queen while Kate fills the cooler with Dilly Bars. Zeb and Anderson plow through a quart of leftover ice cream. I've gotten to the point that I know as much about closing up here as any of the employees. Kate and I have been dating more than two years now, so I've had plenty of practice. I can cut a good twenty minutes off the amount of time it takes the girls to get out of here, and that's twenty minutes Kate and I can spend alone before my eleven o'clock school-night curfew.

"You two better never break up," says Zeb, watching in wonderment as Anderson shovels in spoons of ice cream. "I don't think The Disposal would ever get over it."

Anderson speaks. It's tough to understand him, but I've gotten pretty used to deciphering what he says when his mouth is full. I'm pretty sure I make out, "It'd be tragic."

"Don't worry," says Kate. "Patrick would make us write to the Pope and ask permission to break up. He'd want to get our going steady annulled. It'd be too big of a hassle."

"Good man—the Pope," Anderson slurs.

I've known Kate nearly my whole life. We met in CCD classes when we were four. Most of Doggett, including Zeb's family, is Baptist. We Catholics are a minority, so we all tend to know each other pretty well. Now, even though I say I've known Kate forever, that doesn't mean I've liked her the whole time. She was always the one in the CCD classes who would make the teacher run crying to the priest. Then we'd have to stay after and listen to the priest defend transubstantiation to all of us six-year-olds. I thought Kate was weird. She thought I was naive.

Anyway, she quit going to church with her parents last year. That's not an option in my family. I'm there every Sunday. Not that I mind. There are some things I have questions about—

journalists always have questions—but I buy into it for the most part. Kate and I get in big arguments sometimes. She's always going on about how the Pope won't let women become priests or how the church's anticondom position leads to overpopulation in poor Catholic countries like Mexico.

"Condoms in Mexico?" I remember telling her. "You ought to be more worried about condoms in Cordoba."

You see, I drive a Cordoba, and sex, well, that's starting to become an issue with us. We're both scared, but Kate says she's willing to conquer her fear.

"That's easier for you to do," I respond. "You wouldn't have to tell Father Madigan about it."

"No, but I know you would. You think he wouldn't know who you were having premarital sex with?"

Confession is a powerful motivation to stay on what my father calls "The Path." But it's not just "The Path" I'm worried about. What if I got Kate pregnant? I mean, we Catholics aren't allowed to wear a condom, and besides, I've heard of condoms breaking. On top of that, I've heard the way some guys talk about the girls here who have sex. I don't want Kate to have a reputation. In the end, though, it may just come down to this: When I lose it (assuming I don't wait until I'm married, and it's looking more and more like I won't be able to hold out that long), I want it to be perfect. And I'm not convinced it can be perfect when you're parked on some deserted farm road, squeezed into the backseat of a 1981 Chrysler. Kate's got three brothers and a sister, so there's never a time when her house is empty, and while my sister moved out of the house years ago, I just know I would be too scared to try anything in my parents' house. I mean, there isn't ten square feet of wall space in the house that doesn't have a crucifix hanging on it. Kate and I have agreed that senior prom night, which is still a good three months away, might be the perfect opportunity. The prom is in Lubbock, and everyone gets rooms at the Holiday Inn and spends the night. I think that wanting something for that long will only make it better.

Kate starts turning off the lights. I look up at the clock and see that it's 10:32. That'll give us almost twenty minutes to fool around in her driveway.

As I walk in the door at home, I'm surprised to see my parents are still awake. They're sitting in the living room, and they seem to be having a very intense discussion. If I didn't know better . . . an argument. They become dead silent when they see me. I check my watch. I've gotten in big trouble when it's been as little as five minutes past curfew. Papa will wake from a dead sleep when he hears the screen door. "Eleven o'clock," he says, "means eleven o'clock." Fortunately my watch tells me it's two till. I wonder what's up.

"There's a number by the phone. They'd like you to call tonight," says Papa.

I look down at the scratch piece of paper. I'm expecting it to be either Anderson or Zeb, but the number is long distance. The name that's written down is Libby Saunders.

"Who is it?"

"Someone from *Classroom Direct*," says Papa.

Suddenly I feel dizzy.

I pick up the phone next to the staircase and try to dial, but I'm having trouble focusing on the numbers. There's only one reason that I can think of that they might be calling. I remember that I'm not allowed to make long-distance calls.

"Is it okay if I . . ."

"Go ahead," Papa says without enthusiasm.

I concentrate and dial the numbers. A woman answers on the second ring.

"This is Libby."

"Hello, ma'am. This is Patrick Sheridan. I'm returning your call."

"Patrick!" she says. "Are you ready to move to Los Angeles?"

When I wake up the next morning, I know I have a lot of explaining to do. Papa said he didn't want to talk about it right when I got off the phone. The result was that I didn't sleep very well, but at least I'm approaching the breakfast table with my thoughts well organized. I've been offered the chance of a lifetime, but I'm aware that unless I convince my father of that fact, it will simply be an opportunity lost.

Back in September I was sitting in government. The class was, as usual, out of control during the airing of *Classroom Direct*, which is the television news show that is sent by satellite to high schools and junior highs all across the country. They say that ten million teenagers see it every morning. More teenagers than watch the

Super Bowl. It's sort of like CNN, but they try to make it appeal to young people. The anchors are young. They wear the latest clothes. (Clothes no store in Doggett sells.) They talk young, like "Yo, was-sup?" No one here says that either, but we've seen kids on television talk like that. Anyway, the controversial part is that they also show commercials for stuff like Doritos and Pepsi and pimple cream. Stuff we buy. That's why Papa was the one member of the school board against allowing it into Doggett. He said that he didn't think we should be showing ads to a captive audience. Plus, oppo-nents of *Classroom Direct* made a presentation at the school board meeting that had examples of them getting the name of a senator wrong. It showed a story they did on abortion and one on AIDS. By the end of it, I had no doubt which way Papa would vote. But in exchange for showing the program every day, *Classroom Direct* offered the school a satellite dish mounted on top of the school, twelve hours of commercial-free educational programming a day, and a free television set in every classroom, all linked together as part of a closed-circuit system. It was too good a deal for the rest of the school board to turn down. I remember I was so excited about it, but then, I love the news. The *Classroom Direct* decision was one of the few things I remember Papa and Kate agreeing on.

"But what's wrong with it?" I asked her. "It's not like there aren't ads in the football program, on the back fence of the baseball field. Don't forget the Dairy Queen ad there on your book cover."

"Yeah, but did you see the show, even the bits of it that the people from *Classroom Direct* put on? It just seemed, I don't know . . . fake."

Maybe she'll feel differently if I'm working for them.

Anyway, during the first week of school, *Classroom Direct* ran a promo saying that if you were a senior and wanted to be a student reporter for them, then you should send in a one-minute video audition of yourself reading the news. They also wanted you to send in a recommendation letter from a teacher and a portfolio of written work. I knew my video audition wouldn't be that impressive. I've never read the news, only written it, but I figured I had the other two categories nailed. Mr. Daugherty, I know, wrote a great letter for me. He showed it to me. In it he mentioned all the journalism awards I had won, and what a pleasure I was to work with. He even said that I was his best student in twenty years of teaching. Plus, I had my clippings. Even if there were a hundred people better at reading the news, I knew not many of them had written quite as many stories as me. That must be what iced it for me. Still, I had given up on it. The applications were due in October, and we're already a week into the second semester.

Before I make it all the way into the kitchen, I can once again hear my mother and father arguing. I probably haven't heard them argue two other times that I can remember. Now I've caught them twice in eight hours. I realize that they must be deciding whether they'll let me go. I try to listen, but the floorboards of this old farmhouse tend to be squeaky. Papa yells out at me. "Don't stand out there like a sneak, Patrick. Come in here and let's all talk about this."

I enter the kitchen and take my regular seat at the table. Mama's got breakfast going, as usual, and Papa's on his third or fourth

Winston. I can tell from the ashtray Mama cleans out every night.

"I got to tell you, son," says Papa, letting smoke ease out of his nose as he talks, "that my inclination is to keep you here. Do you mind telling me why you didn't let your mother or me know that you were applying for this position?"

Sometimes—heck, most of the time, Papa's too intimidating for me to talk to, but I've been working on my nerve all night, and this was one of the questions I was expecting.

"I didn't really expect them to want to hire me, Papa. Did Miss Saunders tell you that they got nearly nine hundred applicants? I just thought it would be good experience trying for it anyway. I figured why argue about whether I could apply, since it wasn't likely I'd get offered the job."

Papa taps his orange juice glass on the table and stares at me. Mama brings over the bottle of orange juice, but Papa waves her away.

"Now, your mama isn't keen about the prospect of you moving to Los Angeles for the remainder of your senior year—"

"They'll fly me home for prom."

"Don't interrupt me, boy." He drags on the cigarette before returning to the point. "And real frankly, I don't care much for the idea myself. I'm concerned with a number of things here. First, and foremost, your education. Now I know they said they'd hire you a tutor, and that you'd graduate on time, but that doesn't sound like a substitute for full-time studies to me. Next, I'm not sure I'm comfortable with this lack of supervision. They told me you'd have your own apartment in Hollywood. What seventeen-year-old—"

"Nearly eighteen."

"I'm not going to tell you again." He taps his coffee mug on the table. This time he does want a refill. Mama pours him a new cup. "What seventeen-year-old boy lives on his own in a Hollywood apartment?"

I wait before attempting an answer. I'm not sure if he wants me to go for it or not. He starts up again.

"Now, perhaps most importantly to your mother—and it's important to me as well—is who's going to tend to your spiritual well-being? We can't really send Father Madigan with you, now, can we?"

"I'm sure there's a Catholic church or two in Los Angeles," I blurt out.

"But none *we've* been to," says Mama.

"Margaret, let me handle this," says Papa. "You got anything you want to say, boy?"

So I launch into my speech. The one I practiced the night before. I had guessed all their concerns, so I felt well-rehearsed. I told them what Miss Saunders had told me about the apartment complex. About how it's the same place where all the kids in TV shows stay: Tad Bronson, from *The Hills*; Candy Taylor, who plays the daughter on *California Riviera*; and Robin Ferris, the star of *Prairie Girl*, one of their favorite shows. I point out that they wouldn't let these important celebrities stay there if there wasn't tight security. Then I mention that, as far as schooling goes, what could be more educational than covering news around the country; heck, the world. Not only would I be taking my core classes, but I'd get a head start on everyone my age for a journalism career. How many kids, I asked, get to interview senators and Supreme Court justices?

"Not many," Papa admits. "If you do get that opportunity, try to get their names right. Would you?" That was my first clue that he, at least, was willing to let me go.

"Now, as far as church goes, Mama, I'll ask who else around the office goes to a Catholic church, and I'll find someone who'll let me tag along."

"Every week?" Mama says.

"Every week," I promise.

Four days later, my parents are seeing me off in Lubbock. Mr. Daugherty has come along, and he's taking a bunch of pictures. Anderson, Zeb, and Kate drove up in a car as well, but Mama wouldn't let me ride with them because she needed to spend some time with "her baby." She broke out in tears a couple times on the drive, and I was tempted to tell her we could just call the whole thing off, but the temptation didn't last long. I think I know, at least partially, why she's so upset. You see, I have an older sister. She's a lot older than me, maybe fifteen or sixteen years, and my parents probably haven't seen her, or heard from her, in the last decade. I've never gotten the exact story, but I know it must have been ugly, because there's not even a picture of her up in the house. Mama must have ten photos of me on the walls. She hangs a new crucifix every time she hangs a picture of me. I think she believes it would be sacrilegious to have more images of me than of Jesus.

Papa said something once about Bridget not being able to live by "the rules of the house." Anderson and Zeb say they couldn't have lived by the rules of my house either. Anyway, I've seen pictures of Bridget when I've dug out old family albums, which I've only done when my parents weren't home. I can vaguely remember her being around, but I must have been five or so at the time. I just remember her being nice to me. I'm adopted. I know that. It doesn't bother me, and besides, I look so different from my parents that it's common knowledge. I've got darker skin than my ruddy, Irish-blooded parents. My hair's black and kind of curly as well. I like to think there's Cherokee blood in me, but around here, it's more likely I'm part Mexican. Anyway, I'm just guessing that Mama's worried about losing her other child.

It's kind of strange, really. There may not be many Catholics in Doggett, but it only takes six families, including the twenty-four Estebans, to fill up the church. The Sheridan clan is, by far, the smallest. "But the proudest," Papa always says. Of course, one of Father Madigan's favorite sermons is called "The Sin of Pride," so I don't repeat Papa's claim too often.

As the woman at the gate starts calling for preboarding, Zeb hands me a small notebook. "It's for autographs," he says. "Every time you meet a star, get them to sign it for your rube friend back in Texas."

Anderson hands me the half-eaten bag of chocolate chip cookies his mom made for me, and I decipher his parting words as, "For the plane ride." Mama busts out in tears . . . again, so I hug her . . . again. Papa says to go knock some sense into "that business you're so fond of." A flash goes off as I shake Papa's hand, and I can already see Mr. Daugherty's photo in *The Ashes*:

School board member Roman Sheridan bids farewell to his son, Patrick, former editor of *The Ashes*, who departed Tuesday for Los Angeles to work for *Classroom Direct*.

Finally I have to say good-bye to Kate.

Anderson and Zeb have already conscientiously strolled away to the magazine racks along with Mr. Daugherty, and Papa puts his arm around Mama and leads her back a few steps.

"They said I could call you all I want for free from the office," I remind Kate. I can see tears forming in her eyes.

"Can they send you back here for twenty minutes a night out in my driveway?" she asks, giving me a sad smile.

"I'll be back for prom."

"That's three months."

"I love you."

"You better," she says, wiping her eyes. Then she kisses me in a way I'm sure my mother has never seen me kissed.

Chapter One
LOS ANGELES, CALIFORNIA

THE WOMAN IS DANCING. AND SHE'S NAKED.

I look around the room. So far the only person I know is Harris—I'm not sure yet if that's his first name or last name—and he's got a folded dollar bill sticking halfway out of his mouth. The naked lady dances over to him and straddles his lap. Then—and I swear I'll never forget this for as long as I live—she uses her breasts to extract the dollar from his mouth. She has to use her hands to press them together, obviously. It's not like she's got some special breast muscles, but as she does it, she makes her breasts rub all along the sides of his face.

I remember listening to some guys—seniors when I was a sophomore—b.s.ing down at the Dairy Queen. They said they'd been up to Lubbock, to some place called The Sugar Shack, where women dance naked. The way they described it, though, sounded much different from this. They said the ladies who worked there were old or fat, and, thankfully, wore some kind of skimpy bikini bottom. This girl here doesn't look much older than me. A couple years maybe. She's not wearing a stitch, and she looks like she just stepped out of an Aerosmith video.

I've been in Los Angeles less than five hours. Harris is the guy who picked me up from the airport and the first person I've seen in real life with a nose ring. He said he was a P.A., which he explained stood for production assistant. That sounded pretty important to me, but he said it was really just a glorified gofer. Then he thought about it for a second.

"Not even glorified, really," he added.

Harris took me to my apartment complex, The Sunset Villas, and got me checked in. The apartment itself wasn't really what I had expected. I thought it would be a real apartment, you know, with a bedroom and a kitchen and a bathroom. At the front desk they called what I had "an efficiency." When I saw it, I knew why. You could efficiently cross the whole thing in about five steps. The bathroom had its own door. Everything else was just one small room, like a tiny motel room, but with a miniature range and refrigerator separated by a four-foot-long bar. The couch was also my bed. (It folds out.) It's not like I wanted to turn around and head back to Texas. I realized how lucky I am; it just wasn't what I was expecting. That's all.

Before he left, Harris told me about a bachelor party a bunch of the guys from *Classroom Direct* were having for Stu Chestnut.

"Wow. Stu Chestnut is getting married?" I said. Stu Chestnut just might be the most popular of all the anchors for *Classroom Direct*. All the girls at Doggett, except Kate, think he's hot.

"Yep, it's safe to let your daughters wander American high school hallways again," answered Harris.

While I waited for Harris to come back to pick me up, I watched a couple hours of HBO. It's a good thing Papa didn't know I'd have it in my room. He would have never let me come. Sitting there, I couldn't help feeling nervous. I was about to meet all these people I had seen on TV, and on top of that, I had never been to a bachelor party before. My hands were already sweaty when a buzzer sounded in my room. It took me a minute to find the panel and then figure out which button to push before speaking.

"What are you doing up there?" It was Harris's voice. "Maybe you'd like a little more time alone tonight."

"Where are you?" I asked.

"Front gate," he said.

"I'll be right there," I said. But I didn't get right there. I couldn't find my way out of the complex. Finally I had to ask someone who was getting out of a lavender MG.

"Could you tell me how to get out of here?" I said to the girl.

"Let your ratings go to hell," she said.

"What?"

"Just go past the main office, past the pool, and take a left," she said.

As I turned around and began sprinting for the gate, I realized why she looked familiar. I had been talking to Robin Ferris, the *Prairie Girl* herself. Whoa. I thought about how Zeb would freak out and Anderson would say, "Robin who?" I probably should have run back and gotten her autograph for Zeb. But I didn't. I finally found Harris smoking against his beaten-up Toyota pickup.

"Is that what you're wearing?" he said when he saw me.

"I've got a suit," I said, assuming maybe it was more formal. I looked down at my Wranglers. My button-down was starched but a little bit wrinkly, but I didn't think I had anything that wouldn't need ironing.

"That's fine, Garth. No need for your Sunday best."

But now, with the naked girl dancing ten feet away, I wish I had worn something that wouldn't show off my sweat so much. The girl is climbing all over Stu Chestnut. It looks like maybe she likes him. Or is it that he's got dollar bills sticking out of all his pockets, his teeth, and—oh, my word—there's one sticking out of his fly. The dancer pulls it with her teeth. Am I the only one here who's embarrassed? Checking out the men around the room, I would guess so. The amazing thing to me is that some of them don't even appear interested. They're standing around the edge of the circle that's formed, and they're having conversations with each other. I don't even catch them glancing. There's Earl Woodbie. He's the black male anchor. Kate says that to get the perfect on-air diversity for the *Classroom Direct* anchor staff, the producers must have raided the "It's a Small World" ride at Disneyland. Anyway, Earl's one of the ones not paying attention, which seems strange because we're in his living room. Another weird thing: Stu Chestnut is getting married, and Earl Woodbie owns a beautiful home at the base of the Hollywood Hills. I always thought these guys were just a year or two out of high school. I stare down into my Sprite—the Sprite I finally poured after being offered a beer for the fifth or sixth time. It's a trick I learned at parties. People always think you've got a drink if you're holding a Sprite. I don't drink, and people have a problem with that sometimes.

There's plenty of noise in the living room. Laughing, whistling, and the hip-hop music from the stereo that the naked lady is dancing to. But above it all I can hear Harris's voice when he says, "Garth needs a lap dance!"

People start hooting, and within seconds people are balancing dollar bills on my legs and shoulders and even on my head. I look up in time to see the naked lady dancing toward me. She's so beautiful, but I don't feel close to turned on. Just flustered. What did I do that she should be willing to take her clothes off in front of me? What would Kate think if she saw me right now covered in money? Then the music stops.

"All right, you fucking degenerates, leave the boy alone."

The man who gives the order is standing next to the stereo with his finger on the volume. People start snatching dollar bills back off my body.

"Happy, Dad?" says Harris. "Think we can get the music turned back up?"

I glance up at the naked lady, just at her face, and I notice that, for the first time, she looks uncomfortable. The music gets turned back up, and her blank expression returns.

The man who gave the order motions for me to follow him onto the porch. I pick up my Sprite and join him outside. He's lighting up a cigarette when I catch up.

"Thanks—" I begin.

"So you're the new two percenter," he says. I can tell he's sizing me up.

"The new what?"

"The talent."

"I'm the new student reporter," I say.

"Oh, so that's what they're calling it—reporter." He chuckles. "Now there's a good one." He pulls out a small liquor bottle and swigs from it. He doesn't offer me a drink, which makes him the first person who hasn't. He still seems to be enjoying his observation, so I take the opportunity to study him.

Mr. Daugherty used to say that the sparkle of a good feature story came from the details. "Imagine," he would say, "that you're doing a feature story on a prominent scholar. Now, it's one thing to mention that he has two dogs. Some people might find that mildly interesting. But if you include the fact that they're pit bulls named Johnny Rotten and Sid Vicious, then all of a sudden we've learned something about this man. Now we've got a story."

Since then, I've always tried to notice details. I decide that the man in front of me doesn't worry much about impressions. His hair, which I can tell was cut short, now flops carelessly down over his ears and sticks out in random directions as if it's been slept on. His clothes, supporting this observation, appear to have been likewise worn to bed. He's wearing a rumpled sports coat over a Flint, Michigan, YMCA T-shirt, along with some off-brand blue jeans. An odd thing jumps out at me—he's wearing a watch on each wrist. Each of them looks like a standard-issue Timex. When he turned down the music inside, he struck me as a big man, but now that I'm standing next to him, I realize he's short, maybe five five, if that. He still gives the aura of being big, though. He's barrel-chested, with a bit of a beer gut. I guess him to be about thirty-five to forty. I watch him take another swig from the bottle. This time—with my eyes on the lookout for details—I make out the Southern Comfort label. He wipes his lips with his jacket sleeve and offers me his hand.

"Billy Trundle," he says. "News producer."

"Patrick Sheridan," I say, aware of the strength of his grip. "So what does a news producer do?"

This makes Billy laugh some more.

"A news producer does it all. He tells the cameraman what to shoot. He tells the reporter what to say. He sets up the interviews. He writes the stories. He cuts the stories. He gets the student reporter a glass of warm milk and checks for monsters under his bed. And when a piece falls all to hell, the news producer takes the blame."

"How do you cope?"

I intentionally say it with too much enthusiasm. Papa is always telling me my smart mouth will get me in trouble someday, but I've already decided that Billy Trundle can take it as well as dish it out. He proves my theory true by laughing.

"Boy, the first time some cornpone principal in some pissant town is halfway up your ass, screaming, 'y'ain't castin' mah school in a positive light,' you'll come running for Dad. Mark my words."

"Is that why Harris called you 'Dad' in there? Did he have to come running for you?"

"No, Harris calls me 'Dad' because I'm friendly with his mother."

Then Billy Trundle laughs some more, and the Southern Comfort reappears. He tilts the bottle all the way back, then throws the empty into a nearby bush.

"You shouldn't be here," he tells me. "Why don't I give you a ride home."

I consider the empty bottle in the bush. I'm sure it began the evening full, but I'm not sure anyone else at the party will be in any better shape. Besides, if I take Billy's offer, I won't have to go back inside the house. Another good reason to leave is that, tomorrow being my first day at work and all, I want to be alert. I know that I made a deal with Kate that we wouldn't ever ride in a car with someone who's had too much to drink, but I'm living in Los Angeles now. She'll have to understand that I'm going to have to bend the rules some.

"A ride would be great."

In his car on the way home, I ask him why he called me a two percenter. He tells me that two percenters are always the last to know.

The only taxi I had ever ridden in before was in Austin when I went there for the high school journalism conference. We took one from our hotel out to dinner, but Mr. Daugherty paid, and I didn't really pay much attention. Now I'm watching the numbers click by on the meter, praying that the ten-dollar bill in my wallet is going to be enough to get me to work. The meter is at nine dollars and twenty cents when it pulls up in front of Cinescope Studios. I hand him the ten and tell him to keep the change.

Yeah, I know it's not much of a tip—I'm not a total hick—but it's all I have.

There's a guarded gate just like you see in all of those movies that show studio entrances. I'm suddenly frightened that they might not let me in, but the guard just takes my name down and points me in the direction of Studio 10. I'm relieved to see the familiar *Classroom Direct* logo painted behind the receptionist's desk as I enter. Before I can say anything, the woman behind the counter speaks.

"Well hello, beautiful."

I hope everyone in Los Angeles is going to be this friendly.

"Um, uh, hi." I'm squirming. The woman behind the desk is young and dressed like a *Cosmo* cover girl. I'm used to the Mrs. Cornish—Papa's blue-veined, trifocaled receptionist down at the law office—prototype. "I'm Patrick—"

"Sheridan. I know. They showed us all your tape. You're even more gorgeous in the flesh," she says. "Could you do me a favor?"

"Yes, ma'am."

And that about does the woman in. She brings the back of her hand up to her forehead dramatically, as though my response has wounded her.

"Libby! Libby! Come out here and get a load of this!" A similarly *Cosmo*-esque black woman emerges from an office. "He called me 'ma'am.' Isn't he just adorable? Let me take him home. Please, please, please." She grabs the woman's wrist. The woman—Libby Saunders, I assume—laughs.

"You'll have to have him back in the morning."

While this is going on, I'm feeling awfully self-conscious. People are walking through the reception area, and I feel like I'm on some sort of stage.

"Say that thing you say," the first woman pleads, but I have no idea what she means by that. "You know . . . that thing."

Libby fills me in. "She wants you to say, Thanks, y'all, for listening."

"Oh," I say. That's what I said at the end of my audition tape *after* I was finished reading the news—just as a way of being polite. It really wasn't even part of the audition. But I guess if it'll make her happy.

"Thanks, y'all, for listening."

The receptionist screams like those teenaged girls you see in early clips of the Beatles. Libby pats her on the head. I stick my hands in my pockets and consider escaping into the men's room. The door is only a few feet away.

"Isn't that just precious?!" she says to Libby. Then she turns to me. "I'll bet those little Texas girls couldn't keep their hands off of you."

But she'd lose that bet. Until I started dating Kate, I never had any luck with girls. I had a couple girlfriends, but I always seemed to be the more interested party in the relationship, if you can call what you have as a sophomore or freshman a relationship. They always seemed to end the same. We'd be at a pep rally. The band would be playing. The cheerleaders would be cheering, and I'd see my girlfriend staring down at the football players, all lined up in their red and black game jerseys. She'd sigh. Then I could begin the countdown. Sometimes it would take a week. Sometimes less. But I would find myself a single man again, and my ex would be walking to class with some guy who looked like Thor. Kate says it served me right for falling for girls who knew what "illegal procedure" meant. No, if you're from Doggett, girls don't fall all over you unless you give your body to Coach Woodacre.

"Not really," I say.

"And shy too." The receptionist uses a notepad to fan her face.

"Patrick, this is Nicola," says Libby. "I'm Libby. We spoke on the phone. Prentiss wanted to see you as soon as you got in. I'd like to promise you that it would be safer in his office, but for a completely different set of reasons, I'm not sure it will be. As soon as you get done in there, they'll send you back to me. We'll get all your paperwork done, and I'll introduce you to your tutor."

Libby leads me back through hallways lined with photographs: Earl Woodbie interviewing Al Gore; Apurva Yoshee wading through a flooded school building; Stu Chestnut pointing to graffiti on a Cairo building; Nan Spencer surrounded by Mississippi high school students. I can't believe I'm going to be doing some of these same things.

"You don't need to worry about Nicola," continues Libby. "Her bark, as they say, is much worse than her bite. Now, Prentiss, on the other hand . . ."

We walk through a door at the end of a hallway. In the sizable office, two male receptionists greet Libby in unison.

"Hey, Libby," says the one in the Happy Mondays (I guess it's a band) T-shirt.

"Ms. Saunders," says the one wearing a dress shirt. "Mr. Scott is expecting you and Mr. Sheridan. Go right in."

We pass through another door and into the largest office I've ever seen. A quick detail check of the room uncovers three Lava lamps, eight speakers, and ten television sets—all of them tuned to different channels. The rest of the building is carpeted in standard flat gray office carpet; Mr. Scott's office has hardwood floors. Black vertical blinds provide the darkness by blocking out the ceiling-to-floor windows that stretch across the curved north wall. Three high-backed leather couches arranged in a U shape make up a seating area in front of the largest of the screens. The face of a pretty teenaged girl occupies most of the screen, and her voice emanates from eight different sources around the room, giving it an ethereal perfection.

Libby circles the couches until she's standing between the screens and a head that's barely visible over the high back of the couch. A voice comes from the head.

"Ah, Libby—good. I was just going through these tapes." A hand shoots into view and points at the screen. "This one's too Southern. Too white-bread. We've got that already," he says. "Show me something else."

Libby ejects the tape from a bank of VCRs and inserts another.

"Uh, I've brought in—" As she tries to speak, the large screen goes black. This seems to make the head furious.

"Libby, do you know what would've happened at MTV if I had brought in a tape to show my boss without cueing it up first?" The head doesn't wait for a response from the woman before answering his own question. "I'd be selling 'Hooray for Hollywood' pencils on the corner of Sunset and Vine and offering to spit wash tourists' windshields."

"It's rewound, Prentiss," Libby says. "Some of these kids just give a little too much leader. By the way, like you asked, I've brought in—"

As she says it, the face of another pretty teenaged girl, this one big-haired (even by Texas standards) and Italian-looking, appears on the screen. The head sticking above the couch, which I assume now to be Mr. Scott's, leans forward. The face freezes on-screen.

"Goddamn it! I want the tapes cued up—not just rewound!"

"Patrick Sheridan," Libby says, finishing her sentence.

"What?" says the head.

"I've got Patrick Sheridan here."

The head pivots and stands, and I get a full view of *Classroom Direct* executive producer Prentiss Scott, the man whose name fades dramatically in at the end of every broadcast. He puts on a mile-wide smile and, as he skips around the couches, he extends his hand out to me.

"Patrick! How's it hanging, buddy? Glad you made it in okay. Did everything go fine with your flight?"

I assure him it did, and then I answer several other questions about stuff like checking into my apartment, how my parents were handling me leaving, if I was scared, and so on. I think I do an okay job answering all of his questions—I mean, I don't get too nervous and just start taking off on tangents like I do sometimes around Papa—but as I'm responding, I'm mainly thinking about how young Mr. Scott must be. I mean, he looks closer to twenty than thirty. He's wearing Converse All Stars—red ones— blue jeans, and a USC sweatshirt. His blond hair is cut very short and gelled flat. He asks me what I did after I got in, and I tell him about Harris taking me to the bachelor party.

"Oh, really?" he says, but he doesn't ask me any more about it.

"Say, Patrick," says Mr. Scott, "what do you say you help us pick out your partner for the rest of the school year? We're just looking over some of the finalists now."

"Sure," I say. Libby told me on the phone that they were having a tougher time finding a girl student reporter than a boy. Each semester they hire one of each. Since we'll be going to tutoring together and living next to each other over at The Sunset Villas, I'm just hoping for someone I'll like.

Mr. Scott has me take a seat next to him on the couch before he takes the Italian girl off pause. Miss Saunders continues to stand by the tape players. The girl reads a story about herself getting chosen as a *Classroom Direct* reporter. "Catherine Delusio says she was surprised by her selection." And so on. Not too clever, if you ask me, but I didn't want to jump to conclusions. I ask if I can see her portfolio and recommendation letter.

"You got those handy, Libby?" says Mr. Scott, pausing the tape once again.

"In my office. You want me to get—"

"Oh, that's all right. You don't have to—" I say.

"No. She doesn't mind," says Mr. Scott. "We should have those handy."

Miss Saunders exits, and Mr. Scott unfreezes the Italian girl. The audition ends, and Catherine dissolves into the soap opera she recorded herself over.

"What do you think?"

I have a feeling there's a right answer, but I'm not sure what it is, so I tell him she wasn't bad.

"But we don't want 'not bad,' do we?"

"No, sir."

That starts Mr. Scott off laughing. "No, sir—do you know the last time anyone here has called me *sir*?"

"No, uh, sir."

"Come to think of it, I'm not sure anyone ever has." Mr. Scott hits stop on the remote control. "We want a tape that jumps out at you. That's what your tape did. It jumped out at us. Didn't even have to think about it."

"Thanks."

"You know what was wrong with that girl?"

"No, sir."

"Nothing wrong with her looks. We would have had most of the boys in New Jersey reaching under their desks"—does he mean that the way it sounds?—"but her voice is all wrong.

"That's something we can't fix here with coaching, wardrobe, or makeup. A bad voice and you might as well settle for a life of print journalism. What you do, when you're going through tapes, is close your eyes. If you can imagine the voice on the radio, then it's good enough for TV."

Libby brings a box into the room and sets it at my feet. Inside are the letters and portfolios of all the girls. For the next hour we look at tapes of finalists. Mr. Scott rejects some of them within two seconds of their appearance. The second one was a bit chunky.

"What were you thinking, Libby? We'd have to install wider-screen TVs across the country for that one."

But I'm reading the girl's recommendation letter, so I have an idea what Miss Saunders was thinking. The letter says the girl, Destiny Weaver, has already been accepted into Northwestern's accelerated journalism program. She's won a slew of writing awards, and she founded her school's television news program. But Miss Saunders doesn't even respond to Mr. Scott's question. She just inserts another tape, so I start reading a story the girl wrote about interracial dating. It's amazing. She interviews a dozen sources. The quotes all have what Mr. Daugherty calls "bite." She's gotten firsthand interviews with college sociology professors. It's better than anything I've ever written.

I look up to discover that Mr. Scott has finally found someone he likes.

"Now, Libby, why didn't you show me this girl earlier? We've wasted a bunch of time here."

"Well, there's a little problem with her grades, and did you notice her grammar?"

"That's why we hire writers here. Let me see her again."

This time I'm paying attention. The girl says her name is Shayla Roberts. She's from Washington, D.C., and she's black. Like the others, she's pretty, but it's her voice that makes her stand out. I close my eyes like Mr. Scott told me, and I listen. When she says

"Roberts," it sounds like Zeb's twenty-five-pound tabby purring. I have to imagine whether her voice would be right for the radio. In Doggett all we get are AM stations from Lubbock that offer either right-wing talk radio—Papa listens to those—or country western, which is what everyone at Doggett High listens to. I found some jazz albums once on a shelf in Bridget's old room, Miles Davis and Ornette Coleman. I used to listen to them once in a while when I was ten or eleven. Those records and a Partridge Family record were the only albums in the house that weren't Christmas records. The day Mama caught me she got rid of the records and the turntable. The point is, Shayla's voice sounds like it would be perfect for a jazz station. When she says that she's one of two girls at her school who "be reading" the morning announcements, I'm kind of jarred back into reality.

"She's the one," Mr. Scott proclaims as Shayla's tape ends.

I'm looking through the box for her portfolio and letter of recommendation.

"She didn't send in anything but the tape," Miss Saunders says.

"Run some background on her," instructs Mr. Scott. "Talk to her principal, maybe a couple teachers. If she's not selling crack to orphans, I want her out here by Monday."

Miss Saunders collects her tapes and leaves. Mr. Scott tells me to go back and talk to Libby about my paperwork. As he's telling me this, he punches a button on his desk and the vertical blinds on the far wall begin to spin and separate. I feel like I'm witnessing a reverse eclipse. The view that remains is of the Hollywood Hills. I look off to the right and find the Hollywood sign.

"Clear day," says Mr. Scott.

I walk out, but as I do, I can hear him on his intercom asking for someone to send Harris into his office.

I spend most of the rest of the day in Libby's office. She tells me I can call her by her first name. I have to fill out a ton of forms, not only to get paid (I can't believe they're paying me for this), but for my tutoring, studio health club membership, parking space (even though I don't have a car), and press card. When I'm done, she gives me a stack of taxi vouchers. She says I can use taxis all I want, and they'll bill *Classroom Direct* for them. When we're done with that, Libby takes me to my desk. Above the door to the office, there's a placard that says TALENT.

"What does that mean . . . talent," I say.

"Don't let it go to your head," she says. "Anyone who's on-air here is called talent—whether they have any or not."

It's obvious in the way she says it that she believes a few of the reporters are lacking in that department. Stu Chestnut is the only one in the office when we go in, but he's asleep, and snoring loudly, in his chair.

"Ah, another day, another thousand dollars," says Libby. She pulls out a chair at a desk on the other side of the room. "Here you go."

On the desk there's a nameplate that says PATRICK SHERIDAN—STUDENT REPORTER. I hunt through all the drawers, but discover they're empty.

"What are you looking for?" asks Libby.

"I don't know. Jimmy Hoffa, Shroud of Turin—usual desk drawer stuff."

"Oh, you're going to fit in here all right."

"You think?" I say.

"Yeah, but I wouldn't be so happy about it."

They tape *Classroom Direct* in the afternoons, then it's seen all across the country the next morning. They call the studio The Hut. Don't ask. It doesn't look anything like a hut. Kate says that Pizza Hut must have slipped them an extra million to name it that.

I think The Hut is supposed to look like the basement of the richest, coolest kid at your school, except if you live in Doggett, where there's no one this rich or this cool. Band posters hang from the fake walls. All the furniture is overstuffed. There's a CD player that really works, giant speakers, a Foosball table, a Macintosh with all sorts of games loaded on it, a soda machine (except they've replaced the giant Pepsi logo with a *Classroom Direct* logo. You can get a cold Pepsi out of it, though). And, of course, TV monitors everywhere. All of this is surrounded by school paraphernalia: a little plastic football from the Grace Buccaneers, a sweatshirt from the Lee Rebels, a banner from the Cromwell Cowboys, a plastic seat cushion from the Sunnyside Grizzlies.

Not every *Classroom Direct* reporter is on the show every day. I knew that from watching the show back in Doggett. There are six full-time reporters—seven, if you count Lane Tauber, but he's hardly ever in Los Angeles.

"He's always trying to get himself shot"—that, according to Anderson. I almost forgot. There is one other thing that interests Anderson besides food, and it's the reports by Lane Tauber. He's my favorite too. If I wanted to work in television rather than print, Lane Tauber is who I would model my career after. He's the one they always send to war zones and to countries that hate America. He's the only one reporting for *Classroom Direct* I've seen wear a bulletproof vest. It wasn't just for the effect, either. You could hear shooting going on in the background.

Anyway, today Earl Woodbie and Apurva Yoshee are anchoring. I guess I always knew the show was taped, since we could watch it at any time of the day at Doggett, but I didn't think about how it was taped. It's like watching a movie being filmed, take after take after take. I guess I always thought it was taped live. Knowing it's not is a great relief to me. I just knew that on my first day, something would happen in Afghanistan, and I'd be the one who would have to report that some Hbkbrr Yhltshn was ousted from power.

I'm watching from the control room. Mr. Scott came down from his office a little while ago, and he introduced me to the "stage crew" and the director, Connie Hiatt, who was screaming— swear to God, screaming—at just about everyone. Plus, she was using just about every word that was on the Sheridan mouth-washed-out-with-soap list.

"Jesus Christ, camera two! You may only be interested in Apurva's tits, but we'd like to see her mouth, and if it's not too much of a burden, her whole head! Get your head out of your ass!"

Then . . .

"Can I have a bit of fucking quiet in here? What is this? Fucking happy hour?"

But when she talked into the microphone that led to Earl's or Apurva's earpieces, her tone of voice changed. She sounded like a kindergarten teacher.

"That's great, you guys. We're just going to take it one more time. We had some problems in here. Earl, honey, this time, could you hit the word 'caused' just a little harder before you toss to Apurva? You're the man. Let's do it."

Even though less than three minutes per show features the anchors—the rest of the time is devoted to preproduced stories that fit in the holes—it takes nearly two hours to tape today's, or rather, tomorrow's episode. I just lean against the back wall of the control booth, try not to get in anybody's way, and watch. When the show is nearly complete, Mr. Scott approaches me.

"We want to use you on Friday. Think you'll be ready?"

"I'll try," I say.

It's nine o'clock when I get out of the studio, but I go to my desk and call Kate and tell her about my first day and tell her that I miss her already. Then I go stand in front of the studio and wait for a taxi.

My alarm clock hasn't even gone off yet, and there's someone pounding on my door. I get up, wrap the comforter around me, and answer it. A stranger stands in the hall. She looks down at a slip of paper.

"Patrick Sheridan?"

"Yeah," I say.

"Let's go shopping."

Seventeen hundred dollars later, Vivienne, who's in charge of public relations, is satisfied. I'm not sure I am though. We've been in five or six Beverly Hills clothing stores and bought everything on what Vivienne referred to as "company plastic." I admit the shopping was kind of a rush. I felt strangely like Julia Roberts in *Pretty Woman*. But it's what Vivienne bought that scares me. She dressed me like some kind of Los Angeles version of a cowboy—shirts with rhinestone buttons, ostrich-skin boots. We even went into a store called Beverly Hillbillies, where I got my first ten-gallon hat. Then we bought a lot of "leathercessories"—Vivienne's term—a vest with fringe, a couple belts with big shiny buckles, and a necklace "like Jon Bon Jovi wore in that 'I'm a Cowboy' song." Then, to cap it off, a gold pocket watch.

"Couldn't we just get a chain and run it to my pocket?" I ask as I looked at the $225 price tag. "It's not like I'm ever going to have to really know the time with it."

"You never know with Prentiss. One day he'll want you to check your watch on the show, and I'd like to still have a job when he does. Besides, this whole look is his idea."

When we get back to the studio, I hang all my new clothes in a wardrobe closet next to the stage, then head to the conference room for the noon show meeting. Libby explained to me yesterday that, no matter what else you're doing, you're supposed to make it to the noon meeting.

"It's where we critique the day's show, scream at each other, whisper petty backstabbing comments, and make power plays. Bring a healthy self-image with you."

But I figure I'm safe today. I haven't even appeared on the show yet.

The conference room has been built to resemble a standard high school classroom. There are even the same kind of slide-in seat/desks we have at Doggett. Libby comes and sits down next to me, and I ask her why the room looks like this.

"It's another one of Prentiss's ideas. He wants us to look at the show in the same way students see it. He tells people to move around. Watch from the front on some days. Watch from the back on others."

The room fills with the *Classroom Direct* staff. Fifty, maybe. Most of them enter carrying coffee cups and notepads. A few glance at me, but no one stares. Billy Trundle fires an imaginary gun at me when he sees me. I look around for Harris, but I don't find him. Maybe P.A.s aren't required at the noon meeting. As soon as Mr. Scott enters the room, the line producer plays the show. I saw most of it taped last night, but I didn't see it with the stories plugged in. The first two are voice-overs. Last night I learned those are the stories when the anchor just reads copy over edited tape. One's on a possible airline pilot strike; the other's on a bill that would ease copyright laws. Then there's a package (that's a story when we actually have a reporter out "in the field" covering the news) with Stu Chestnut reporting on juvenile detention center overcrowding. At the end of the show, Earl asks Apurva what stories she's working on, and she says something about her look at carpal tunnel syndrome airing on Thursday.

"Sounds tight," says Earl.

Then Mr. Scott's name fades onto the screen as rock music kicks in.

"Comments, anyone?" says Mr. Scott. He scans the room, but no one looks eager to speak. When his eyes reach me, they stop. "Why don't we let our newest staff member, Patrick Sheridan, give us his impressions."

I try not to panic, but I have no idea what to say.

"Perhaps I should introduce Patrick first," Mr. Scott says. "Patrick, stand up." I do. "Many of you have already seen Patrick's audition tape, so you know what a find we have here. Patrick's from Dogpatch, Texas."

"Doggett."

"I'm sorry, Patrick." Mr. Scott smiles, and I decide he was kidding. "Doggett, Texas. So, Patrick, what would the students of Doggett have thought about today's show?"

I feel everyone looking at me. I don't want to sound stupid, but it's an impossible question. I mean, some students like the news, and they always listen. Some you'd have to smack in the back of the head with a two-by-four to get them to shut up during the show. I try to explain this.

"Well, different students would have thought different things."

"What about the typical Doggett student, Patrick?"

Mr. Scott isn't letting me off the hook. I don't know who a "typical" Doggett student would be, but there were a couple things about the show that bothered me. I didn't want to mention them, but I don't see any way out of this without looking stupid.

"I think the story on the airline pilots would have lost the attention of half, maybe more than half, of the kids I go to school with."

"Really?" says Mr. Scott, scribbling a note to himself on his pad. "Why?"

"Not many of them have ever flown anywhere, and the only time anyone flies is during the holidays."

A woman I don't recognize speaks up. She sounds defensive. "Prentiss, teenagers fly all the time. We've all seen them. They usually sit next to me and turn their Walkman all the way up. It's news that may affect them."

"Yeah, but I don't think anyone would have listened past the lead," I say. "It was something about how the pilots were hoping for a cost-of-living increase in pay. Kids don't care about that unless maybe their dads are pilots. Maybe if we would say something like, 'A planned airline strike might make getting home to see Grandma impossible for thousands of families this Easter,' more students would have listened. My journalism teacher, Mr. Daugherty, says that if—"

"Prentiss!" says the woman.

"I think he's right, Lydia," says Mr. Scott. "Anything else, Patrick?"

"Well, yeah. One thing I've always wondered. The word 'tight'—I've never known what it meant."

That makes everyone in the room bust out laughing. Earl Woodbie shouts at me over the noise. "Yo, G. 'Tight.' It's like 'cool.'"

"Oh," I say. "That's what I thought." I've kind of always wondered what "G" meant, as well, but I decide not to ask.

When things simmer down, the woman named Lydia gets Mr. Scott's attention. "Prentiss, I was just wondering why you decided on another white male two percenter for the student anchor position. Don't you think we've got that demographic pretty well-covered with Stu and Lane?"

Some people groan, but the room quiets down quickly. I decide that I dislike being called a two percenter by Lydia even more than I disliked it from Billy Trundle.

"Calm down, Lydia," says Billy. "Lane's no more than a fifty percenter."

That makes everyone laugh some more, but, of course, I don't get it. Mr. Scott cuts the laughter short.

"Lydia, our biggest state in sheer numbers is Texas. A million Texas kids a day see us. And where do our marketing reports say we score lowest in customer satisfaction?" He answers his own question. "Rural schools. You know why? Because they don't know what the fuck 'tight' means!"

The ten-gallon hat back in my wardrobe closet starts to make more sense to me, and I wonder, if I were from Vermont or Oregon, whether I would be sitting here right now.

*   *   *

Libby introduces me to my tutor, Kim, after the meeting. I can't believe my teacher is telling me to call her by her first name. That sort of thing would land me in detention at Doggett. I like her, but the work she shows me looks too easy.

"We're just supposed to make sure you graduate and that you meet all your state requirements," she says. "But if there's something special you want to do, let me know. I'll do my best to teach it. I know Spanish, French, and Italian, but they're not required for you."

"Really?" I've always wanted to learn Italian. I don't know why, especially. I've just always liked the sound of it. Maybe that's what the mystery blood in me is. The only language they offer in Doggett is Spanish. The college-bound students learn it as a requirement. The farmers learn it so they can talk to the migrant workers who work in their fields. I tell Kim that I'll keep that in mind. We decide to meet in the mornings from 8:45 to 11:45. I only have to go to school three hours a day. Man, Zeb and Anderson are going to ride me about that.

After Kim and I get our schedules worked out, I visit Ms. Saunders's office. I'm wondering if they've decided to hire Shayla. It'd be nice to have someone around here my age. Ms. Saunders isn't in her office, but I do some poking around. The office is full of tapes. I find a box that has the words MALE FINALISTS printed on the side in felt tip. There's a VCR in the office, and I decide it might be fun to check out the competition. I dig through the box and look at some of the names. Then I find my envelope, the one in which I sent my portfolio of work and my letter from Mr. Daugherty.

It's still sealed.

On Friday I put on the clothes that Vivienne has picked out for me, then veteran anchor Shino Takawai tells me to follow her to makeup. I climb up on a stool in front of a big lighted mirror and a woman starts pounding my face with some kind of pad. Before I know it, I resemble a Doggett dance teamer on game day. I stare at my face in the mirror. It looks like a painting.

"Nervous?" asks Shino.

"Very," I say.

"Don't worry. They make you look great."

But it's not how I look that I'm nervous about. I'm afraid I won't be able to read off the teleprompter, or worse, I'll sound like I'm reading. Maybe people will be able to see my eyes move back and forth. What if I start sweating, and I end up with big sweat stains under my pits? I'm afraid they'll decide halfway through that they hired the wrong person, and that they'll send me home. I need to get my mind off my nervousness. I ask Shino what a two percenter is.

"Did someone call you that?" replies Shino.

"Yeah."

"Well, don't worry about it. It's just another way of saying you're handsome. They're saying that you're in the most beautiful two percent of the population."

"That's really what it means?"

The makeup woman pauses with her eyeliner pencil next to my tear duct. "For the most part," she says.

The studio lights have been turned on by the time I've gotten out there. I've already taped my voice-over—a story about new nutritional requirements in school lunches. I went into a little booth and read a script. It was tougher than I thought it would be. Lydia had written the story, and she was also the one coaching me from the booth.

"Think about what you're saying," she kept telling me. "You're not an actor, don't perform. Just say the words like it's important information that you're explaining to a friend."

It sounded easy, but it wasn't. The story was only a minute and a half long, but it took an hour until Lydia was satisfied with my reading. She wasn't very nice, either—not like everyone else has been. She wasn't mean exactly. Just cold. I knew she was being sarcastic when she asked me if the script met my approval, so I just ignored her. She didn't congratulate me or anything when I finally got it. She just said, "You're done."

Now I'm about to have Connie in my ear. I'm glad that I won't be able to hear what she's saying in the booth. Someone comes up behind me and starts untucking my shirt. I spin, out of reflex.

"Relax," says some longhaired guy. "I'm sound."

"Okay."

"Reach down your shirt and grab this."

He runs a wire up my shirt, and I take it. He pins the tiny

microphone up near the top button of my shirt. Then he puts my earpiece in. "Nice hat," he says, but I know he's joking. It's so stupid.

Connie the kindergarten teacher says hi in my ear. The stage manager, a woman named Heather, puts Shino and me in position, and I hear the assistant director start the count in, "Ready in five . . . four . . . three—"

"Hold on," says Connie. "Patrick, can I get you to tilt your hat back? We can't see your face."

"This is how they wear them."

"This is how who wears them?" she says.

"The people who really wear ten-gallon hats. They wear them down like this. Yankees wear them tilted back."

When the intercom comes back on, I can hear people in the control room laughing. Mr. Scott talks to me this time instead of Connie.

"Patrick, those other people aren't on television, and I'd be willing to bet they don't have faces as nice as yours. Now, we're not going to have you in the hat every time, but we think it would be a nice touch for this first show."

"How's this?" I say, tilting the hat back a bit and facing camera three.

"A little more," says Connie. "There. That looks good."

And we begin. An hour and a half later we're shooting the closing shot. I've only messed up a few times that I can tell, and I'm feeling pretty good about myself. At the end of the show, the *Classroom Direct* anchors always chat casually. "Happy talk" is what Libby called it. Anyway, I had always assumed that they just made that part up, but as I look into the teleprompter, I see that's not the case.

> Shino: HEY, GREAT DEBUT, PATRICK. TELL ME THE TRUTH—WERE YOU NERVOUS?
> Patrick: NO, NOT AT ALL.
> Shino: PATRICK?
> Patrick: ALL RIGHT. A LITTLE BIT.
> Shino: (LAUGH) I THOUGHT SO. THAT'S IT FOR *CLASSROOM DIRECT*. HAVE A GREAT WEEKEND!
> Patrick: THANKS FOR LISTENING, Y'ALL.

Connie's voice is in my head again.

"Patrick, when you say 'a little bit,' hold up your index fingers about an inch apart. Then, Shino, on your laugh, spread his fingers about a foot wider."

"Gotcha," says Shino.

"That's comedy," says the sound guy.

"Uh, do you really want me to say this at the end? The 'y'all' part," I say.

"Is there something wrong, Patrick?" It's Mr. Scott.

"It doesn't sound, I don't know, like . . . the news."

"We're always breaking barriers here, Patrick. That was one of the charming elements on your audition tape."

"I was just trying to be polite."

"I think this show could do with a good dose of manners, Patrick. You ready for a take?"

I can feel my head starting to sweat, and I have to fight the desire to take off this hat and scratch my scalp. I want to get this over with.

"Sure," I say. "Let's do it."

"Rahz and shahn, Tex!"

I was sound asleep when the telephone started ringing.

A second voice.

"Ah'd lahk to thank y'all fer answerin' the phone."

And then they bust up. It sounds like they're close to crying, they're laughing so hard.

"Kiss my round, off-white, hairless butt," I tell Anderson and Zeb, and they crack up some more, then I remember that it's two hours later in Texas. "Aren't y'all supposed to be in class?"

"Mr. Gale sent us out. We couldn't stop laughing. We're at the pay phone by the gym," says Zeb.

"Did I look really dumb?"

Zeb stops laughing. "No. In most ways it looked really good. You were a lot better than those student anchors they had last year. It was just funny looking at you in those clothes—"

"And that hat!" Anderson yells into the phone.

At the end of tutoring I ask Kim if she'll start teaching me Italian. She gets all excited.

"*Si!*" she says, then something in Italian.

"What does that mean?"

"It means maybe we'll even get you to test out of a year of it when you go to college."

"That sounds great."

I loiter a little bit in the empty office where I have "class." I'm not anxious to get to the noon meeting, but I decide I can't put it off. I walk down the hall. The show has just started to run when I get there. I take a seat and stare up at the screen. Fifteen minutes later, I'm wishing I hadn't shown up. I was awful. I mean, the difference between Shino and me was light-years. She sounded so confident, and she spoke just like Lydia tried to get me to speak, like she was explaining an interesting story to a friend. I, on the other hand, sounded like a zombie reading his "What I Devoured This Summer" essay. I feel myself shrinking in my desk. When TV me says, "Thanks for listening, y'all," some people laugh, others whistle or clap. Billy Trundle slaps me on the shoulder.

"Comments, anyone?" says Mr. Scott.

Today there are plenty. Some people didn't like the way the show was blocked (how the director positioned the cameras and the anchors); some people thought Lane's report from Lebanon sounded too "pro-Arab"; some people thought that we shouldn't use Nirvana music anymore because it glorifies suicide. The meeting drags on and on. The people who do mention my performance say nice things. Are they blind?

Eventually everything gets sorted out, and I think I'm safe. That's when Lydia speaks up. People groan.

"Prentiss, what's with the way Patrick was dressed? Don't you think we have enough trouble already getting taken seriously? People already call us 'kiddie news.' Surely this sort of pandering isn't going to help. And 'Thanks for listening, y'all'? It's embarrassing."

Mr. Scott takes a deep breath and lets it out slowly. The murmuring that seems to be standard background noise at these meetings dies down. He addresses Lydia at first, but then he begins sweeping the room with his eyes to let everyone know he's talking to them too.

"When I was hired away from MTV by *Classroom Direct*, my mission was made very clear to me. Keep feeding the kids news, but make it palatable. A spoonful of sugar, as they say. Now if I can get a few kids' heads off their desks by dressing our anchors a certain way, or by playing rock music, or by running an occasional piece on Michael fucking Jackson, I'm going to do it." Mr. Scott is getting worked up. "We could give kids Bosnia updates every day, but they wouldn't learn anything, because they wouldn't watch shit that boring."

The room is silent. Mr. Scott surveys his staff before continuing.

"So I guess this is as good a time as any to let everyone in on a new weekly feature we're instituting beginning next Friday. We're going to have a guest anchor work with one of our regular anchors each week."

The room's familiar buzz returns. Billy Trundle speaks up. "Hey, Prentiss, I'm almost afraid to ask, but who do you have in mind as guest anchors?"

"I'll turn that question over to Vivienne. She's done a great job of lining up the talent. Vivienne."

This reminds me. I'm supposed to get together with Vivienne as soon as possible to get a bio written about me and get my head shot done.

"For autographs," she told me, but I'm sure she was joking.

Vivienne stands up and reads from a list. "So far we've got Pierre LaFont from the L.A. Kings booked."

"He's only nineteen," Mr. Scott says. "How do you think that'll play in Minnesota and Wisconsin, places where they still think hockey is a major sport?"

Vivienne continues, "Then we've got one of the guys from Boyz Boyz Boyz, that hip-hop group. Oh, yeah, and I just got a confirmation today from Robin Ferris's manager."

A couple guys whistle.

Lydia speaks up. "Are we having to pay these people?"

"No," answers Vivienne.

"Then why are they doing it?" asks Lydia. "This *is* Hollywood."

"I'll handle that question, Vivienne," says Mr. Scott. "They're doing it for the recognition. We do provide a pipeline to nearly ten million teenagers."

"Robin Ferris was on the covers of *People* and *Seventeen* last month. She must be really insecure," says Lydia.

"Ah, but her new movie, *Slave Daze*, comes out this spring," says Billy. He scratches his head sarcastically. "Could there be any connection?"

"Prentiss, I'm hoping you don't expect us to include plugs in a news show," says Lydia.

"Not plugs, so much," Mr. Scott says. "Just a mention. At the end of the show, we can have one of our anchors ask the guest what he or she has been up to. That's all."

"That's the definition of a plug," says Lydia. "Can you see Peter Jennings reading the news with Jim Carrey and then, at the close of the show, saying, 'So, Jim, when can your fans expect the new *Ace Ventura*?' Has our culture sunk this low?"

"Lydia, commerce creates culture, and let's be honest here. It's not like our current anchors are, for the most part, trained journalists—"

"That's hardly something that—" interrupts Lydia, but Mr. Scott keeps going.

"So I don't think we're treading on thinner ice, journalistically speaking. The question is how many of our kids sit all the way through a half hour of network news? Let's ask Patrick. Patrick, would more students pay attention to the news if there was some celebrity they liked reading the news?"

Oh man, do I want to disappear. I don't want to get in the middle of this.

"Come on, Patrick," he says. "There's no right or wrong answer. Just tell us what you think."

I *think* the idea is crazy. On top of that, I think there is a right or wrong answer. I'm still reeling a bit from the knowledge that the anchors aren't trained journalists. But the question Mr. Scott asked—"Would more students pay attention to the news if there was some celebrity they liked reading the news?"—is not really a question of standards, is it?

"Yeah, more would watch it."

"And that, staff," says Mr. Scott, "is our mission here."

The busiest place at *Classroom Direct* is the newsroom. It's where all the writers and news producers have their cubicles. There is a constant onslaught of noise. Five television sets are mounted high along one wall where everyone can see them. The first three show the major networks. The fourth one runs CNN, and the last one is the feed from our wire service, which provides the video we use when we don't have our own people out covering a story. Everyone has a speaker on his or her desk that can be tuned to any of the five monitors. That explains a lot of the noise, but not all of it. You also hear producers begging for one more minute for their stories about leaking oil tankers in the Gulf of Mexico or proposed antihazing legislation in Ohio. When deadline is still hours away, the producers will share anecdotes about hotel bars in Singapore or covering the Jesse Jackson presidential campaign. Then there's the clacking of fingers on keyboards as stories are completed minutes before deadline. That's why I spend most of my time in here.

I started off hanging out in the talent offices, but there isn't much to do in there except my homework, and that doesn't take me very long. I have gotten to talk to the other anchors when they haven't been on the phone to their friends or their agents. They've been nice. Real nice. I've gotten autographs from everyone but Nan Spencer and Lane Tauber for Zeb's autograph book.

Nan's in South America doing something on the rain forests, and Lane's still in the Middle East. David Saldaña invited me to go to a Lakers game at the Forum, and Stu Chestnut said he'd take me up to Magic Mountain some Saturday. I still don't know what the reporters are supposed to be doing when the camera isn't on them, but I'm going to find out soon. Mr. Scott has warned me that they are going to send me "into the field" any day now.

I try to stay out of everyone's way in the newsroom. I'm sitting at the desk of one of the producers who's out of the country, and I'm daydreaming. I'm picturing myself leaning into a howling wind, with rain pelting me, assuring students that the worst of Hurricane Roman has passed. That's when the managing editor snaps me out of it. "Patrick, you ready to earn your keep?"

"Yes, sir."

"We're sending you to Seattle tonight. A school up there wasn't going to allow girls to attend some formal dance together. The girls sued, and a judge ordered the school to change their policy. Yesterday the student body voted to cancel the dance rather than let the lesbians attend. Billy's your producer. Get together with him, and he'll give you all the travel details."

"Yes, sir."

"And Patrick?"

"Uh-huh?"

"Prentiss told me to remind you to pack your clothes from wardrobe."

Chapter Two
SEATTLE, WASHINGTON

BILLY AND I FLEW OUT THREE HOURS LATER. ON the plane, I asked him if I should start working on a list of questions to ask students. He told me not to bother. We spent the night downtown at the Roosevelt Hotel, where we each had our own room. Lying there in that hotel room bed, I felt lonely for the first time since leaving Texas. All week I've been going home from *Classroom Direct* so tired that I've just fallen right asleep. Plus, I've been able to call Kate from the studio and talk all we want for free. I couldn't do that from the hotel. I watched TV until Letterman was over and then figured I'd have to masturbate just so I could nod off. I started out thinking about Kate. I always do. But my mind invariably wanders, and I end up having my mental way with girls from Doggett who I know do the deed. Girls I don't even like. That's part of the reason that I think Papa is right about lustful thoughts—that they're evil. Last night was weird, though. Last night Robin Ferris popped into my mind. I didn't see her as the *Prairie Girl* though. She was getting out of her MG wearing that miniskirt and those sunglasses. I didn't last very long after that, but I used my trick. Right as I got to the point of no return, I replaced Robin's face with Kate's. That always makes me feel less guilty.

The next day Billy and I are standing in the rain across the street from Bayside High School waiting for our camera crew to arrive. I'm trying to decide whether Papa ever masturbated. His real name's not Roman; it's Cormac, but Grampa started calling him Roman when he was little because of how serious he was about his Catholicism—much more serious than Grampa Sheridan. I sometimes find myself really missing Grampa. He spoiled me like grandparents are supposed to. He was the only one I had left alive—my parents are as old as most of my friends' grandparents—but he spoiled me enough for four. That's for sure. He used to tell me stories about growing up in Ireland. He had a thick accent, but as a kid, I thought all grandparents must talk like that. He said he read an article in a newspaper when he was eighteen about people getting rich on oil in western Texas, so he borrowed enough money to sail from Ireland to Boston and from there to Galveston. He hitched his way to Lubbock, looked around at the flat, brown land, fell to his knees, and started bawling. But he knew there was no turning back. Everyone in the family had given him money. He never did strike it rich, but he became a foreman at a refinery and made enough money to pay back his relatives and send Papa to law school. He always talked about returning, but he never did. He died when I was ten.

The crew shows up. I've learned that *Classroom Direct* doesn't have full-time photographers and sound technicians for the field. They hire freelance crews wherever they go to save money on travel and so on, but it looks like Billy has worked with these guys before.

"Bobby! Greg! I was hoping they'd splurge and pay you your outrageous fucking rates. What are you charging now?" says Billy.

"A K a day," says the guy holding the camera.

"And worth every penny," says Billy.

"What happened to you?" says the sound guy. "I thought you were still with CNN. Since when have you been doing kiddie news?"

"Ten months now," says Billy. "Ever since CNN instituted that new 'no assholes' policy."

"You must have seen the writing on the wall."

"Got out before they had a chance to fire me." Billy points to me. "Fellas," he says. "This is Patrick, and I'll warn you—the boy's a virgin."

It's that obvious?

"And they picked you to pop his cherry?" says the soundman, who I now know is Greg.

"I promised I'd be gentle."

At least I figure out what they're talking about.

"So what do we got here?" says Bobby.

That's when Billy gets to work. He tells the crew the story, then explains that the principal won't allow any cameras on school grounds, but that he wants wide shots of the school, a tight shot on the granite plaque with the name of the school on it, B-roll of kids exiting the school and getting in cars and buses, and nat sound of "the noisy little fuckers scrambling to get out."

"Now the rest of the stuff, if you get it, would be a bonus. I'd love a shot of that fat fuck principal covering his face with a notebook and hightailin' his ass out to his car. I could use shots of couples making out in the parking lot. And goddamn it! If you could get me a couple queers hugging on each other, I'll stuff my tongue down your throat myself." While he's talking to the crew, Billy pulls a pad out of his pocket and hands it to me. "Then we're going to trap some of the little homophobes, and Patrick's going to ask them a couple questions."

The pad includes only two questions. *How did you vote? Why?* Man, Mr. Daugherty always told us never to show up anywhere with less than ten questions. I decide not to mention this to Billy. The crew gets busy shooting the exterior of the school, so I take the opportunity to ask Billy a couple questions. "So why don't you like the principal?"

Billy looks at me like he's trying to decide whether I'm being smart-mouthed.

"Because he never should have let the student body vote on this. He should've had the balls to make this decision and live with the consequences. When I talked to him on the phone yesterday, he hid behind this student election like he was some kind of Thomas Jefferson. Besides, why should anyone give a shit if a couple girls want to tongue-kiss in the middle of the gym. It's time for these kids to grow up."

I'm nervous about asking this next question, but curiosity is either one of my qualities or faults, depending on who you talk to.

"When you feel so strongly about a topic, is it tough to remain objective?"

Billy starts laughing.

"Objectivity is a myth. Whoever told you that journalism means being objective is full of shit. Just by choosing to cover this story, we're making a subjective decision. We're telling kids across America that it's not normal to vote to cancel a dance rather than let gay kids come. We're saying it's newsworthy."

"But what about presenting both sides of the story? Are you still able to do that?"

"Yeah, sure. For the most part." He scratches his head. "I try to get sound bites on both sides of an issue. I try to make sure I present all the facts. But true objectivity, you'll never find it. Do you think that there was a reporter covering the O. J. trial who *didn't* have an opinion about whether he was guilty? But most of them were able to tell the story in terms of the facts. That's what we're going to try to do."

The other two questions I have are simple terminology. I find out that nat sound is short for natural sound, which is any audio that isn't people being interviewed: dogs barking, car horns blowing. Similarly, B-roll is video of anything except people being interviewed.

The crew returns, and Greg hands me a microphone.

"Better show him how to work that thing," Billy says.

Greg isn't sure whether Billy is serious, but he demonstrates anyway. He makes me practice holding it three or four inches under my chin, then three or four inches under his.

"That about covers it," he says. "Just don't forget to move it back to your mouth when you're asking a question."

A few minutes later the final school bell rings, and the exodus from Bayside High School begins. While the camera crew scrambles around on the sidewalk just outside of the school grounds trying to get all the shots Billy requested, Billy is grabbing kids, literally, and asking them how they voted. I'm standing right there as he does it. The ones who stutter or sound brain-dead he shoves along. Anyone who sounds fully functional he orders to wait beside him. I'm standing there in my leather vest and bolo feeling terribly out of place.

One of the kids who Billy has waiting leans over to me. "So what station are you with?"

"*Classroom Direct*," I tell him.

"Never heard of it. What station is that?"

I don't know how to answer that question. It's not, after all, really a station at all. You either get it or you don't. I just assumed that any school we visited knew about the show. I decide to lie.

"Uh, it's cable. I'm not sure what station it's on in Seattle."

That seems to satisfy the guy, who continues to wait with the rest of the half dozen Billy has gathered. Eventually the crew returns, and it's time for me to go to work. I feel kind of stupid with only two questions to ask. But I ask them. And I remember to keep the microphone four inches below their chin. And I remember to point it at me when I'm speaking. It's cake. The responses to the questions vary not only in terms of opinion, but in eloquence. One girl says she voted for cancellation of the dance because it would "gross her out" to see two girls there together. "What about heterosexual rights?" she beseeches. "We're the majority!"

The next boy compared America's permissive society to Sodom and Gomorrah. Billy was standing in my field of vision, and I saw him shake his head and make the jacking-off motion. It hurt to keep from smiling. The girl who spoke next said that it was embarrassing to go to a school that persecuted people based on their sexual preference. "Are the people who voted to cancel the dance afraid it's contagious?"

The next boy just seemed unhinged by the whole situation. "I already put money down on a tux," he said. "It's not fair."

After we had gone through all six, Billy asked the Bible-quoting boy and the embarrassed girl to hang around. Then he told Bobby he needed cutaways.

"Aye, Cap'n," he said.

"Now, Patrick, pretend like they're answering your questions. Just stand there and nod while they're talking."

The cameraman moves behind Gomorrah boy and starts taping me while I nod along in silence.

"Good," Billy says. "Now the girl."

When that's over, I tell Billy that I had never thought about how that was done.

"Well, now you know. It's one of the many magic tricks that you're going to learn in the next few months."

"Why haven't any of these people known who we are?"

"Are you joking? This is a negative story. This is a story the school in question would prefer we didn't cover. We only shoot these stories at schools where they don't subscribe to *Classroom Direct.* If the story is on gang problems or drugs in schools, you can bet we're not doing it at one of our schools. They'd pull the plug. On the other hand, if the story is some bit of fluff about the winner of the national spelling bee, I can guaran-fucking-tee you, it's a subscriber school."

"That doesn't sound right."

"Well, boys," he says to Greg and Bobby, "his cherry's officially popped."

A couple hours later we're in the living room of one of the two girls who wanted to go to the dance together. They're sitting next to each other on the couch answering the questions that Billy jotted down for me. They tell some awful stories about getting harassed at school by boys who expose themselves and say things like, "Try it. You'll like it," or girls who stick "Sinners Repent!" pamphlets into their gym lockers.

After we wrap up the interview and we're out on the driveway, Billy asks me how objective I'm feeling.

"Not very," I admit. I try to decide whether the situation would have played out any differently in Doggett. Probably not. "Billy, I don't think I've ever met a lesbian before."

Billy laughs, which is the reaction he has to about every other thing I say, whether I intend to be funny or not.

"No, Patrick. You've met a lesbian before."

Chapter Three
LOS ANGELES, CALIFORNIA

ON MONDAY MORNING I DISCOVER I'M NO LONGER Kim's only student. Shayla Roberts was brought in while I was in Seattle. Kim introduces us, and Shayla tells me I was good last week.

"Really?" I realize I shouldn't sound so surprised. She probably wouldn't tell me I sucked without really knowing me first.

"Yeah."

"Oh, well, thanks. I saw your audition tape. I thought it was great. You've got a great voice," I say, but as the words are coming out of my mouth, I can't help thinking about Destiny Weaver's portfolio.

At the noon meeting, Lydia wants to know why Billy cut to a close-up of the two girls' intertwined hands during their interview. Billy explains that it was a visual way of showing the two were a couple, not simply girls bent on fighting the system.

"Would you have cut to the hands if it had been a boy and a girl on the couch?" she asks.

"Lydia, don't you think you're being a little hypersensitive here?"

"I don't know, Billy. Can you answer my question?"

Billy shakes his head. "No, I probably wouldn't have used the shot of the hands. I wouldn't have needed it."

"Then what you're doing is turning these girls' private lives into some sort of freak show."

Billy says, "Fuck this," and walks out of the meeting.

I'm still trying to debate the journalistic point in my head when I figure out who Billy had been talking about.

After the noon meeting, most of the *Classroom Direct* staff heads to lunch, either to the studio commissary or one of the kosher, Italian, or Thai places that surround the grounds, but Lydia always packs a lunch and eats it in front of her computer terminal. That's where she's sitting when I ask her if she'll help me with my news reading.

"Now that's something I haven't heard from a two percenter," she says. "What makes you think you need help?"

"I want to sound natural, and I don't sound close to that now."

"It's hard work sounding natural," she says.

"That's not a problem," I say.

"You're brimming with confidence."

The way she says it—harrumphing and as a statement rather than a question—makes me think she considers my answer predictable. I look around Lydia's cubicle for clues to why she dislikes me. Phone memos and Post-it notes obscure potential evidence and turn her cubicle space into a sort of Concentration board. I'm able to make a deduction based on a framed certificate that reads "As- - - - -ted P- - - - News Wr- - - - - -ward, L- - - - Estevez, Wash- - - - - - -ost."

"You worked for the *Washington Post*?"

"Impressed?" she says, sounding surprised.

"Of course. What brought you here?"

"The same thing that leads all decent print journalists to the dark side—money."

"I want to work in print," I say.

"Well, that's something of a shock, given how well you seem to have bought into Prentiss's grand plan around here. You've sounded like a true TV head in the staff meetings."

"It's the way he words the questions he asks me."

"Never answer the question Prentiss asks you," she says. "Answer the question behind the question Prentiss asks you."

"I'll keep that in mind."

"When do you anchor again?"

"Thursday."

She clacks away at her keyboard.

"I just printed out an old story we did on earthquakes. Get it out of the printer and underline the words or phrases that you think are most important. Usually, you'll only underline one per sentence. Don't memorize the story, just become familiar with the main points. Once you know what words to hit, we'll go down to the studio and work with the teleprompter."

"Great," I say. "Thanks."

I walk toward the printer, but I decide to push my luck. "Lydia, what's a two percenter?"

She gazes up at the fluorescent lights for a moment before turning her attention toward me. "*You're* a two percenter, Patrick."

"I've been given a definition. I want to know what it really *means*."

"It means, Patrick, that you have the luxury that you can get by on your looks. It means that you're one of the beautiful people for whom everything comes easy. It means you'll never have trouble getting a job, getting promoted, making friends, getting a loan, getting laid. Being a two percenter gives you the power to just bullshit your way through life."

"But, I don't . . . bullshit my way though life."

"It's not even something you control, Patrick. People do it for you. Or to you—whichever way you want to look at it. Think about it. We got five hundred audition tapes from boys wanting the job you've got now. Now, I don't know a thing about your experience, or your work ethic, or your talent. You seem like a bright kid. But I can promise you: The best thing you've got going for you, like it or not, is that face."

The mirror in my bathroom at The Sunset Villas has those exposed frosted lightbulbs that encircle the mirror and turn all who use it into stars. I keep staring into it, trying to find answers. I decide to run a detail check on myself, something I've never done before. I start with my eyes. They're green. Green like . . . green like . . . no simile jumps to mind except "green like a green crayon." Mr. Daugherty would never accept that. My nose is too thin, I think. Kate calls it a snob nose. I try smiling. Things start looking up here. My smile is wide, and it shows off my straight teeth. Years of Mama harping on me about brushing has kept them toothpaste ad white. I think the contrast with my skin's pirate swarthiness adds to the effect. Skin used to be my major flaw. In fact, it's only been in the last year or so that my complexion has cleared up. I was easily the most crater-faced eighth grader in Doggett, but I went to a dermatologist in Lubbock who prescribed Accutane. I take a pill every day. If I forget for two days, it's zit city.

I have one of those heads where it's easy to imagine a skull being inside. I think this is caused by the way my cheekbones kind of jut out and dare my skin to stretch over them. My hair is black and cut short. What's left of it attempts to curl into nickel-sized rings. I swivel my head and try to catch myself in profile, wondering if what people say about having a good side has any truth to it. I can't tell the difference.

I've always known I wasn't ugly. I never really hated the way I look. But then, I've never really given it a whole lot of thought. Kate calls me handsome every once in a while, but no one's ever thrown a fit over me. I decide that Lydia and Billy are wrong. No one's ever handed me anything because of the way I look.

Until now.

There's a knock on the door of my apartment, and for some reason I'm embarrassed about spending so much time in front of this mirror. It's Shayla Roberts. She's holding a copy of *Ethan Frome*, which is what we're supposed to be reading for English. She looks upset.

"This make sense to you?" she asks.

"Some," I say.

"Then explain it to me."

We sit on my couch and talk about Ethan Frome. Shayla doesn't have much sympathy for the farmer's plight.

"You know my favorite thing about it?" she says. "It's short."

Pretty soon we're talking about our hometowns. She asks me if people ride horses to school in Doggett. At first I want to laugh, but then I remember that Chet Webber rides his mare in and keeps her in the ag barn. I tell her no anyway. I explain that most everyone drives pickups to school. She says no one drives to her school. There's no parking lot, and besides, she says, no one has a car.

"Do you play gin?" Shayla asks.

I tell her yes, and she's out of the room and back in a matter of seconds with a deck of cards. She starts shuffling like my champion bridge player mother, and within twenty minutes I've lost three hands. Normally I'm a pretty decent gin player, but I'm having trouble concentrating on what she's picking up, let alone my own cards, because, as we're playing, Shayla's telling me about her life. It turns out that Shayla's not even sure her mother knows she's living in Los Angeles. She says she gave her older sister's name instead of her mother's.

"Cassandra and me take care of the family anyways," she says. "Sometimes my mom's gone for days. She lost it for some trumpet player and just abandoned ship. She stops in sometimes when the dude's playing in the city, but Cassandra says she's gonna

change the locks. I don't really care one way or another—she's
been pretty worthless since Daddy left anyways—but Cassandra's
real mad 'cuz she had to drop out of D.C.C.C.—that's District of
Columbia Community College—and go to work full-time. We
got a ten-year-old brother and an eight-year-old brother, so there
wasn't much choice."

Cassandra picks up the eight of hearts I just discarded and lays
down gin.

"You sure you've played this before?" she asks.

"I'm rusty."

"Like a tin roof." Shayla takes the cards out of my hands and
begins shuffling.

Shayla and I share a cab into the studio the next day. On the
way there, she tells me about how great her shopping trip with
Vivienne was.

"Do you realize we get to keep these clothes when we leave?"
she asks.

I tell her I didn't know that. But it doesn't fill me with the same
excitement as it does Shayla.

As we walk into the studio, Nicola's sitting behind her desk
wearing a huge grin.

"Oh, Patrick," she sings, "there's a letter for you. It's from a
girl."

She gives the word "girl" eight syllables, then presents me the
letter as if she's bringing me news from the front. I can smell the
perfume before it's even in my hand.

"You go, boy," says Shayla.

I try sticking it in my back pocket, but Shayla and Nicola aren't going for that.

"Oh, no you don't," Shayla says, trying to reach behind me.

"All right. All right," I say, fending her off. "What a couple voyeurs."

"Voy-who?" says Shayla.

The return address is Boise, Idaho. I don't know anyone in Boise. There's a little heart drawn in red-colored pencil on the back of the envelope. I show it to Shayla and roll my eyes. The letter itself is printed in the same red pencil in blocky, half-inch-tall letters. I scan it before speaking.

"Hmmm, Alicia Silverstone wants to know if we can get together sometime."

I get no reaction from my audience, which has now grown to include Libby, so I go ahead and read the letter out loud.

> Patrick,
>   You are the cutest actor on *Classroom Direct*.
> ["Out of the mouths of babes," says Libby.] My
> friend Jennifer thinks Stu Chestnut is cuter, but
> your cuter. If your ever in Idaho, will you call me
> up? I have put in a picture of me. I dont have
> braces any more. Is it fun on TV? I think it is.
>   Were you scared you might get AIDS when
> you talked to those gay girls? You looked brave. I
> would have thrown up when they were holding

hands. Can you send me a picture?
Your friend,
Shelli Coombs
Yeats Junior High

Billy Trundle has joined the group by the time I finish reading. "Some girlie out in TV land want to grab your wang, Sheridan?"

"Billy, please!" says Libby.

"Says here she's your sister," I say.

Billy smiles. "Fuck off," he says.

Libby covers her ears and snaps, "Boys!"

David Saldaña has two careers. He's explaining this to me at a small table in the Forum Room, the swanked-out bar inside the Forum. We've just watched the Lakers dismantle the Mavericks, and it's hard for me to concentrate on what he's saying because every direction I turn I'm seeing someone famous: Danny Glover, Kareem Abdul-Jabbar, Steve Martin, and that woman no one knows but they always show on TV at Lakers games—she's here too. I'm thinking it might be funny to get her autograph for Zeb. I'm having my first alcoholic drink ever other than the beer I downed on a dare from Anderson in eighth grade. David got me a rum and Coke. He said it was good for someone just starting out. I told him I just wanted a Sprite, but he said he had worked too hard convincing the doorman to let me in to order a soft drink. I'm sipping very slowly. It's not as good as a plain Coke, but it's not bad, either. Not nearly as gross as that warm can of Coors four years ago.

"So, like I was saying." David waves the waitress over and orders another scotch and soda. He looks at my three-quarters-full glass and tells her that'll do it. "South of the border, my career is music. Latin hip-hop. Down there I just go by . . . David."

He pronounces his name Dah-VEED, and he elongates it as if it's being announced to a screaming throng.

"I move a lot of product in TAY-Has."

"Cool," I say, hoping I sound enthused.

A couple expensively dressed Hispanic women approach the table shyly and begin speaking to David in Spanish. From my year of it at Doggett, I understand that they're big fans, and that they own all his records.

"*Señoritas*, we're in America now!" says David. "Let's speak the language of the land. We don't want to offend *mi compadre* here, do we?"

They giggle and ask for his autograph in English. He obliges and is happy to pose for a picture with the two of them. I'm the designated photographer. As they jiggle away, David explains to me that he's working on his Spanish.

"Man, growing up in Bel Air, the only time I heard the language was when our maid was talking to our gardener."

Over the next few minutes I learn that David learns his songs phonetically ("It's not that hard, really") and that his father is a plastic surgeon to the stars ("The stories I could tell you"). I avoid asking whether he's ever gone under the knife, but there's something suspicious about his face. It looks different close-up than it does on TV. The flesh sinks and bows in spots that don't seem natural. He asks me if I have a personal trainer. I tell him I don't, and he snatches a business card out of his wallet and slides it across the table.

"If you're looking for career advice, there it is," he says.

"I want to write for a newspaper after college," I say.

"You're kidding."

"Maybe a magazine."

David grins at me. Then he shakes his head, and his long hair falls down in front of his shoulders. "Keep the card," he says, "in case one of your sources tries to rough you up."

I glance down at it.

    IRON DICK

     A good man is hard.

I finish my drink and stick the card in my shirt pocket.

"You want another?" David asks.

"Why not," I say.

Chapter Four
AUSTIN, TEXAS

A WEEK AFTER I LEAVE MY PORTFOLIO OF CLIPPINGS from *The Ashes* in Lydia's box, we get sent to Texas together. My home state, at the urging of the governor, is considering a bill that will allow judges to sentence teens convicted of vandalism or petty theft to time on a chain gang. Last fall, the governor's campaign ads accused his opponent of being lenient on crime. He followed this denouncement with a solid promise to his would-be teen constituents.

"If I'm elected, and you get busted . . ." Here, they cut away to stock footage of grim-faced black-and-white-striped convicts holding picks and shovels. "I'll have *you* busting rocks."

"Busting Rocks!" became the bumper sticker of choice during the campaign, with most people thinking of "rocks" as a verb, but the ACLU and a ragged coalition of liberals, enemies of the new governor and legislators who fear the teen work camps will end up in their districts, have been fighting a fierce battle to defeat the plan.

I'm looking out the window of the plane. The pilot has just announced that we're flying over Lubbock. I think I see Doggett—

looking even smaller than normal from this vantage point—and I try to imagine what my mother is doing right now. Kate and Anderson and Zeb are still in school. I'm struck by a desire to jump out of the plane, with or without a parachute, and just float down and land on the football field. The fifty-yard line. There would be a pep rally. I'd say a few words into the microphone that the principal would hand me. Tell the student body funny stories about Stu and David and Earl. I imagine my ex-girlfriends sitting up in the stands with their football-playing boyfriends.

Sighing.

"Have you read up on all of this?" says Lydia, looking up from her notes.

"Read it? I lived it. In Doggett, if you didn't vote for the governor, you were either communist or queer." As soon as it comes out my mouth, I want to shoot myself. I forgot about Lydia. "I mean, that's what some people thought."

Kate may have been the only person I knew in Doggett who would speak up in support of his opponent in class. She didn't catch much flak over it though. You don't win a war of words with Kate Mosely. Everyone knows that.

Lydia doesn't seem perturbed by my observation. She just says, "Texas," as if that's a put-down in itself.

"Do you want to come up with some questions?"

"Yes, ma'am."

"You ever call me ma'm again, and it'll be the last time we work together."

"Who are we going to talk to?" I ask.

"Who do you think we should?"

I think about it for a minute before answering. "How about people who are already spending time in juvenile homes or who are on probation. We can ask them if knowing they would have been sent out busting rocks would have kept them from committing whatever crime they committed. Then we ought to talk to some state legislators and see which way they're voting and find out why, and what do you think of talking to some high school students to get their reaction?"

Lydia hands me a piece of paper. It's an itinerary mapping out our movements from the time we land until we get on the plane back to Los Angeles. She's already scheduled interviews with everyone I mentioned. Tomorrow we visit the Central Texas Detention Center for Boys, the state capitol, and Austin's Reagan High School. As soon as we land, we're meeting our crew and driving an hour out to a limestone quarry.

"That's where I want to shoot the stand-up," she says. "We'll only have a bit of sunlight left by the time we get there, so don't screw up. Especially not now that I'm starting to think you could have a future in this business."

"Did you read my portfolio?"

"Yep."

"Then you're the only one here who has."

"That shouldn't still come as a surprise to you. You've been working in television for more than a month now. Get jaded, for chrissakes. Cynicism, you should know, is one of the primary attributes of a quality journalist."

"So I should believe the worst about everyone?"

Lydia appears to struggle to come up with a response to that. She dispatches a couple of grapes that came with her vegetarian meal before speaking.

"Forget what I said about being cynical. It's bullshit. I've just lived in Los Angeles for too long. I think what I mean is, you should be skeptical without being cynical."

"So what did you think of my portfolio?"

I'm nervous about asking this. Lydia doesn't sugarcoat, which is apparent at all the show meetings. She dishes out criticism to other producers and the talent, but she also takes what people tell her very seriously. I've seen her jot down all the comments staff members make about the pieces she produces. Even the silly things that the people from the school relations or business department suggest.

"It's good stuff, Patrick. I have to admit I was a bit surprised. But I think you ought to concern yourself more with quality rather than quantity. It might be fun to be able to say you wrote fourteen stories for one issue of the paper, but I think you would learn more and the paper would be more interesting if you concentrated less on the square-dancing club's officer election and really got inside some serious teen issues. I realize that in your hometown you're probably not inundated with gang troubles or teen suicides, but what about issues like working with pesticides, or the decline of the family farm. Maybe even something on the football madness these wastelands spawn. I'm sure that in a small town like yours there's not much for teenagers to do. Is drinking and driving an issue?" I nod. "I know it's been covered a lot, but I think you could put a small town slant on it—the car culture, the boredom, the acceptance of teen drinking. I think you could come up with something fresh.

"One last thing—your style."

"Uh-huh," I respond.

"You don't have any."

"Okay."

As a journalistic term, style refers to consistency within a news organization. The *New York Times* uses courtesy titles like Mr. and Ms. before names. The Associated Press doesn't. But I'm pretty sure that's not what she's talking about.

"It's like you've memorized all the writing rules: the inverted pyramid, the quote transition format. Your stories flow well. The facts are put together better than most of the *Classroom Direct* pieces—"

"But . . ."

"But there's no flair. No individualism. Have you ever seen those personalized greeting card machines that they have in some supermarkets or Hallmark stores?"

I saw something like that in Lubbock once. I nod.

"You feed it the names of the principal characters. You click on the correct holiday, press a button, and out pops your 'personalized card.' But, you see, they really all sound the same, and none of them have any real depth of feeling, any soul."

"And that's how I write?"

"Don't sound so upset about it, Patrick. There aren't many

teenagers who write as well as you. Style is one of the most difficult qualities to achieve, because you can't teach it. On the bright side, it's not something that at birth you either have or don't have. The more you write, the more you read, I'd even say the more you live, the more likely you are to find it."

"Well, that's just great. I haven't written anything since I left Doggett."

"You want to try writing a stand-up for this story?"

The stand-up is the part of the story where the reporter is on-screen talking directly to the viewer.

"Really?"

Lydia slides a legal pad over onto my tray table and hands me her pen. By the time the captain tells us to prepare for descent into Austin, I've completed my first attempt at writing for television. I read it over before handing it to Lydia.

Here in Texas, a new governor is trying to make good on his promise to send teenaged vandals and petty criminals out to bust rocks on chain gangs, but the plan is meeting with opposition from lawmakers and concerned citizens who believe the sentence doesn't fit the crime.

I hand the legal pad back to Lydia, who reads through it.

"So it's the concerned citizens who are against the plan? Doesn't that imply that the people who are for the plan aren't 'concerned citizens'?"

I see what she's getting at. "Okay. Anything else?"

"Remember that you're going to be saying this. We normally speak in short sentences. Longer sentences are more difficult to say and more difficult to understand."

"All right."

"One more thing. Don't forget that you're writing for television. That's an advantage you've got to utilize. A picture really is worth a thousand words, but only if you tell the viewer what she's seeing."

Lydia returns the legal pad. I decide against asking her if the stand-up has "style." Our crew meets us at the gate. The photog says his name is Knobby, then he points at his partner, a sheepdog of a guy wearing a T-shirt that says KILL BONO.

"Harper's got sound," says Knobby.

They lead us out to the rental car. I work on a new stand-up in the backseat as we drive out into the Hill Country. The legal pad goes back and forth from my hands to Lydia's. Each time, she points out something else she doesn't like, but she refuses to make suggestions. I'm about ready to give up when we arrive at our destination. I look around me, and I know what to write. I jot it down and push it in front of Lydia.

"That works," she says.

We get out of the car, and Harper starts to wire me up. He's running a line up the front of my blue denim shirt (Lydia isn't making me wear the hat) before he seems to take any notice of me or my age.

"I must be getting old," he says, shaking his shaggy head and adjusting dials on his receiver. "Give me a level—your voice has changed hasn't it?"

I answer with my thickest accent, "Yes, sir."

"Ah, fuck me," says Harper. But the level checks out.

Lydia gives instructions to the whole crew, and I take my position.

"Any time," says Knobby. I begin.

"A hundred years ago, Texas murderers and thieves, sentenced to long prison terms, were sent to rock quarries like this one. Here they carved out the limestone that was used to build the state capitol building and the governor's mansion." I start walking along a sheer limestone wall toward the camera. *"If the governor currently living in that limestone mansion gets his way, Texas's new generation of rock busters will be teenagers convicted of vandalism and petty theft."* I stop walking right in front of the camera. *"But the governor's in for a fight."*

"One-take Sheridan!" says Lydia. "Knobby, show me the replay."

By the time we're heading for Reagan High School to interview students, I'm dragging. We've already been to the capitol building, where we found legislators more than willing to talk to us. Then we visited the juvenile delinquents, who weren't big supporters of the governor's plan. Surprise, surprise.

I whine to Lydia about how tired I am.

"Talking to the scum of the earth takes a lot out of you," she says. "And those little creeps in the detention center weren't much fun either."

The principal of Reagan High School meets us out in front of the school. He keeps saying how excited the kids are to have us visit their school. It's weird, because he talks to me like I'm the one in charge.

"I hope you don't mind," he says, "but I told our television kids they'd get a chance to interview you before you left."

I glance at Lydia, who checks her watch before shrugging.

"Sure," I say. "No problem."

Lydia chose this school because of its demographics. It's an urban school on Austin's lower-income East Side. Since I've been living in L.A., I've gotten used to black faces, but Reagan is so different from Doggett, where we have mainly white kids and Mexicans, lots from migrant families. More than half the kids here are black. I see their faces as they turn and stare at me as the principal leads us through their bustling courtyard. I hear a bunch of *that's hims* and *check it outs*. Plain as day, I hear a girl say, "Why couldn't they send Earl?"

Two girls approach me. They look a bit embarrassed, but one of them holds out a textbook. "Could you give me your autograph?" she says.

Weird. I've never signed one of these in person. The girl is pretty cute. Not Kate cute, but certainly attractive. I take the book from her.

"Could you make it 'To Danylle'?" She spells her name for me. I have to cross out my first attempt and try again. A crowd has started to gather, mainly girls, but a few hulky guys in letter jackets are starting to mill around the perimeter. People start talking to me, asking questions about the other anchors, telling me it's cool they got someone from Texas, wondering out loud where my hat is. A bell sounds, and they begin dispersing.

"Can we get back to work now?" says Lydia.

"*Subito!*" I say, using the Italian word for "at once" Kim taught me. Lydia stares at me quizzically, so I shoot her my other Italian phrase. "*Conosco una buona discoteca.*" She decides to ignore me—she doesn't seem much like the dance club type anyway.

We follow the principal into a classroom. A half dozen of Reagan's best and brightest have been assembled for the interview. Knobby assembles the group in an easily framed six-shot while Harper gives three students stick microphones and instructs them on their use. Then he speaks to them *very* slowly.

"If you don't have a microphone, no one can hear you. Ask your neighbor if you can borrow his." The students stare blankly at him. I imagine they're all silently saying, "Duh." I think Harper must get this impression as well.

"Good. Don't screw it up, then," he adds.

Today Harper's T-shirt says THE OPIATE OF THE MASSES. Below the slogan is a TV set that looks remarkably like the *Classroom Direct* model mounted high up on the wall in the corner of the room, reminding me of home. Lydia and I came up with the list of questions last night at the hotel. Afterward, I stayed in her room watching SpectraVision until she was forced to tell me that she needed to get some sleep. Being this close to Doggett makes me lonelier than usual. I'm okay as long as I'm doing something, but too much of this job is sitting around hotel rooms waiting. That's the worst.

The students start out kind of slowly, but soon enough, we've got them jumping in, yammering away, trying to snatch the microphone away from each other. A freckled, redheaded boy gives a moving account of how his father's convenience store gets tagged every couple weeks.

"My dad says that if he ever catches one of them, he's going to blast away with a shotgun." The boy looks at me seriously. "I'd rather have them out busting rocks than getting shot outside our Friendly Mart."

I'm admiring the quality of the sound bite when I catch Harper out of the corner of my eye. He's slapped himself in the forehead and slumped backward in his seat. Then I realize—Red wasn't using a microphone.

"Uh, Lydia, we didn't have that miked," I say.

The other students start razzing their lone white compatriot.

"Dude, you're making us look bad," says one of the boys.

"*Pendejo*," says another.

"Watch it, Jesús," warns the principal.

"Can't we just have him say it again?" I ask Lydia.

"Forget it," she says, "it's gone."

No one forgets to use the microphone after that. The rest of the interview goes well. I recognize several usable bites. I notice another crew—this one composed of students—has entered the classroom while we've been taping. Their camera is pointing at me. Lydia has Knobby shoot cutaways of me over the shoulders of the students. I do my best concerned nodding. When we're done, I sign autographs until a bell releases the students from school. I take the Reagan Raiders sweatshirt that one of the girls hands me and promise to wear it on-air someday soon.

The student camera crew continues to follow my every move.

I face away from them and whisper to Lydia, asking her why we couldn't have that boy repeat his sound bite.

"After the first time, it's not real," she answers at normal volume.

I want to ask her what she means by that, but I feel a tapping on my shoulder. I turn. Standing behind me holding a microphone is a boy with the worst case of acne I've ever seen. His zits come in two varieties. Ripe or scabbed. It's tough to see where the disorder ends and his lips begin. The condition spans his cheeks and continues to fester all the way down his neck before mercifully disappearing into the collar of his sweatshirt. I never had anything close to this. I catch myself feeling guilty. Guilty over my Accutane.

Am I staring at his face? Look in his eyes, Patrick.

"Patrick, I'm Christian Hanson. This is Eron, with the camera, and Seph, on sound. We were told we could have a few minutes of your time."

He doesn't give any sign that he caught me staring. Maybe he's used to it.

"Yeah, did you want to do the interview here?"

He says no. I'm led across campus to a portable building behind the gymnasium. Lydia doesn't come with us. She wants me to meet her back at the rental car when I'm done. Above the portable's door frame is a handmade sign that says THE CAVE-SHOOT OR DIE. I can't believe there are high schools with television news classes. We just got computers at D.H.S. last year.

Without waiting to be told what to do, Christian's underclassmen crew gets busy—Eron positioning lights on what passes for a set, and Seph hooking me up with a wireless. Their equipment all looks like secondhand Radio Shack gear that's been spliced and taped together. Eron asks me to sit in a chair, and Seph turns off the lights. A monitor is positioned back toward the stage, so I can see myself. Christian sits facing me.

"You ready," he says.

"Shoot," I say.

He's got a list of questions in his hand but doesn't refer to it.

"Give us your impressions of *Classroom Direct*," he says.

I have to think for a moment on that one.

"It wasn't quite what I expected," I say.

Christian orders an espresso and convinces me to order a caramel cappuccino. ("It's good if you're just starting out.") He has to repeat his order to the girl behind the counter because a jet roars over Flight Path Coffee Shop, sounding as if it has designs on landing on the roof.

"Gives the place atmosphere," he shouts at me. I nod.

Christian came by the Hilton and saved me from another night of TV movies. It was my idea. A few minutes into this afternoon's interview I had quit noticing what he looks like. He was so well prepared. He asked me questions about the difference between living in Doggett—"a town with a population under six thousand"—and living in Los Angeles. He wanted to know how much input reporters had in the content of the show. (I told him about my limestone stand-up.) He asked about the tutoring and the difficulty of missing out on my senior year. He didn't ask what any of the other anchors were "really like." He didn't ask about the hat. He didn't ask for my autograph.

When he came to pick me up, and we were walking out of the hotel lobby, we passed the concierge. She visibly blanched when she caught sight of Christian. He remained oblivious. The girl behind the counter here at Flight Path refers to Christian by name. He leans over to me again.

"That's kind of embarrassing. You know you don't have much of a social life when they know you by name at the late-night coffee shop."

I don't know what to say to that.

Chapter Five
LOS ANGELES, CALIFORNIA

IT'S PROBABLY JUST AS WELL THAT I HAD TO GET OFF the phone with Kate so soon. Calling from my apartment is expensive, and I have to pay for it. She said she and Zeb and Anderson were driving into Lubbock to go to the movies, but not before telling me she loved me and missed me, which was really all I was calling to hear anyway. I mean, I talk to her nearly every evening from the studio anyway. This is my fifth Saturday night here, and Saturdays in L.A. suck. There's just nothing for me to do except watch TV and feel sorry for myself. I flip through the channels and I catch the last few minutes of *Prairie Girl*. From what I can tell, Robin Ferris has been able to nurse a wounded wolf pup back to health, and she's forced to let it go in the end. Tears trickle down her cheeks as she tells the pup that "Ma and Pa's chickens are off-limits, you." How do my parents watch this?

I wander down the hall and knock on Shayla's door. I can hear her jam box from out in the hall, so I know she must be in. I knock louder. She opens the door, and I can see her schoolbooks all spread open in the middle of her floor.

"Patrick, wassup?"

"Wanna get something to eat, or maybe play some cards?"

"Sorry, I can't. They're sending me to Kansas City tomorrow, so I got to get my schoolwork done before I leave."

"You're boring," I tell her. She knows I'm kidding.

"Like Ethan Frome," she says.

I don't go back to my room. I head out the security gate and start walking west on Sunset. I'm a block away before it occurs to me that I should have worn a sweater. I keep going to spite myself. I hug myself as I walk to keep warm. I get to Vine and turn right. I pass newsstands that offer every sort of porno magazine you can imagine. I swear I see one called *Beastie*, but I'm afraid to look at what's on the cover. It's starting to get dark, but I don't want to go back to the apartment. When I reach Hollywood Boulevard, I keep heading west.

As I round the corner, I nearly run over a guy who's facing into a doorway of what looks like an out-of-business souvenir store. I can't figure out what he's doing until I see the stream flowing out onto the sidewalk. I cross to the other side of the street and begin walking faster. The exercise begins to warm me up. Within a few minutes I've reached the Walk of Fame, but I don't recognize half the names. I tromp over the Duran Duran star and it makes me wonder what the criteria are for making it on the walk. A double-decker tourist bus drives by. I look up at the faces pressed to the windows and wonder how many of them are thinking they could have gone skiing instead of this. I pass by Frederick's of Hollywood. The mannequins in the windows are dressed in red lace bras, see-through teddies, and crotchless panties. A couple wearing matching University of Wisconsin sweatshirts enter the store. By now I can see the lights of the El Capitan Theatre and Mann's Chinese Theater. I press on. I join the swarm of video camera–toting tourists who are wandering around the plaza in front of the Chinese Theater comparing their hand and shoe sizes with the stars'. It turns out that Jimmy Stewart is my closest match.

I continue up to Fairfax and cut back down to Sunset, but I keep heading toward the Pacific. I stop at a place called All America Hamburgers and get two large orders of fries. I dump them open in a bag, open a packet of salt into it, and shake the bag. It takes me five or six blocks to finish them off. I'm wiping my hands on my jeans when someone asks me if I'm lonely.

Two women—maybe they're girls—are standing in front of me, leaning on the back of a Plexiglas bus stop shelter. The one with the blond hair, red stretch pants, red spiked heels, and unzipped bomber jacket is doing the talking.

"Huh?" I say.

"Come here," she says, arching her body toward me, but still leaning back against the bus stop. I'm pretty sure she's a prostitute, but I'm not sure, and I don't want to look rude. I don't want to get mugged either.

"Don't be shy," she says. "Come here."

I'm unable to resist this order. I walk up to her. The other girl watches expressionlessly. Once I'm within arm's reach the blond girl reaches out and grabs me by the belt and pulls me close to her. I nearly fall into her, but I put my hands up on the Plexiglas to keep myself upright. My face is right next to hers, and I can smell her. She's covered in perfume, but I can distinguish cigarette smoke in her hair and her ripe body odor. She begins whispering in my ear and reaching in my pants.

"What's your name?" she asks.

I can't think fast enough to lie.

"Patrick."

"I think you like that, Patrick." She licks my ear. "In fact, I *know* you like that."

She's not pretty. Not especially. And I'm kind of grossed out, but I can't deny that what she's doing down there is starting to feel nice.

"Patrick, for fifty dollars I can take care of this little problem of yours. Excuse me—big problem." She eases her hand out of my pants and laughs at her own joke.

"Wait a minute," interjects the girl's friend. "I know you. You're that guy. You're on some TV show. God, I know I recognize you. Let me think."

But I don't let her think. I start sprint-walking up Sunset. Again, heading west. I know the ocean is out there somewhere. I walk for half an hour. Signs let me know I've entered West Hollywood. Billboards for all the latest movies line the street. I pass in front of The House of Blues and the Playboy office building. The billboard now looming in front of me shows two clean-cut men locked in a romantic embrace. It's an advertisement for health insurance that provides relief, ". . . in case one of you isn't there anymore." I stand at the base of the Hollywood Hills, which can be seen from Prentiss's office on clear days. I think of trying to find Earl's home and warming up. I know it's down here some-where, but I decide I don't want to see anyone. I should have told that prostitute to get her hands off me. I should have had the strength to just keep walking. What would Kate have thought of my performance? Did that other girl really recognize me? That would mean she's in high school. Jesus.

Without warning I throw up a stomachful of french fries. Two Hispanic men holding hands sidestep the sidewalk in front of me. I use the toe of my shoe to try to sweep the vomit into the gutter. I swear I can smell the ocean. I know it's out there somewhere. I keep going.

I go in Book Soup because the door is open, and it looks warm. The spectacled clerk behind the cash register looks me over dispar-agingly before returning to his magazine. In the humor section, I pick up a paperback called *How Texans Talk*. It defines words like: *all: 1. n. a fuel pumped from the ground used in automobiles. "Have y'all seen mah all field?"; 2. contraction representing the first-person future. "All tell mah waff y'all need hep."* I set it down and walk through the shoplifting detectors on my way out. I jog across the street and go into the giant Tower Records. The only place I've ever bought music has been at the Doggett Wal-Mart. This place is like a fantasy land. I wander over to the Spanish music section and find David's CDs. He's shirtless on the covers of all three. His abs look like they've been chiseled, and his hairless chest shines. I have to get out of here.

It occurs to me that I've been walking for hours. I look at my wrist, but then I remember that I'm wearing one of my "outfits." I dig out my pocket watch. It's ten thirty. In Texas it's twelve thirty. There's no way I can call Kate this late. I've been walking for three hours. I stand in the light supplied by the massive Tower Records sign and shiver. The sweat on my shirt is no longer warm, and I'm colder than I've been. Across the street a green neon sign catches my attention, and I walk toward it. There's a line of people standing in front. Loud rock music leaks out from the club. I recognize the place from MTV News. I'm standing in front of The Viper Room.

Every time a group comes out of the club, the doorman lets in an equal number, but twice while I'm watching, limousines pull up and the passengers are ushered in. As I get closer to the door, I see the vases of flowers that people have left there. They look fresh. Are people still mourning for River Phoenix? Does the club set them out here? Eventually I reach the front. The doorman looks at me, shakes his head, and asks to see my I.D.

"I'm eighteen," I say.

"You're out of luck, then," he says, "though I have to say I admire your honesty."

"I'm on television," I say.

"I own a television," says the doorman. He waves in the two people behind me. I stay where I am.

"You might want to think about going home," he says, not in an unfriendly way. It just sounds like advice.

"It's all I think about," I tell him.

I wave down the next taxi. I've got plenty of vouchers.

*   *   *

For the first time since arriving in Los Angeles, I make it to church. I've lied to Mama when she's asked me about it. That's one of the things I'll be talking to my new priest about this morning. There'll be a full menu of sins, actually. St. Mary's is within walking distance of The Sunset Villas, but I take a cab anyway. There is one sitting outside the apartments; I really don't feel like doing any more walking. I get dropped off in front of the church, and I'm forced to make my way through a gauntlet of street people who apparently do good business in front of the churches on Sunday morning. I give a pocketful of change to the first old man who approaches me, but that makes me the object of a feeding frenzy. Three or four beggars block my progress up the church steps. I take out my wallet and find I have twenty-three dollars. I pull the ones out and hand them to the first three bums. The first two say, "God bless you," but the third one just snatches the bill from my hand and runs after another mark. I'm left with a twenty-dollar bill and one remaining wretch stooped over with his hand out.

He looks down into my wallet, then up at me. "I can make change," he says.

By making change, he means he can give me sixteen dollars back for my twenty, but I don't realize this until the deal is almost complete. Live and learn.

The church is huge, but we get more people to Immaculate Conception back in Doggett than they get here. People are spread out everywhere. I would guess that no one sits within twenty feet of anyone else. If we wanted, we could all fit in the first two rows, and the priest wouldn't have to use the microphone. I'm the youngest one in the crowd. In fact, I might be the only one under forty in the building. Mostly it's old women. The priest leads us through all the same rituals we go through back home. Somehow making these same responses to the priest's words is comforting to me. The service is short, which would not sit well with Roman. He typically equates the length of a sermon with its quality. Papa will rave about Father Madigan's lecture if it's caused him to doze through part of it. After it's over I camp out next to the confessional and wait for a priest to make his way over. When I see one walking this direction, I take a seat in the confessional. I don't want him getting a good look at me. I'm thinking this might be one of the advantages to living in a big city. The odds aren't very good I'll run into my priest four or five times a week like I tend to with Father Madigan.

I hear the door outside open, then the panel slides across and I hear the voice of the priest. "Have you sins to confess?"

"Bless me, Father, for I have sinned. It's been six weeks since my last confession."

"Go on."

"I looked at myself in the mirror for an hour."

There is a long pause before I get a response. "Were you getting ready for something important?"

"No," I say. "I wanted to know if I was handsome."

"What did you decide?"

This is the hard part. I know it's not a sin to look at yourself in the mirror.

"I decided I was."

*   *   *

Because *Classroom Direct* airs Mondays through Fridays, that means we tape shows on Sundays through Thursdays. It also means that I have to make it into the offices on Sundays, and since I have class on Fridays, I really only have one day a week off. I'm fine with that. I find a cab outside the church after I say my required Hail Marys and Our Fathers.

Sundays are kind of fun around the office. None of the normal Monday through Friday people are here. The business department, the school relations department, the personnel department, and the travel department all fit that category. That leaves just the editorial staff, who are less inclined to display any sort of corporate dignity. Today's show meeting is delayed by a spit wad fight between the talent and the news producers. It subsides when Mr. Scott walks in the room, but as soon as the lights go off and the show begins to run, I get nailed with a nasty hunk of wet tissue. I hear giggling from the back of the room, coming from where Billy Trundle and another producer are sitting. When I turn around to look, I see Billy slide his hand across his crony's palm. The other producer is just back from the Middle East. It's rumored that Lane Tauber, who returned with the producer, will make an appearance in the office soon.

Naturally I swear vengeance, but my desire to watch the show forces me to put it off. I'm anchoring with Earl, and I can tell that I'm starting to do better. Lydia spent hours with me last week. At first she just had me read scripts to her. Then, when she thought I was sounding decent, she took me down to the studio and taped me. Then we'd watch my performance, and she'd give me more pointers. One of the best things that came out of the sessions was that I found myself getting bored in front of the cameras when we taped. Bored is a lot better than nervous and sweaty. When I told Lydia this theory, she told me not to get *too* bored. Once again they required me to say, "Thanks for listening, y'all," at the end of the show. After I say it, Earl looks into the camera, waits a beat, and adds, "Yeah—what he said." The staff room falls apart, and a fresh new barrage of spit wads rains down on the talent.

Since I'm not anchoring today, I'm not really required to do anything else. They tell the anchors that they want us to keep normal hours, but as little as I see most of them, I know that's not a commandment written in stone. As I walk into the talent office, I see a reimbursement voucher on David's desk. It catches my eye because my name is on it. When I look closer, I realize that's he's putting in for the cost of the tickets and "refreshments" at the Lakers game. In the column labeled CAUSE FOR REIMBURSEMENT, David's penciled in, "entertaining student reporter per memo of 1/15."

I sit down at my desk and find a box sitting on top of it with my name on it. I pry it open with my thumbnail. Inside are a hundred photos of me. They took half with me in my hat and half with me without the hat. Naturally, they chose one in which I'm wearing it. I take one out and stare at it. It's a head shot, but they took it in front of the video wall, so behind me the *Classroom Direct* logo is blazing away, in all its glory. I'm smiling, and I take note again of how monumentally wide my smile is. I'm showing all my teeth. Maybe even some other people's teeth. I pull a big envelope from my desk (Libby let me raid the supply closet), and I stick a photo in it to send to Kate, signing it, "To my good friend, Kate—Tex Sheridan." Then I call Zeb. I tell him everything about my walk.

"She stuck her hand in your pants?" he says after I finish the story.

"Yep."

"She touched it?"

"Uh-huh."

"Was she pretty?"

"She was all right."

Zeb doesn't say anything for a long time. "You can't catch anything from that, can you?"

I hadn't actually thought of this, but I tell him I'm pretty sure you can't. After he's digested all of that, we get to the stuff I'm really interested in—Doggett gossip. The basketball team is winless, but that's not unusual. Even though Doggett's tiny, Coach Woodacre won't let any of his football players play basketball because they'll lose weight. I learn that the guy Kate dated when she was a sophomore, Blaine Mathews, flunked out of SMU and has been spotted at the Dairy Queen. This gives me some reason to be nervous as Blaine never really quit calling Kate after he dumped her. Zeb saves the biggest news for last: Anderson has found himself a girlfriend.

"You won't believe who it is," he taunts.

"I give," I say without even thinking about it. If she walks upright and is warm-blooded, I'm going to be in a state of shock.

"Laurie Wilcox!"

"No fucking way!" I say, and I fall off my chair, laughing. Laurie Wilcox is nearly six feet tall. She's the star of our girls basketball team, and she's never dated anyone either. I try to picture the two of them kissing, but the thought makes me laugh harder.

"Do you eat out of that same mouth you talk with?" says Zeb, doing a nearly perfect impression of my father.

"Blow me," I say.

After we hang up, I pull my fan letters out of my desk drawer. I'm up to four. All from girls. I write a small note to each of them, thanking them for their letters. Then I sign a photo—for grins, I sign them "XXXOOO, Patrick"—and stick them in with the notes. I feel like a goof. I'm sealing the last one when Lane Tauber enters the room. He doesn't acknowledge me. He sits down at a completely barren desk, lights up a cigarette, and starts breezing through the headlines on one of the computer terminals.

I take Zeb's autograph book out of my desk and roll my seat over to the desk where Lane's sitting.

"Excuse me, would you mind signing this for a friend of mine?"

Lane doesn't respond. His eyes just keep scanning the screen. I watch for a moment, wondering if he heard me. When he gets to the bottom of the story, he asks me who I am.

"I'm Patrick Sheridan. I'm one of the student . . ." For the first time that I can ever remember, I'm embarrassed to call myself a reporter. "I'm one of the students who's on-air."

Lane takes the book from my hand and signs it. He hands it back to me and leaves the room without saying another word. When I'm sure he won't come back into the room anytime soon, I stab his cigarette out and open Zeb's book to the last page. There he's written, "Patrick, never ask a colleague for his autograph— Lane Tauber."

The story he was so intently reading is still on the screen. I scroll up to the top before realizing it isn't a story at all. He's been studying the latest stock market figures.

Chapter Six
SANDYMOUND, OHIO

THERE AREN'T ANY DECENT HOTELS IN SANDYmound, Ohio. At least that's the assessment of Cal Sherman, the producer who's in charge of the story we're doing on Sandymound High's renowned dance squad. They've won national championships six straight years. We're at the Youngstown Airport with our crew, waiting for the squad to return from a six-day tour of Japan, where they danced for the prime minister. Cal's acting pissy because he was kept awake by a snorer one room over at Snooze Village. The plane has been delayed, and I've taken the liberty of jotting down some questions. I don't think he's going to mind. Mr. Scott brought Cal with him from MTV, and from what Libby says, he was added to the staff to give the show "flash." Libby made quote marks with her fingers when she told me to indicate that "flash" was Mr. Scott's word. I told her I would have known that without the visual.

"The visual?" she said, shaking her head. "You are learning quick."

I asked her if Cal was short for Calvin, and she laughed and said, "No, California." She thought that was very funny. Anyway,

Libby explained that Cal was generally given the stories where the use of music and a million cuts, bizarre camera angles, and random handheld photography was appropriate—"Anything with the news impact equal to or less than that of a new panda being born in captivity," she said. It turns out it was Cal who was sent to Washington in a crunch and subsequently turned in the piece with the misidentified senator in it.

"He doesn't get sent there anymore," Libby said.

Stu Chestnut told me I'd have fun working with Cal. "He doesn't sweat the small stuff." That's evident. He's now got the top six scores on the Mortal Kombat game, and he's working on number seven. I ask him if he minds if I write a stand-up for the story.

"Knock yourself out," he says.

I read through the information packet that the school relations department put together for us. It says that the squad has performed in Moscow and Toronto the past two years. Tonight they're performing at halftime of the Sandymound High boys basketball game. I jot down a couple ideas and walk down to the Sky High Lounge, where our crew has parked themselves in front of ESPN. I get their attention from the "Minors OK" side of a barricade of plastic ferns.

"Hey, y'all. Cal wanted me to do a couple stand-ups from down by the gate."

They don't exactly pull muscles getting off their butts, but after throwing a couple bills down on the table, they gather their equipment and follow me down to the gate where the girls are supposed to arrive in forty-five minutes. My idea is to set up a shot of the bleary-eyed girls slogging off the plane, then to cut to a shot of them wearing those giant dance team smiles as they dance tonight.

"Stick or wireless?" asks the soundman.

"Stick," I say. He hands me the microphone, and I slide a *Classroom Direct* mic flag on it. "Cal said to start with a wide-shot that shows all of the parents waiting around, then, as I walk toward the camera, close down to a one-shot."

"Should we get Cal?" asks the cameraman.

"He's busy," I say.

It takes us five times to get the shot I want, but it's not my fault. All the parents started turning around and watching the camera, so instead of the "anxious family members" I mentioned in the stand-up, we kept ending up with what would have been more accurately described as "gawking yokels." Finally they get bored with me repeating myself, and they return to staring out the giant window behind me. I watch the replay in the monitor. As it begins, the shot captures the bored parents staring out toward the runway. I walk up the gangway and begin speaking.

"Seventeen hours. That's how long the Sandymound Rangerettes will have been on the plane that's just minutes away from landing here in Youngstown, Ohio. Anxious family members have been waiting for the girls, who will have very little time to recuperate. Tonight they're back in action."

"That looks like a keeper," says the soundman.

"Here's Cal. Let's ask him," suggests the cameraman.

"Ask him what?" says Cal.

The cameraman rewinds the last take and shows Cal.

"What the hell is this?" Cal looks at me.

"You said to knock myself out." I tell him about my idea for cutting from the tired girls to the shots of them dancing later. "What do you think?"

"Well, that's one approach," he says. "It's kind of, I don't know, local newsy."

Around *Classroom Direct*, the worst thing you say about anyone's piece is that it reminds you of local news. I suck on my bottom lip and shake my head. Papa always says he wants to take me out to the woodshed when I do that, for what he says he knows is going through my head.

"Come on now, Patrick. I didn't say it was bad. Just a bit traditional. Maybe we can work it into the piece somehow."

"I'm fine, Cal. Really."

"Good. Okay, then. Gentlemen. Let me tell you what I want."

After the basketball game, I'm back at Snooze Village, and I'm on the phone to Kate. I'm telling her how cool this story is that we're going to break.

"I started out interviewing these girls, asking them all these softball questions Cal had written for me. You know, 'What did you do in Japan? Did you like the food?' Yadda Yadda Yadda."

"'Yadda Yadda Yadda'?"

"It's something they say out here. It's what you say instead of saying something long and boring. So anyway. Where was I?"

"You were asking them about softball."

"No. Softball questions—that means they were easy questions."

"Gotcha."

"Yeah. And I was getting all these predictable sound bites—'It was expensive'; 'It was crowded'; 'Everything was so small.' Then this one girl just blurts out, 'It was a blast until we got busted.' Can you believe it? It turns out that sixteen of the girls were arrested in this department store in Tokyo for shoplifting."

"What happened then?" Kate says, starting to sound interested.

"The shit hit the fan. Some of the girls started crying. They talked about how embarrassing it was. You know what? The Japanese authorities took their passport numbers, and those girls aren't allowed back in Japan for ten years. They told them that."

"I really miss you, Patrick."

"I miss you too. You should have seen them dance, though. I swear they were as good as the Laker Girls."

"When did you see the Laker Girls?"

"Oh, I didn't tell you about that?"

"No."

That's when the knock on the door comes. I tell Kate to hold on a minute. I figure it's Cal wanting to run through a script with me, but it's not. It's three of the girls I interviewed this afternoon—Sabrina, Tandy, and I can't remember the last one's name. They're standing outside my room, and when I open the door none of them say anything. They just start giggling. Finally the one whose name I can't recall catches her breath enough to speak.

"Howdy," she says. Then they practically fall down from laughing. They're carrying a twelve-pack of Budweiser, but I'm pretty sure they must already be drunk.

"Just a sec," I tell them, and I run back to the phone, fearing the worst. There's already a dial tone. Kate's hung up. I turn around, and the girls have invaded my room. As if I needed another cause for distress, Sabrina is entering my bathroom. She comes out without delay, carrying one of the sanitized glasses provided by Snooze Village. I start dialing Kate's number as the girl with the glass opens a tab on a can of beer. I make the *ssshhhhhh* sound and hold my index finger in front of my mouth. The girls quiet down, but it doesn't matter: Kate's taken the phone off the hook. Her family has Call Waiting. I shouldn't get a busy signal.

"Oh, my God! There it is!"

Tandy, a tall, dark-haired girl with the largest breasts I've ever seen on a skinny girl, points to the TV. But it's not the TV that's caught her attention. It's my hat sitting on top of it. She walks toward it as if she's discovered the Ark of the Covenant. When she reaches it, she doesn't put it on like I expect her to. Using both hands, she lifts it gently by the brim, walks over toward the bed, and places it down on my head.

"It's really you," she says.

At first I think she's saying that the hat looks right for me, but there's something creepy about the way it came out of her mouth. It was almost like she thought I wasn't me unless I was wearing the thing.

"It's really not," I say, but I leave the hat on anyway. It seems to make her happy. "So, wassup?"

"Nothing's ever up in Sandymound," says the girl whose name I still can't remember, though I'm starting to think it started with a K. Or maybe that's the whole thing—Kay.

"That's why we're here bugging you," says Sabrina. "Any good at quarters?"

"I've never played."

They start laughing like I've just made a joke. Then Sabrina speaks. "We'll go easy on you, then. Come on."

In my head I know I should ask them to leave, but I don't really want them to. I'm tired of not being around people my age, so I hesitate. That's when Tandy reaches down and takes my hand. She leads me over to the little table by the window, where Sabrina and K? are already sitting.

"Usual rules?" says Sabrina, who appears to be the leader.

Tandy and K? offer "Uh-huhs."

"What were those rules again?" I ask.

"Listen to how he says 'Uh-gih-yin,'" says Tandy. "It's just like on TV."

Sabrina ignores Tandy's observation. "'One in' means you can make anyone drink. If you call 'Dare,' you have to get three in a row or you drink. If you get all three"—Sabrina slides beers in front of each one of us—"you can dare anyone to do anything."

"Within reason," says K?.

"Patrick should go first," says Tandy. She places a quarter in my palm. I look at the beer in front of me, then around at the three fine girls, the sort of girls who would have never been interested in me in Doggett. Then I bounce the quarter into the grill of the air-conditioning unit.

"No one plays this in Texas," I lie.

Sabrina regards me suspiciously, but Tandy's got a new quarter out of her pocket almost immediately. She bounces it expertly into the short glass. "Drink, Patrick," she orders. This doesn't come as a surprise.

I lift my Budweiser, hold my breath, and take a few swallows. The aftertaste makes me want to gag. Something I didn't know about playing quarters—it's make it take it. Tandy keeps going. Four times in a row she sinks the quarter, and each time she indicates that I have to drink. I'm halfway through my first beer before she misses. I give up trying to hold my breath. It's nasty stuff, but it's not unbearable.

"Kayla's up. You're safe," says Sabrina. I register the third girl's name, relieved. Defying her reputation, Kayla manages to rattle in the quarter by rolling it down the bridge of her nose. Miraculously, she gives me a break.

"Drink, bitch," she says to Sabrina, who complies, but the nose trick works only once, and Sabrina's finally up.

"First," she says, "payback." She bounces in the quarter and points at Kayla. "Now, this gets fun. Dare." Kayla and Tandy both groan. With robotic efficiency, Sabrina sinks three in a row.

"I think Patrick ought to shotgun a beer. He's too far behind us tonight."

I've seen this done, but I've never attempted it myself. It's always looked impossible to me. I watch in fear as Sabrina digs a fresh Bud out of the twelve-pack. She lays the can flat and uses one of her keys to punch a hole in the side. Then she presents it to me.

"Tell me you know how to do *this*," mocks Sabrina.

I shake my head. I feel Tandy's hand on my knee. Sabrina

explains. "Cover the hole with your mouth. Tilt your head back and let it rip."

So I do. Beer rushes in my mouth and I try to swallow, only I can't do it fast enough. Budweiser starts erupting out of my nose and the corners of my lips. I cough and hack, but what I'm surprised to find is that within a few seconds the can is empty. And I'm dizzy. And I want to throw up. I burp, and I can taste the beer that worms up the back of my throat. Sabrina grins and calls Dare again. She drains her first two shots before rimming out the third. She drinks without having to be told to, then forks over the quarter. This time my shot fails to gain any altitude, and the quarter slides harmlessly into the side of the glass.

During the course of the next round, Tandy makes me drink twice before she misses. Kayla isn't able to get her nose trick to work, and Sabrina calls Dare. The three tosses seem automatic. I prepare myself to shotgun another beer.

"Tandy," she says, rubbing her palms together and grinning slyly. "Kiss Patrick."

I expect to get a quick peck on my cheek or for Tandy to get embarrassed and protest. Instead, Tandy takes my chin in her hand, spins my head toward her, and leads with her tongue. Her forehead bumps into my hat and knocks it off the back of my head, but that doesn't stop her. Everything's moving in super slo-mo. Her breath smells like beer. Her lips connect, and I can taste the vanilla of her lip balm. Over the top of her head I watch as Sabrina leans over and whispers something to Kayla. I'm aware of Tandy's wonder-breasts bulldozing into my arm. It seems like I can't think quickly enough to do anything to stop her. Her tongue pries apart my lips and begins investigating rumors of a similar appendage inhabiting my mouth. *Then* Tandy pulls back. *Then* she acts like she's embarrassed.

"God," she says, putting her face in one hand. "I can't believe I did that."

But her other hand is still on my leg.

Things go downhill from there. Sabrina chooses Dare again, and I end up shotgunning another beer. I've now downed three, but it's been less than fifteen minutes since we've started. The girls keep taking unprompted gulps from their own cans. The highlight for me comes when I'm able to bounce one in. I make Kayla drink, primarily because I think she's the one least capable of wreaking vengeance on me. Later, Tandy completes a trifecta and dares Sabrina to show me her tattoo. Which she does. It's a small and otherwise unremarkable butterfly. Location, in this case, though, is key, and to exhibit it for me, she's forced to stand up, turn around, undo her belt and drop her Guess? jeans a good six inches. I'm staring right at the top half of one of her butt cheeks, wondering why I can't just turn my head.

"She could get thrown out of dance team if our sponsor ever found out," Kayla says. She's looking at the tattoo with what I consider a little too much admiration.

"Miss Richter is a Nazi," says Sabrina as she rebuckles her belt.

"Are all of those girls who got caught in Japan going to get kicked off the squad?" I ask. I realize that I don't remember if any of these girls were in the shoplifting group. I interviewed them before the big confessional. For a moment it occurs to me that they could be coming here to ask me not to run the story. They're in for disappointment if that's the case.

"Probably not," says Sabrina. "Two of the girls were officers, and besides, Miss Richter would have to answer why she wasn't 'supervising' us in the department store. They treat her like she's God around here. She's not going to give anyone the impression that she's not. She actually said something about how not being able to go back to Japan would teach us a lesson.

"Let's see"—Sabrina holds up two hands like they're scales—"Japan." Her right hand sinks. "Hawaii." Her left hand elevates above her head.

"Some lesson."

Fortunately, the more we drink, the less accurate Sabrina and Tandy become. It's when we're down to our final Bud that Sabrina is able to get three in a row to fall. She tells me I have to kiss Tandy. I'm vaguely aware that I'm responsible for drinking at least half of the twelve-pack, but it's an awareness that seems very removed from anything I'm saying or doing. I lean across the table to kiss Tandy, knocking over my empty Bud can as I do. Tandy leans in as well, and I'm determined that this kiss is going to be as passionless as aunt kissing. We bump foreheads and then just settle for leaning our heads against each other's. I pucker my lips and press them against Tandy's.

Simple.

But I stay there. More of my weight seems transferred to my skull. We're like two Leaning Towers of Pisa, reliant on each other to keep upright. I pucker, and we kiss again. This time our lips remain there, resting on each other's. I can feel the heat of her breath and, for a moment, I'm able to place Kate's face on top of Tandy's. I open my mouth and invite her inside.

I'm only remotely aware of the door opening and Sabrina and Kayla exiting. Before I know it, I'm on top of Tandy on the bed and my hand is up her shirt. But as my hands glide over the Grand Tetons, even with my eyes closed, I'm unable to keep Kate's image locked in place. Back when I went through confirmation, Father Madigan handed me a book of saints for me to pick out a patron saint. I remember reading this story about Saint Maria Goretti, this Italian teenager, who died rather than have premarital sex. I could use her help. I ended up picking Saint Thomas the apostle, because Mama's father, who I never met, was named Thomas. It made Mama cry. At the time I was pretty proud of myself, but right now it's not seeming like the wisest of choices.

"Just a second," Tandy says, and I'm hoping she's going to call an end to this nonsense. "I've got to go to the bathroom. I'll be right back. Don't move," she says, and taps me on the nose. She stands, then leans back down and kisses me. "You are so beautiful," she adds.

When she's locked herself in the next room, I start praying. I start off with a few *lead me not into temptations*, but I decide it's too late for that, so I switch to a mental chant of *deliver me from evils*. I know I'm not sober. I'm drunk for the first time ever, and I'm glad about it. I don't think I could deal with myself sober. But then again, would I have gotten into this position if I were? I did *start* the evening with all my senses. Now everything seems pleasantly unclear. I'm not so sure about what's right and what's wrong. If I could just stay here . . .

The toilet flushes, and I hear the sink being turned on. In a moment, Tandy someone—I don't even know her last name—is going to come out here and crawl into bed with me. Tandy—what kind of name is that? I'll bet she spells it with an *i* at the end. Kate would laugh about that. No she wouldn't. Kate wouldn't laugh about any of this. What makes Tandy agreeable to my molesting her, running my hands all over that amazing body of hers? She doesn't know anything about me. She wouldn't know it would be my first time. I wonder if she's willing to go that far? Three months. A bit less, even. That's how long I have to wait for Kate. And that will be perfect.

The bathroom door opens, and footsteps pad up to the bed, but I've got my eyes closed and my breathing is heavy, bordering on a snore.

Deliver me from evil . . . Deliver me from evil . . .

My head hurts. Bad.

And my tongue's dried out. I want to swallow, get this taste out of my mouth, but I can't gather the saliva necessary. Water. I must have water. But I try to move my head, and it pounds. I can't even think about opening my eyes. Maybe I am dead.

"Patrick?"

Whose voice is that? Who's speaking to me? Where am I?

"Patrick, someone's knocking on the door."

Now I'm aware of that sound. I thought it was internal. My head is covered with a pillow. I squeeze it around my skull, which seems like nothing more than a watermelon-sized pain receptor. Using any of my senses results in suffering. If I'm not dead, it's a state that's holding some appeal to me. The knocking becomes louder.

"Patrick. The door."

Someone's shaking my shoulder. A girl's voice. It's coming back to me slowly. Details of last night. Talking to Kate. Then a knock. Jesus. There's a girl in bed with me. I pull the pillow off my head. Sweet Jesus.

I look at her. She's in my cowboy-cut, rhinestone-studded button-down. I hope she's got underwear on down there. In daylight, with all her makeup off, she looks sort of scary. I do a quick inventory of the clothes I'm wearing. White T-shirt. Wranglers— yes! Wait a minute. I don't remember taking off my boots, but they're not on me. It hurts too much to try to remember last night. The knock on the door has turned to pounding. I recognize Cal's voice coming from behind it.

"Yoo-hoo, Patrick," he sings. "We have a plane to catch."

Shit.

I sit up and try to ignore the pain. I struggle to the door and turn the handle. Cal's been leaning on it, so he practically falls into the room. He catches his balance, then takes in the room, as well as my guest. Beer cans are spread out across the floor, and sundry articles of girl's clothing, including a black bra, are draped over the chairs.

"Well, well, well . . . ," he says, a massive grin blooming across his face.

The room is uncomfortably silent for what seems like a long time to me.

"Cal, this is . . ." Then I go blank. I just stand there with my mouth open. "Uh, uh, uh—"

"Tandy," she says. She gives me an evil look, and she doesn't get off the bed to shake Cal's hand.

"You kids today," Cal says, not helping matters any. "I hate to break up this interlude, but we're on the nine-twenty to Chicago. I don't think you've even got time left to shower. I'll meet you at the car in ten minutes."

I nod and Cal exits. I turn back toward Tandy and try to apologize. "I'm sorry. I knew your name. I'm just having trouble thinking this morning."

But Tandy sneers, then rolls over and picks up the telephone. The movement causes my shirt to hike way up. Her legs just keep going and going. She asks Sabrina to come pick her up. I hear her say, "Nothing to tell," but I'm still staring at her body. I can't seem to help myself.

I thought I felt bad when I woke up in the motel room. Now that I'm at twenty thousand feet, all my symptoms have worsened exponentially. Cal asks me about what went on last night, more like he's jealous than angry. I just groan.

"That sweet thing you had in your room this morning had quite a set on her. Yes, sir," he says. "Quite a set."

I scramble to pull the airsickness bag out of the pouch in front of me. Then I fill it.

Chapter Seven
LOS ANGELES, CALIFORNIA

BY THE NEXT DAY AT THE OFFICE, MY LEGEND HAS grown. No. I should say my legend has begun. Billy Trundle applauds and whistles through his fingers when I walk into the newsroom during our tutoring break.

"Ladies and gentlemen: Patrick Sheridan, television star."

A few of the producers slap me on the back. Billy holds out his hands like he wants skin. I give it to him; it's easier and more believable than telling him nothing happened. Behind him Lydia isn't even looking up from her computer screen. I know she's heard all of this, but I doubt she's quite as impressed as her peers. In what's left of my break, I check my mailbox. It's stuffed. There must be fifteen letters. What's more, the box has been garnished with an assortment of condoms. Everyone here must have participated, because they're all different brands. I hear giggling, and I look up and catch Billy, David, and Cal peeking around the corner. They succumb to hysterics. I flip them off, which only makes them laugh harder.

I take the stack of stuff from my box and haul it off to my desk. The fan mail I throw into the big bottom drawer. I'm probably fifty letters behind in answering it. I notice one piece in there that doesn't look like an envelope. It's not; it's a pamphlet: *Preventing AIDS*.

Very funny.

I catch more hell at the show meeting. I try to decipher the look Mr. Scott gives me. Why is it that he can appear so much younger than most of the staff and act like he's twenty years older? The legend of Mr. Scott as told to me by Libby goes something like this: He was born in West Virginia, the youngest of seven children. His father worked in the coal mines, and the family lived in a shack.

"No running water, I'll bet," I said.

"Just a shovel that he would draw on with little lumps of coal," responded Libby with equal skepticism.

"Isn't Prentiss sort of a weird name for a coal miner's son?" I asked Libby.

"Now there's an example of good journalistic instinct," she said. "Prentiss isn't his real name. At least, it's not the one he was born with. His real name is Hank P. Scott. Originally the *P* didn't stand for anything. All the boys in his family took that letter as their middle name. When Prentiss started campaigning to get into USC, he decided that Hank was too much of a working-class name, so he changed it to H. Prentiss Scott."

Little Prentiss was twelve before he saw his first television show, but he knew instantly that this was his life's work. The next part, Libby said, sounds a little far-fetched, but the press materials claim that he built his own TV.

"Someone probably gave him a broken set, and he replaced a

tube or something," said Libby. "Otherwise you'd think he'd at least be able to work the coffee machine."

Anyway, he knew that if TV was going to be his life, he was going to have to be in Los Angeles. He began writing to the USC department of television and film weekly. He began a campaign to get himself accepted, over which the faculty still marvels. Weekly, he sent them treatments for sitcom pilots, sample scripts, budgetary memos concerning his proposed shows. He would clip items from any newspapers he could get his hands on that he thought would make "doable" movies of the week.

He got in, but he stayed there only for three years. His internship at ABC, which originally consisted of seating studio audiences and sorting mail, became full-time after one of his superiors recalled a note from Prentiss suggesting developing a sitcom around middling comedian Jerry Seinfeld. The executive brought him into his inner staff two years later after *Seinfeld* reached number one for NBC. Seven months later twenty-two-year-old Prentiss Scott was the executive producer of *Sunset & Vaughn*, a drama centered on a cowboy wanna-be white cop and his urban black partner. It lasted less than half a season, but what it lacked in substance it equally lacked in restraint. The music was louder, the clothes flashier, the lingo hipper than anything else seen on TV. Mr. Scott was out of a job for less than a week. MTV needed a savior.

As the executive vice president there, he revamped the network. He relegated heavy metal to a late-night ghetto. He fired every VJ older than himself. He brought in more nonvideo programs: *The Real World, Beavis and Butt-Head, Singled Out, The Week in Rock.*

He was quoted in *Rolling Stone* as saying, "The new MTV doesn't really need bands."

But he wasn't The Man, the executive producer, and Mr. Scott had ambition. That's why, when he was approached by *Classroom Direct* with an offer that would guarantee him final say on all editorial decisions and a seven-figure salary, he bit. That's one of the funny things about these meetings. They're run almost as if the show were a democracy. Everyone jumps in with their opinions, but I don't think I've ever seen anyone change Mr. Scott's mind.

The show starts without him making any sort of comment to me. I'm relieved until I see the cold open. A cold open is when we start out with highlights of what we'll be covering later on in the show. Today we're taking a look at the U.S. deficit reaching an all-time high, a train wreck that killed seven in Arizona, and Sandymound, Ohio's, award-winning dance team. But how is that possible? I haven't cut a voice-over for the story. I haven't even seen a script yet. Usually with feature stories, unless there's really a timeliness peg, no one busts their asses to get them on-air. Cal is sitting behind me. I turn in my seat and try to get his attention, but he pretends not to see me. He keeps his eyes on the screen.

I squirm my way through the first two stories and commercials from Noxzema, the Army, and the new Robin Ferris movie. The dance team piece lives up to my worst fears. Not only is there no voice-over from me, there's not even a stand-up, despite the fact we taped a couple during the basketball game performance. Not to mention the one I wrote at the airport. It's not like I don't appear in the story though. Nope, there's shots of me yukking it up with the locals in the stands at the game, stuffing a hot dog in my mouth, signing autographs, teaching one of the dance team girls how to two-step. It's mixed in with a montage of shots of girls dancing, girls walking off the plane, girls trying on my hat. Cal's set it all to the music of a song that the girls weren't even dancing to. The beats match, but I'm not sure they're going to appreciate our switching them from that "We Go Together" song from *Grease* to the Nine Inch Nails song Cal chose. Stu Chestnut and Shayla are anchoring, and I hold out some hope for a mention of the girls shoplifting in Japan in the tag. But that turns out to be wishful thinking. As they speak, I visualize the teleprompter scrolling through the words.

> Stu: IT LOOKS LIKE PATRICK HAD A GREAT TIME. HAVE YOU EVER SEEN DANCING LIKE THAT?
> Shayla: (HORRIFIED) LIKE PATRICK'S?
> Stu: (LAUGH) LIKE THOSE GIRLS'.
> Shayla: THEY HAD IT GOIN' ON.
> Stu: BUT WE'VE GOT TO BE GOING OFF. SEE YA TOMORROW!
> Shayla: LATER.

"Comments anyone?" says Mr. Scott.

"It sucked." I don't really think before I say it. I feel the people in the room swivel to stare at me.

Mr. Scott scratches behind his ear with a ring finger. He looks right at me when he speaks. "Care to elaborate, Patrick?"

"Well, I just don't see why I even went on the trip. There's no reporting in it. It's just a video. Do we really need a shot of me eating a hot dog? Where's the news in that? I also think it's dishonest to change the music. And, the worst thing about it is that when we were there we found out that a bunch of the girls were arrested for shoplifting when they were in Japan. We don't even mention it. The whole thing just sucked."

"Tell us how you really feel. Don't hold back," says Billy Trundle.

"Patrick, the story was on this amazing dance team. We weren't there to blow the lid off the Ugly American syndrome." Mr. Scott laughs dismissively. "I remember some of the crazy things we used to do on field trips when I was a debater. I must have hotel towels from every hotel on the East Coast."

Lydia comes to my rescue. "But these girls were arrested in a foreign country while representing the USA. There's a big difference between that and—"

"Additionally, I *loved* the way Cal established the reporter presence in the story. It showed panache," Mr. Scott said, cutting off Lydia.

"What does that mean?" I ask. "'Established the reporter presence'?"

"It means that we've won the war simply by getting our talent out on location. It's not always important what we do with them as long as people get the sense they're involved."

The way Mr. Scott uses the third person when you're right in front of him gets on my nerves.

"Just think of yourself as being part of the royal family," Lydia says sarcastically. "At least we're not sending you out to cut ribbons at shopping malls. Right, Prentiss? I mean, we're not, are we?"

I'm thinking Lydia might be pushing her luck, but Mr. Scott ignores her.

"Look. This story accomplished its mission. We've always said that we're going to run pieces on exceptional programs at exceptional schools when we have slow news days. It keeps our subscribers happy. It keeps the kids' attention. Cal, do you have anything to add?"

"Only that I tried to call Patrick three times last night when I was cutting the story, but the phone was always busy. I assumed it was off the hook because he didn't want to be disturbed. I figured he wanted to sleep." He takes a sip from his coffee mug. "Or maybe he had company."

Some of the people in the room try to stifle their snickers. Most don't even make the attempt.

The sound of hysterical laughter reverberates out of Libby Saunders's office. My first thought is that I'm the subject of conversation, but I can also hear a television set. My knock is ignored, so I open the door.

It seems like the entire editorial staff as well as most of the talent has gathered in Libby's smallish office. They're all squeezed in front of the TV watching a tape. I see the title, *Freaks and Misfits*, on a video box next to the set. On-screen there's a girl with a speech impediment who would "wove wooking fo' *Cwasswoom Diwect*."

The crowd cackles and wails. A junior high kid is next. He's sitting importantly at a desk in someone's trophy room. I doubt he realized that the position he's sitting in makes it look like a pair of antlers is growing out of his ears. I can't help it. I start laughing too. The entire video has been set to disco music—"Le Freak." The next guy is obviously stoned. He's lying in a field of bluebonnets, talking slowly, and he's supplying his own camera work, spinning the camcorder around and around. He drops the camera, and you can see it land on his nose and hear him say, "Oh, shit." He picks it back up, points it at himself, and says, "Uh, ignore that take, start watching now." He's followed by a creature that no one in the room can guess the sex of.

As I'm maneuvering for a better position, I sense that I'm no longer standing on carpeting. I glance down and discover a six-foot-long fax has uncoiled down to the floor and that I'm in the process of destroying it. I pick it up and look at it. It's been sent by a marketing research company in New York City called Zeitkids. The entire sheet is filled with feedback about the day's episode. Part of it is called "anecdotal response." The rest is referred to as "survey results." I'm not sure if I'm supposed to see this, but I feel like I'm safe. No one is going to tear themselves away from the video and catch me. I start with the survey results. One hundred students have been asked to grade the show on a scale of one to ten, with ten being great. Today's show received a 7.6. Then the survey asks for students to grade each piece individually. Lydia's deficit story received a 2.2; the train wreck garnered a 7.1; and those Midwestern dancing girls topped the charts with a 9.2. After that, the talent's up for review.

Anchors:

Shayla Roberts	5.6
Stu Chestnut	8.9

Reporters:

David Saldaña	8.8
Patrick Sheridan	8.6

And I didn't even have to speak.

I read through a few of the anecdotal responses. It's easy to see where Mr. Scott gets his views on the show.

• *You need to do more stories like the dance team story. Stuff we care about!*

• *Are those Patrick's real eyes, or does he wear colored contacts?*

• *The deficit—yawn.*

I let the fax fall back down on my feet and turn my attention back to the screen. At first I don't see what's funny about the ensuing audition. A girl is sitting on a couch explaining why she would make a good reporter. She's not bad, but nothing special. Then I catch it. There's a mirrored closet door behind her angled out across the hall. Plain as day, a stark naked toddler walks by. The next snippet is of a girl singing her résumé to the tune of "Here Comes Santa Claus."

"I'm in drama! I can charm ya! Voice coach says I'm great!
From Salvador Dalí to Boutros-Ghali I enunciate.

The next misfit is a guy my age with severe acne. He's telling us that he wants to be a reporter for *Classroom Direct*. Tears pour out of Stu Chestnut's eyes, and he holds his sides, but he's laughing too hard to make any sound.

I watch as Christian Hanson describes the qualities that make him a good reporter.

"No, but what was she *like*?"

Zeb never calls me in Los Angeles. Why should he? I can call for free. But this morning's show, the one we taped last night, featured me and Robin Ferris as the anchors. The first time Zeb asked the question, my response was that she had a little problem with the teleprompters at first, but that she picked it up pretty quickly. Apparently, that wasn't what he wanted to know about.

"She was nice."

"Nice? Your mother is nice. Mother Teresa is nice."

"Well, she was professional," I say, hoping this will satisfy him.

"What does that mean?"

"It means she just came in here and did her job and left. She had a manager with her and a PR person."

He sighs. "What's a PR person?"

"Public relations—they handle your appearances, fan mail, stuff like that. They make sure you're in the news as much as possible. Anyway, she really only talked to those people. She was polite to me, but we didn't get all palsy-walsy." I examine the pile of Taco Bell garbage on the coffee table in front of me. I'm sure I have another burrito in here somewhere. Zeb tries another approach.

"Was she hot?"

"Like an atom bomb," I say, knowing I'm stealing the expression from Shayla, whom I've been calling Queen of the Similes. There's a long pause.

"Damn, you're the luckiest person I know."

"So what's the news from back home? How's Don Anderson Juan making out with Laurie Wilcox?" There's news I'm more interested in, but I don't want it to seem like I'm too anxious.

"I think they're doing it."

"Did he tell you that?"

"No, but man, wait until you see Anderson. You'll see what I mean."

"You're saying you can just tell?" I have my doubts about this.

"Patrick, he's starting to gain weight. He's getting a roll on him."

Now, this *is* news. The way Anderson eats, you'd think the boy would be a blimp, but he's always been rail thin. There may not be any scientific basis for this, but most guys I know—me included—believe that the loss of virginity coincides with a radical change in metabolism. Hence the clearing of one's complexion, the lowering of one's voice, the ability to view erotically suggestive material without being thrown into evening-long masturbatory frenzies.

"Damn," I say.

I ask him how his tennis season is coming along ("Kicking ass, taking names"), and I give him an edited version of my night in Sandymound, leaving out the juiciest bits. It's not that I'm afraid he would tell Kate, or anything. I just think it's somehow less disrespectful to her—the fewer people that know and all. It feels weird not telling Zeb everything.

"So what's up with my favorite SMU dropout? Have you heard anything about Blaine Mathews?"

"Oh man, that's right. I knew I had something else to tell you." Zeb sounds like he's working himself up. "The other night I show up to the Dairy Queen, and—"

A knock on the door interrupts Zeb. I tell him to hold on, but I never remember to get back to the phone. There's a woman standing at the door. I sort of expect her to go into some sales pitch, but she just looks at me.

"Can I help you?" I ask.

"Patrick," she says. "I'm your sister."

I don't want to invite the woman in. My housekeeping skills have really started to decline recently. In addition to the Taco Bell remains, I've got a sink full of (petri) dishes, and there's underwear stashed around the place like Easter eggs. We're standing there awkwardly, neither of us saying anything. She keeps opening her mouth like she's going to add something, but nothing comes out. I haven't said anything yet. Then she spreads her arms like she wants a hug, but I'm frozen there. She tilts her head and studies me, then begins to lower her arms, but I'm finally able to move. I step forward into her arms. But I can't help thinking that the person I'm embracing is a stranger.

"Let's go for a walk," she says.

"Where?" I say, praying she doesn't want to walk through Hollywood.

"Does it matter?" she asks. My silence has to suffice as an answer. "Get a jacket," she says. "I'll show you."

*   *   *

My sister has aged pretty well, I decide. She must be thirty-three by now. She's not the teenager I have the faintest memories of, but she's not falling apart. Maybe she could stand to lose a few pounds, but it's not like she's fat. She's still pretty. Cute might be a better word. Her light brown hair, worn short and straight, reminds me that we're only adopted siblings.

We didn't talk much on the short drive from Hollywood up to Universal City. She asked me my impressions of Los Angeles and how I was liking my job. It was almost like nothing real could be discussed until we arrived at our destination. I don't know if we're there yet. We're strolling down the middle of what they call City Walk. It's like a street in Disneyland, but for older people. Bars, restaurants, arcades, gift shops, pool halls, and an eighteen-screen theater face each other along the prefabricated, neon-illuminated boulevard.

As we stop and watch a street theater group reenact *Romeo and Juliet* using an elderly Florida couple in the title roles, it strikes me that this is what tourists really come to Hollywood to see. It's all make-believe. Nothing like the authentic streets of Hollywood. Prostitutes don't work City Walk. Garbage is scooped up or stabbed seconds after landing on the ground. Magicians and licensed street musicians rather than beggars ply passersby for pocket change. Bridget waves me forward, and we continue through the throng until we end up at an ice-cream and coffee shop. She gets a scoop of something called "wicked as sin chocolate." I order a caramel cappuccino. We sit down, and the pressure on us to speak becomes unbearable. I give in to it in a big way.

"So how did you know where to find me? Did you call Mama or Papa? Are you here on vacation?"

Bridget smiles, but it fades before she answers. "I live here, Patrick."

"Los Angeles?"

"The Valley. Reseda, specifically."

I try to register this news and decide whether I'm happy about it, but I fail to conjure up any emotional response at all. It's just news. There's a stranger who lives in Reseda.

"Oh."

"I'm a high school teacher, and guess what?"

"Your school gets *Classroom Direct*."

She points at me to indicate my guess is correct.

"The day they introduced you, I was checking roll, trying to get all my paperwork taken care of while the kids watched the show. I heard 'Patrick Sheridan, from Doggett, Texas,' and you'll never guess what happened."

"What?"

"I fainted, Patrick. Right in the middle of my second-period art class. The little hooligans didn't even revive me. I must have been out for five minutes before someone decided to get the nurse in there." Bridget shakes her head as if she can't believe the nerve of her students. It's funny, but I think I would have been the one to fetch the nurse. But then, at Doggett, several of us probably would have raced to do it. "Ever since then," Bridget continues, "I've been wanting to look you up."

"I've been out here eight weeks."

"I know, Patrick. Actually, I called a few weeks ago and pretended I was Mama. I said I had lost your address, and they gave it to me. I just haven't had the nerve to do it. I didn't want to just call you. I wanted to make sure I got to see you. But there were other things to consider."

"Like what?"

"Like whether or not I wanted Roman and Marge to know where I was living."

"I won't tell them," I say, wondering why it's important to her, "if you don't want me to."

"I'd appreciate that, Patrick, but it's going to be an awfully tough secret to keep. It'll be easy for you to think you'd be doing everyone a favor if you told them, but you really wouldn't be."

"I'm pretty good at keeping secrets," I say.

"I'm not surprised," she says. "It's a Sheridan talent."

That makes me want to ask Bridget all the questions I've never had the nerve to ask Mama and Papa, but I don't. I've got a hunch that it would be too much to get into. I settle for something a little less personal.

"So what have you been up to for the last"—I look at my watch—"fourteen years?"

"Nothing much," she says.

"Yeah, me either."

Then, for the first time, we both laugh.

"Let me get a cup of coffee," she says. "This might be a long story."

When she returns, Bridget begins her tale with the ambiguous line, "After the apocalypse in Doggett."

"'Apocalypse'?"

"It had an Old Testament quality to it—dead frogs, hellfire, exorcisms . . ."

Ignoring my attempt at a follow-up question about this "apocalypse" business, Bridget forges ahead. "Anyway, after that, things didn't get much better. So I moved out here."

"To go to college?"

"Not immediately. The first plan was to become an artist. Preferably a famous and wealthy artist whose work would attract so much attention that Roman would stumble across an article about my work. The trouble with this plan was that they've rarely done stories on teenaged avant-garde art phenoms in *U.S. News and World Report*. In the interim between my personal exodus and fame, I wanted all the stereotypical artistic experiences." Bridget counts these off on her fingers. "I wanted to be poor. I wanted to live in a studio with amazing morning light. I wanted to suck the marrow out of life. I wanted to cavort within a circle of equally creative bohemians and intellectuals. I wanted to avoid getting a tan.

"The only one I truly succeeded at was being poor, which I don't recommend, in case you're considering that route."

"I want to write for a newspaper."

"Ah, so you *are*."

"I are what?" I ask.

"Considering that route."

"Yeah." Papa's always talking about how little money newspaper writers make, like it's going to keep me from doing it.

"Anyway, two years and seven waitressing gigs later, I applied to UCLA as well as every student loan and grant available. That's where I met Charley and, soon after, decided that getting a teaching certificate wasn't such a bad idea. If you tell Roman any of this, I swear I'll kill you. He was always saying things about how a teaching degree was what a smart young lady should strive for."

"Who's Charley?"

"Charley's my husband. He works in accounting for Disney."

"Congratulations. I know it's a bit late, but . . ."

"There's more. I've also got two children—Shane and Jill. Shane's five now, and Jill's almost three."

"I'm an uncle? Wow."

Bridget looks at me sadly. It's the same way Mama looks when Bridget's name somehow gets brought up in conversation. The expression almost looks like shame. I think all three of them, Bridget and my parents, know that their inability to work out whatever broke them apart deprived me of a sister. But my parents have never seemed tempted to try to mend the rift. It's apparent that my sister is satisfied with the status quo as well. She scrapes the bottom of her cup of ice cream with a spoon, but there's none left.

"What's your last name now?" I ask.

For a second, Bridget appears to have forgotten it. "Rathmore," she says. "Sorry, my mind was wandering. I was wondering what's happened in Doggett since I left. Why don't we have you answer some questions now."

"Since you left, hmmm. We got a new stoplight. It's there at the corner of Sycamore and LBJ."

"Cool," says Bridget. "They've needed one there."

I was being silly in telling her this, but her response makes me think she's truly interested in the news. I decide to continue along the same line.

"And they put in a Wal-Mart about five years ago. It's where everyone goes now. Well, except for Mama and Papa. They refuse to set foot in the place. I think they're single-handedly keeping all the downtown stores in business. On Friday and Saturday nights, everyone from the high school parks in the Wal-Mart parking lot."

"Same stuff. Different decade. I guess getting used to the slow pace of Los Angeles must be tough for you."

"I'm dying of boredom," I say, realizing she'll think I'm also being sarcastic.

"So what do you do? Cruise town? Hang out in the Wal-Mart parking lot?"

"Not much. My girlfriend works at the Dairy Queen, so I spend a lot of time there. Anderson and Zeb—those are my friends—and I, we hang out at Zeb's a lot. He's got a pool and a pool table. It sounds pretty boring now that I say it out loud."

"Not really," Bridget says, "but let's get back to this girlfriend you mentioned. I have some girls who are going to be crushed when they hear about this."

"Her name's Kate. We met in CCD."

"That must make the folks happy."

"We've been going out for . . . well . . . it'll be two years in . . .

in . . . Oh shit! It was two years two days ago. Bridget, you've got to take me home."

Mrs. Mosely tells me Kate's out. I don't have the guts to ask out where. I just tell her to have Kate call. I dial an 800 number I saw on TV and order flowers. I have them sign the card, *I'm sorry, Patrick.*

All things considered, I shouldn't bitch about this part of the job, but I hate it anyway. I've been watching my mail stack up in my desk drawer for the past three weeks. I must be a hundred letters behind. I always thought that letter openers were the stupidest invention, but now I have my own, and I get mad when I've got to go snatch it back out of Stu Chestnut's desk. The letter opener is part of my system. I position everything I need in a half circle on my desk. The unread letters sit at nine o'clock, my pub shots at high noon, and the big *Classroom Direct* envelopes stay at three o'clock. The letter opener, notepad, and black felt-tip pen stay right in front of me. When I really get in a groove, I can answer thirty an hour. That includes answering all their pertinent questions ("I like Green Day too"), signing a photo (time-saving tip: presign the "Love Patrick" part), and addressing the envelope. At first it was kind of fun to get fan mail, but after twenty or thirty letters, they all start sounding the same. I don't even really read them anymore. I just sort of scan them. Maybe I'll read them if the girl sends a picture, and she's really good-looking, but that's not usually the case. Most are from junior high girls. Occasionally I get an invitation to someone's prom, but I just write back saying I wish I could go, but that *Classroom Direct* is sending me to Zimbabwe, or somewhere like that. Guys don't write me. Just doesn't happen. That's why I give special attention to the letter from Drew Hartsock. The name could go either way, but the handwriting is definitely male. I'm becoming something of an expert on female script.

I read his letter. Then wish I hadn't.

Patrick,

I think it says a lot about the sorry state of American education that we're actually doing a letter-writing unit in English Class. I'm a freshman, not a retard. Anyway, we're supposed to write some celebrity that "we admire" a letter. If we get a letter in response we get bonus points, and since I've been blowing off this class in a big way, I thought I'd be more likely to get a letter from some minor news jockey for *Classroom Direct* than someone I really admire. Besides, Kurt's dead, so the extra credit would be tough to come by.

Sorry about calling you minor, but I don't really believe these letters are even read. And if they are read, I don't believe you read them. I'm not even sure you exist. For all I know, you could be some sort of holographic image hypnotizing us all into buying Doritos. But let's pretend for a moment that you're real, that you're really reading this. How would I be able to tell? Sure, I might get a letter back. I can see it already.

Dear Fill-in-the-Blank,

Thanks for writing to me—Patrick Sheridan. I, Patrick Sheridan, take your comments very seriously.

Best Wishes,
Patrick Sheridan

That wouldn't tell me much. It sure wouldn't tell me whether or not you read my letter. But I've got an idea. This will let me know.

Tell me something you hate.

In return, I'll tell you something I hate.

Here goes.

I hate people my age. Not just some of them. All of them. That includes you. I especially hate girls my age. They're stupid and, I'm convinced, evil too. I think they study people—boys and each other—until they figure out everything that's wrong with you. Then they try to hurt you. With me, they don't even have to look that hard. They don't have to look at all. I stutter. Go ahead, laugh. Everyone else does. You know what they say, though, about "he who laughs last"? Well, that's a load of crap. It's he who laughs first and

keeps laughing that comes out on top. After a
while, the person getting laughed at just gives up.

So, holograph, if you care about my grade in
English, drop me a line.

Ch-ch-ch-cheerio,

Drew Hartsock

As I finish reading the letter, Libby sticks her head in the talent office.

"Patrick, Prentiss is looking for you. He wants to see you in his office."

She punctuates this announcement by singing the theme from *The Twilight Zone*. Being summoned to Prentiss's office feels a bit like getting sent to the principal's office. It reminds me of a question I've had on my mind.

"Hey, Libby, whatever happened to that P.A., Harris? The one who picked me up from the airport."

"He was, uh, dismissed."

"Fired? For what?"

"We prefer the word 'dismissed,'" she says in good humor, "and reasons for dismissals are confidential. Let's just say he made some bad decisions."

"Taking me to that bachelor party. Was that one of them?"

"Off the record?" says Libby, stepping inside.

"Off the record," I promise.

"That was strike three."

"It's not like it scarred me or anything."

"I'm not sure anyone here cares if it turned you into Dr. Jekyll, Patrick." Libby rolls Earl's chair over and sits down in front of me. "I've told you already, television is about appearances. If your parents had found out one of our employees took you there, or if some Hollywood gossip writer had reported that *Classroom Direct*'s teen reporter was last seen being straddled by an exotic dancer, we could've ended up looking really bad. Remember, we fight a battle in every school district in the country to stay in the schools. Winning that battle is worth three hundred million dollars a year. Firing Harris may be harsh, but he wasn't the sharpest of tacks around here."

"You mean Mr. Hyde, don't you?"

"What?"

"Well, Dr. Jekyll was the good guy. Mr. Hyde is the monster."

"Around here," Libby says as she stands, "Mr. Scott is the monster, and he wants you in his lair right now."

"Fine," I say.

I'm happy to stop answering mail anyway. I'm not quite prepared to respond to Drew Hartsock. I walk down the hall and into Mr. Scott's reception area. Neither of his secretaries are at their desks, and his door is wide open. I go in and plop down on one of the leather couches, pausing momentarily to pick up the *Entertainment Weekly* with Robin Ferris on the cover off the coffee table. The headline asks the question, "Rockin' Robin: Can Prime-Time's Sweetheart Make the Big Leap to the Big Screen?" I study the cover. She's a two percenter, all right. In fact, she's a half percenter. They don't make girls like this in Doggett.

Inside the magazine are a couple more pictures of her: one where she's wrestling with her golden retriever back home in Vermont, and one from the set of *Prairie Girl* of her hugging the bearded guy who plays her father. The story begins, "Robin Ferris is beautiful, stars in a top-rated show, and has an Emmy nomination behind her. She'll tell you, though, that all she wants is to be a normal teenager."

I can't bear it. I put the magazine down, but when I do, I notice a leather-bound notebook with an embossed Zeitkids logo on the outside. I scramble into the outer office and shut the door. Then I sprint back into Mr. Scott's office and open up the folder. Inside I find all compiled survey results of the entire year to date. Every page is some sort of chart or graph refining one hundred viewers' opinions into tidy colored bars and pie slices. On one long page that folds out, the individual grades given to shows appear as vertical bars. At the bottom, the show date, the stories by producer, and the anchors are listed. Mr. Scott has highlighted in some sort of funky purple all the shows that scored over a nine. Four of the five shows that have graded out that high this semester have had celebrity guest anchors. It's easy to notice this because Mr. Scott has drawn little asterisks by their names. He's also highlighted, this time in yellow, the three shows that have graded out below a three, only the asterisks are by Lydia's name. In each case, she's produced the lead story. I look at the pieces: health care, Bosnia, the deficit. She does these stories because no one else wants to. He must take that into consideration.

I flip through the pages until I find the foldout section on the anchors. We've all been assigned different colors. I'm gold. The full-time anchors' lines start in August. Mine starts at the end of January, and Shayla's the beginning of February. It's interesting because most of the anchors' lines are flat; their rankings having stayed pretty consistent. Stu and Earl have been the most popular anchors, trading off the number one spot over the course of the year. I'm a different story. My line looks like the stock prices of a company you might want to think about investing in. My first few shows, I score below a five, which looks pretty much like a disaster on this chart, but as I keep unfolding the chart revealing the most recent shows, my line begins an incline that keeps heading up. The final fold reveals that the top anchor at *Classroom Direct* . . . is me.

That's when I hear the door in the outside office opening. I fold up the graph as quickly as I can, put the folder down, and cover it up with the magazine. Mr. Scott walks in the office and raises his eyebrows. "Patrick?"

"Libby said you wanted to see me."

"That's right." Mr. Scott adjusts to finding me in his office. "What I'm going to tell you I don't want you to take the wrong way, buddy." Mr. Scott sits down on the couch across from me. "But I think you're going to find that it's nearly impossible to stop people from gossiping around here. We are, after all, a news organization." He chuckles at his own observation, then leans forward. "Anyway, I've heard about your little liaison in Ohio."

He waits for a reaction from me. None comes.

"Now, I'm all for you having some fun when you're out here, but I simply can't have my anchors bumping uglies with students at our subscriber schools—not even our student reporters. If you got a girl pregnant, do you know what that would do to the company?"

Not to mention the girl or me, I think.

"There was no danger of that," I say.

"Now, don't give me that. I wasn't a teenager that long ago, Patrick. I have to tell you that if I find out that it's happened again, I'm going to have to send you home."

"Okay."

"I don't want to do that, Patrick. We're very pleased with your performance here. In fact, there's a possibility we might have a position available for you next year as part of our full-time staff. I've already had my secretary call USC and that other school." (Mr. Scott refuses to utter the initials UCLA.) "They'll be sending you applications. I want you to think very carefully about your future. Don't throw it away for some piece of high school ass. I am serious about sending you home."

But I've seen the survey results—the Bible of Prentiss Scott. They could catch me in bed with a hedgehog. He wouldn't do a thing.

"All right," I say.

Mr. Scott nods, looking satisfied. "Sorry this had to be unpleasant."

I get up and start walking out of the office.

"Patrick?" Mr. Scott calls.

"Yeah."

"I see it didn't take Los Angeles long to get rid of that charming 'Yes, sir.'" He produces a smile that I can't interpret. "I had one last question. Don't you have a girlfriend back in Texas?"

* * *

The Holiday Inn room in Lubbock is bigger than I imagined it would be. It's the honeymoon suite—the only room they have left. The carpeting is white. The bedspread is white. Kate's dress is white. I'm wearing my *Classroom Direct* clothes. My hat's still on. I carry her over the threshold, and she runs and jumps on the bed. She beckons to me with her hands. I lie down next to her and pick up a remote control. For the first time I notice that the entire wall across from the bed is a video monitor. I click on the power. The face of Prentiss Scott fills the room. I click the channel button while Kate starts unbuttoning my shirt. That girl from Ohio appears on the screen. I keep switching channels: Blaine Mathews, Kate's ex-boyfriend, appears, then Bridget, then Papa, then Robin Ferris, then Christian Hanson from Austin, only his face has cleared up. Kate's kissing my chest and telling me to turn off the TV, but I flip the channel one more time. My face appears on the screen. I set the remote control down and turn my attention to Kate. Before I know what's happened, we're naked, and she's on top of me. She's smiling, and everything seems right. Kate says to wait a minute. She leans across the bed, takes a quarter off the nightstand, and puts it in a slot. The bed begins a low vibration that begins to pick up as Kate straddles me. This is it. We're finally going to do it. And it's perfect. But something's wrong with the bed. It's beginning to buck wildly. Behind Kate I see myself on the monitor. I'm eating a hot dog. The bed throws Kate off of it. I look over the side of the bed, but she's gone.

And I'm awake. But the bed hasn't stopped shaking.

I hear dishes in my kitchenette smash against the floor. I look at my digital clock, but the power is off. I stretch my arms across the bed and grab the metal frame on both sides. Then I pray. The hideous painting of garden lilies that's been hanging up across from my bed since the day I moved in smashes to the ground. That's a start. A fine dust of plaster from the ceiling begins raining down on me. Then it's over. Everything is still. I've survived my first earthquake.

As usual, I've thrown my clothes off right beside the bed. I reach down and find them with my hands. I dress without getting up. I put on my shoes and begin the search for a flashlight. Papa made me pack one. As I walk into the kitchen I can feel glass crunch beneath my feet. The flashlight is under the sink. I flip it on and survey the apartment. The kitchen got it worse. The cabinets are all open, and nine out of ten plates, cups, and glasses are now in pieces beneath my feet. A lamp has fallen over in the living room, but it'll survive. My television is teetering on the edge of its stand. I make my way over and restore it to its perch. I'm disappointed to discover the garden lilies print survived, though its frame did not. I take the liberty of ripping it down the middle. Someone down the hall screams. My first thought is of Shayla. I throw open the door and jog down the darkened hall. When I hear the scream again, I realize it's from beyond Shayla's room. The hallway ends, but there are three doors. I shout.

"Hello!?"

It's a stupid thing to yell, but what else am I supposed to say?

"In here," comes a whimper.

I try the door, but it's locked. I look around the hallway and spot a fire extinguisher mounted on the wall. I use it as a battering ram. The door gives way. With the beam of my flashlight I illuminate Robin Ferris. She's lying on the ground. At first I can't understand why, but as I move the beam across her body I see the pool of blood gathering at her feet.

"Help me," she says.

It seems like every male news producer and anchor has gathered around my desk the next afternoon to hear me tell the story of taking Robin Ferris to the hospital. I tell them how, when we got to Cedars-Sinai, the emergency room was packed with people suffering from heart attacks, broken bones, and plaster in their eyes, but when I walked in carrying Robin Ferris . . .

"You were carrying her?" David Saldaña asks.

"I told her she should suck it up and walk, but she kept whining about big chunks of glass sticking out of her feet."

"I thought they might have wheelchairs at a hospital, dickwad," David responds.

"Anyway, when I walk in carrying Robin Ferris, it's like the whole hospital is there just for her. Even the other patients seemed to clear way for me to get through with her. A couple actually asked her for her autograph."

"What'd she do?" asks some random P.A.

"She pretended to pass out." My audience nods along in approval. "So we get to the front of the line, and the nurse starts barking orders, doesn't even ask about insurance. Two orderlies actually lift some old man out of a wheelchair and bring the wheelchair over to Robin. I'm not sure what I'm supposed to do at that point, but Robin asks if I can come with her, and the nurse says yes. They wheel her down into an examination room, and one of the orderlies starts peeling off the T-shirts I had wrapped around her feet."

"Your T-shirts?" asks Cal Sherman.

"Yeah, and they're just drenched in her blood."

Cal gets in a follow-up question. "Did you keep them?"

"They threw them in a trash can, and I thought I'd look like a letch digging them out."

"I would have," says Billy Trundle.

"You probably would," says Earl Woodbie, shaking his head in disgust. "Go ahead, Patrick."

"Then the doctor comes in, and he starts looking her feet over. He says that mostly they're just cut up, but that there appears to be glass in a couple of the bigger gashes. He says he can put her under to remove them, or give her a local anesthetic and do it after it's taken effect.

"The next part is the coolest."

I glance around the circle to make sure everyone's paying attention.

"Robin tells the doctor she hates needles and asks him if he can't just dig the glass out right there and then."

The group makes the appropriate wincing expressions.

"The doctor looks like this idea makes him nervous, but he says he'll do it. He positions this light right on her feet and takes out a pair of tweezers. I'm still standing there feeling useless, but when the doctor first starts poking around down there, Robin grabs my hand and squeezes. I kept looking at her face, but her expression never changed. She might have been lying on a tanning bed, as calm as she looked, but at the same time, I thought she was going to crush my knuckles. I'm sure it must have looked hilarious to the doctor. Robin with her poker face, me looking like the Tragedy drama mask. But it only takes him a couple minutes to get all the glass out, then he bandages her up and asks if he can get his picture taken with her. They actually have a Polaroid camera that they use for something or other. Anyway, I end up taking her picture with the doctor, an orderly comes in with crutches, and I drive her home in her MG."

"Any good-night smootchie-koo?" asks Billy.

"By the time we got home it was morning."

"So . . ."

"Well, we're having lunch tomorrow."

With that news, I'm offered high fives by just about everyone.

I get calls all day from people worried about me. Last night's as-of-yet nameless earthquake, in the estimation of the old-timers around *Classroom Direct*, wasn't nearly as devastating as the Northridge Quake of '94. Only two deaths, but not surprisingly, Mama was sure I was one of them.

"There are ten million or so people out here, Mama. More people were killed in drive-by shootings last night than died in the earthquake."

Of course that doesn't make her feel any better. I wonder whether I take some kind of perverse pleasure in telling Mama that. I don't tell her that I just got off the phone with Bridget, who was also call-ing to make sure I was all right. I ask Bridget the same question, but she says the quake didn't hit the Valley as hard as it did Hollywood.

"We slept right through it," she says.

The plural pronoun makes me think about her family. Does she not want me to meet them? You'd think she would invite me over to meet my brother-in-law and my niece and nephew. She says Reseda is so far away, but people commute from there. Maybe she doesn't want *them* meeting *me*. It's strange, we've had lunch three times now. Every time we meet, she has a present for me. It's like she's trying to cram a decade and a half of sisterhood into three months. But it's okay. I mean, she's really nice and funny. She reminds me so much of Papa. At one of the lunches, I actually brought up "the rules of the house," but she changed the subject right away. I didn't pursue it.

When Kate calls, she's less interested in details about the earthquake than she is in plans for the prom.

"Only twenty-two more days," she says. "I made the room reservation."

"I can't wait," I say, remembering my dream.

"You need to go into a tux shop out there and get your mea-surements, then send them to Doggett Formal."

"You already told me that."

"Sorry. You've just seemed so out of it lately."

"This is a weird place. Billy calls it Hell-A instead of L.A."

"Yeah, I get it," Kate says tersely. "Which one is Billy?"

"The producer."

"Oh yeah."

"So how's Blaine?"

There's a long pause before Kate says anything. "What's that supposed to mean?"

"It means," I say, "that I hear he's been flying around in great big circles above the Dairy Queen, waiting until it's safe to land."

"Patrick . . ." Kate says my name like it's a warning.

"Guess college was a bit too tough for ol' Blaine. Is he working at his mom's video store?"

"Patrick, don't do this," Kate says. "I love you. I don't love Blaine."

I don't know why I want to stay angry with Kate. Maybe it's because it's easier than missing her. All I have to do is think of her back as a sophomore holding hands with Blaine Mathews in the cafeteria, and suddenly those twenty-two days don't seem like such a long time. They almost did it. She told me that once, thinking that the knowledge they didn't would come as a relief. Instead, I ended up with this mental video of the two of them naked and poised that plays every time I start feeling too good about life.

I've been thinking about my future with Kate. Next year, she'll be at Texas Tech, and I'll be eight hours away at St. Mary's, this Catholic college in San Antonio where Papa went to law school. I've visited the campus; it seems nice, but its biggest selling point is that it's the only place my parents will pay for. I've been coming to the realization that long-distance relationships are semi-doomed, and it seems that lately, I haven't been able to get Mr. Scott's job offer out of my head. There's no way Kate could come out here to L.A. Maybe it's time I did some growing up.

"Yeah, forget it. I didn't mean that. You know I love you too."

"Are you sure?"

"Absolutely."

"Is Italian okay?"

I'm riding down Melrose with Robin Ferris. The top on her MG is down, and the lipstick from her kiss hello is still fresh on my cheek. I'd say yes to a restaurant that specialized in cannibalism.

"Great."

"I've got a confession," she says at a red light. Three chunky teenaged girls are crossing the street. One of them spots Robin. They huddle, and a camera emerges. "I didn't recognize you until we got to the hospital." Two of the girls rush over to Robin's door.

"Can we take our picture with you?" says the one wearing a silk Planet Hollywood jacket.

"No prob," says Robin, who continues talking to me. "It's when I heard your accent, after I quit thinking I was going to bleed to death, that I remembered where I knew you."

The girl with the camera is having trouble. First she forgets to take the lens cap off, then she realizes she hasn't advanced the film. The light turns green. "Sorry, you guys," Robin says as she accelerates. The arm one of the girls has wrapped around Robin falls away, and I hear the other one say, "Bitch." Robin doesn't seem to notice. Or care.

"It was very fairy tale–ish, if you think about it," she says. "Damsel in distress rescued by a handsome prince." Robin pulls in front of a pink awning with the words EL FIN—LA TRATTORIA scripted along the front. "That's why I hated it."

"That's why you hated it?"

"Yeah. I don't want to be the damsel. I want to be the handsome prince. I want to kick the dragon's ass."

"There wasn't much ass kicking required," I say.

Robin hands her keys to the young Italian valet, who doesn't seem to care how obvious he is about scoping her out. His whole head moves as he runs his eyes down her body.

"That's not the point," continues Robin as we enter. Now that I'm walking beside her, I realize that she's almost as tall as me. "You know, my first acting was with my sister when we were kids. My mom still has videotapes of us putting on little shows in the garage, and I'm always the cowboy or the astronaut or Captain Kirk. I've got a hero complex, and it got shot down the other night. Besides, now I'm indebted to you for life. Until there comes a day when I can pay off my debt in some similar fashion, I owe you. I can't stand owing people."

"Buy lunch, and we'll call it even."

"It's not that easy," she says. "We're talking about my self-esteem."

As we're shown to a table, I try to imagine how someone like Robin Ferris could have self-esteem problems. After we sit down there's a moment of silence that, naturally, I find uncomfortable. I hurry to fill it. "What would you say if I told you that when I was little I used to put on my sister's dresses and pretend I was Scarlett O'Hara?"

Robin laughs. "I'd say you have a lot in common with a lot of the actors I've worked with."

"So what's Vermont like?"

"I couldn't tell you," says Robin as she scans the menu.

"I thought that's where you were from."

"You've been reading *Entertainment Weekly*." She says it like it's a serious allegation. "Patrick, you struck me as more of the intellectual type. Vermont is just where my dad lives with Old Number Four. I may have spent two days there total, and I don't think I left the yard. Nice syrup, I hear. Or is that Maine?"

"Who's Old Number Four?"

"My dad's spouse du jour. Mom's Old Number Two. She lives here, down on Manhattan Beach."

"Why don't you live with her?"

"And commute forty-five minutes to work? Get real. Besides, we get along much better over the phone than we do in person." Robin waves to someone across the restaurant. "So did you always want to be an actor?"

"Uh, I've never wanted to be an actor at all. I couldn't do that. I'm not very good at pretending," I say. "I always planned on writing for a newspaper." Robin's expression makes it plain my career goal is distasteful to her. "Though lately, I've been giving some thought to being a television reporter."

"I thought you were playing a television reporter already," she says.

"Not intentionally. I'm trying to actually be one, but at *Classroom Direct* that line between the two is pretty fuzzy."

"I don't know about journalists. The other day I caught one going through my trash. You're not one of those, are you?"

"One of whats?"

"One of the ones that picks through my used cotton balls or tries to pay my friends for the inside scoop on my coke habit or the heated backstage battles with my costars. That's the reason I don't have any poor friends, you know. I have to have friends who can't be bought."

Robin smiles. I think she's joking.

"I want to expose corruption, afflict the comfortable, defend the people's right to know, win Pulitzers." I say it with a straight face.

"I don't know, Patrick. You *might* have a future as a thespian."

"I used to believe in all that," I say, tracing the rim of my water glass with my finger.

"A regular Clark Kent," Robin says.

"Something like that."

An impeccably groomed and attired Italian waiter approaches the table.

"*Bella signorina!*" he says, running his fingers through his graying hair. "*Cosa desidera?*"

"*Buon giorno*, Anthony. What's good today?"

"Everything!" our waiter says, but he follows his proclamation by running through a list of the chef's specialties. Robin listens, then orders something completely different. Anthony turns his attention to me. "*Signor?*"

I order my meal in Italian. Fortunately they have the same *medaglioni* dish that I used for the oral test Kim gave me last

week. I can't tell who's more surprised by my performance—
Robin or our waiter.

"*E insalate?*" he asks after a moment.

"*Si, grazie.*"

Anthony scribbles my order down, nods, and departs. Robin
stares at me with her mouth wide open. "You're really from
Texas?" she asks.

"Yes, ma'am."

Robin shakes her head. "Then you can call me Lois Lane."

They're having Shayla and me anchor the show together for the
first time. Apparently they think we can be trusted now. Between
the fact the show is taped, the teleprompters, and Connie whispering in our ears, I'm not sure we could screw it up if we wanted
to. The two of us are sitting in makeup together. I'm working on
my return letter to Drew Hartsock while the makeup woman
works on Shayla.

I hate to say it, but I'm starting to worry about Shayla. Maybe
I've just been more aware of it since I've seen the survey results, but
it seems to me that Mr. Scott doesn't even know she exists anymore.
He doesn't ask her what all the kids in D.C. would think about our
story on rap lyrics, and it seems like she's on the show half as much
as me. She hasn't said anything to me about it, but that's part of the
problem, if you ask me. She doesn't even care. At least I went and
got help, underlined my important phrases, practiced in front of
the mirror. All Shayla does is study. She never goes out. She'll never
get dinner with me. She still wants to play cards sometimes, but

that's about it. Cards get boring after a while. Shayla gets boring after a while. That's mean of me to say, because Shayla's always nice.

"Yo, sister," I say, hoping to get Shayla's attention off her copy of *A Tale of Two Cities*.

Shayla responds without taking her eyes off the page. "Not 'Yo, sis-tirrrr,'" she says, making fun of my accent. "Yo, sistah."

"Yo, sistah," I say, doing my best to copy her inflection. Shayla lowers her book and stares at my reflection in the mirror. "What up?"

"When are we supposed to have that read by?"

"Next week."

"That's right," I say.

"Why're you asking, Patrick? You ain't . . ." She stops herself, then restarts. "You haven't turned anything in for weeks."

"Kim said she didn't care as long as we get everything in before the end of the semester."

"Yeah, well, I think she's just so happy about getting to teach someone Italian that she's letting you slide on everything else."

"I'll get it in."

Shayla lifts the book back up in front of her eyes while she gets her hair worked on. "You're just one of those people everything comes easy to, I guess."

It's then that I have an idea about what to write to Drew.

Drew,

    I have to be honest. This is probably going to sound pretty lame to someone so sure of his own hatred, but I had to really think for a long time to come up with something I hate. There are plenty of things that I don't like: Los Angeles, Blaine Mathews (You don't know him. You're lucky.), AT&T, but something I really hate? That's tough. Here's what I came up with.

I hate it when people tell me that everything comes easy to me.

And you know what? You would probably be one of those people. Of course you already told me you hate me, so I'm not going to feel too guilty about putting you in this category. You know why I hate it? It's because it means that whatever I do, no matter how hard I work at it, it's never going to be enough. It has no value. People will always say it came naturally to me, or it was handed to me because I'm on television or because of the way I look.

The scary thing is, I think I'm starting to believe it.

So yeah, Drew. I'm real.

Patrick (Not a Hologram) Sheridan

The usual sound guy is sick, and they've got this replacement in who doesn't seem to know an IFB from a low-impedance connector. The show is taking twice as long as usual to tape because, alternately, Shayla and I can't hear the booth and the booth can't hear us. Shayla's getting on my nerves too. The girl can't say Sarajevo when the tape is running. She can say it easily between takes, but once we're counted in, it becomes "Sarah-Havo." After the fourth time she screws it up, I ask Connie if Shayla can't just say "the capital city" or, better yet, couldn't she just let me do it.

"Or maybe Patrick ought to just tape the whole show. That way he might actually like watching it," says Shayla.

Connie's voice cuts through the static in our ears. "Kids! Take it easy out there. You're doing fine. Shayla, why don't you let Patrick take this intro. He'll toss to you for the NASA story."

Shayla shakes her head like she's going to murder me tonight in my sleep. "Happy?" she says.

"Like a lottery winner."

I one-take the Sarajevo intro. Jesus, I've heard it enough.

The show proceeds without a hitch until we get to the sign-off. According to the teleprompter, Shayla's supposed to say something about being out of time, and they want me to say, "Shucks."

"Connie, I'm not going to say it. I've never said the word in my life. No one I know says 'shucks.' You wouldn't make Shayla say 'shucks.' Why should I have to? How about if we just stick some straw out of my pocket and have me say something about wanting to bone my sister?"

"Don't get dramatic," Connie says in my ear. "We're all tired. Just say the line and let's all get out of here."

The stage manager counts us in, and Shayla delivers her line. "Looks like we're about out of time, Patrick."

I get a confused look on my face and pull my pocket watch

out. "You're right, Shayla. I'm about to miss my stagecoach."

"Cut!" Connie uses the voice she usually reserves for the people working with her in the booth. "Patrick, quit acting like a prima fucking donna and say the goddamn line. Do you want me to get Prentiss on the line?"

"Go ahead," I say.

A minute passes. The substitute sound guy keeps looking at the Exit sign. Shayla slumps down in one of the couches. Finally we hear Connie's defeated voice in our ears.

"Fine, Patrick. Say whatever you like."

I didn't really get a good look at Robin's apartment the night of the earthquake, the power being off and all. I guess I had figured that all the apartments in the complex were the same as mine and Shayla's. They're not. Robin's is a loft. Her living room is huge. I'm struck with how much it looks like it was decorated by the same person who did The Hut. I guess there's a hierarchy here at Sunset Villas like there is everywhere else in the world. I know one thing ol' Prentiss and I will have to discuss if I decide to stay. Robin handed me a drink and kissed my cheek as soon as I walked in. The drink is frozen and lime. I think it's a margarita.

One of the walls of Robin's apartment has been painted lavender like her car, and the trim has been done in a deeper purple. A huge painting hangs above her couch. The entire six-foot-square canvas is covered with multicolored polka dots.

"What do you think?" says Robin, coming out of the kitchen with her drink.

"It's better than what I've got in my room," I say.

"Which must look something like this."

Robin opens a closet revealing two stashed prints that look remarkably similar to my garden lilies.

"There must be some college somewhere offering degrees in rental property art. For years the school works at draining the students of any taste they might have mistakenly picked up before enrolling. By the time they graduate, the students can instinctively create works that no one will enjoy, but no one will get offended by."

I consider the idea.

"Could they get extra credit for finding art that people actually liked, but that no one was offended by?"

"No such thing," Robin says. "Besides, that defeats the purpose. You don't want people really getting off on the art or out it goes with the towels and mini–shampoo bottles." Robin sits down on the couch. "This is an Ariel," she says, pointing to the polka dots above her. "Have you heard of him?"

"Ariel who?"

"Just Ariel."

"No."

"Well, you'll probably meet him tonight. He's always out. He's got a gallery down on Melrose. I'll take you down sometime if you get tired of the 'scenes from the garden' motif."

"Thanks," I say, finishing off the margarita.

"There's more in the blender," Robin says. I head toward the kitchen while Robin continues to tell me about her interior decorating. "I painted the wall myself. I think it adds something. What do you think?"

"Yeah," I shout into the other room.

"If you wanted, we could do it in your apartment."

I'm pouring when she says this, and at first I think I'm hearing her wrong. Then I realize she's talking about the wall.

"What did the Sunset Villas people have to say about you painting yours?"

"I didn't ask."

"Oh."

I stay in the kitchen waiting for my blood to return to appropriate locations in my body. I check out the old-fashioned cappuccino machine sitting on her counter. It looks like the one they had at Flight Path. I can't believe I'm actually getting to do something on a Saturday night. Saturday night—that reminds me.

"You want to watch your show before we go out?" I shout.

"Are you kidding? I haven't seen a finished episode in two seasons. The novelty kind of wore off. Hasn't it for you?"

"Yeah, I guess so," I say, returning to the living room.

"Besides, it's so bad, don't you think? I mean, who watches that show? No one I know. Did you see the episode where I single-handedly prevent an Indian uprising. I make Chief Black Bow sit down and smoke the peace pipe with Colonel Yellow Hair. Oh, my God."

Robin shakes her head as if she's embarrassed.

"My parents never miss it."

"How old are they?"

"Late fifties."

"Sounds about right," says Robin. She pours some of my drink into her empty glass. "Retirees and horny twelve-year-old boys—that's the show's target audience."

"So how's the movie coming?"

"It's done. It was filmed this summer. In Texas, as a matter of fact. Here, listen to this—*Hey Scraps, what sorta car d'yew drahv?* What do you think?"

"Sounds like home," I say, thinking it sounds more like home than home sounds.

"The premiere's at the Chinese in a couple weeks. Should be the happening thing. They're broadcasting it on *E!*"

"The movie?" I say, a bit confused.

"That wouldn't make much sense, Patrick." She says this very seriously. "No. The arrivals. All of us getting out of our cars and walking in, waving to the crowd. Guys never watch these things, but girls love it. You sit there and make fun of the actresses—how fat they look, how wretched their dresses are. That sort of thing. Then you say which of the actors you'd trade your boyfriend for. It's a hoot."

As Robin's talking, I can see our reflection in a sliding-glass door. Something about seeing myself in this position startles me. And it's not the fact that I'm sitting here in Hollywood, wearing a bolo tie and sipping margaritas with Robin Ferris. I think what amazes me is that it seems pretty normal. I'm not freaking out about it. I've come a long way.

That's when the front door swings open. Two guys—one tall, the other taller—swagger in. Robin bounces up and rewards each of the intruders with a hug and a kiss. They look old to me. Mid-twenties, maybe. Dirty—but not dirty. Sort of an artificial grubbiness they achieve through rumpled designer sports coats, three-day facial growth, and long, oily hair. The taller one notices me.

"Hey now, Rob. You didn't tell us you had another man here. Looks like a cockfight. Everybody whip it out."

Both of the new arrivals begin unzipping their flies.

"Stop it," says Robin. "I don't think the apartment's big enough."

"Damn straight," says the less tall one.

"Julian, Trevor. This is Patrick, my knight in shining armor. Don't worry, Patrick. They wouldn't have gone through with it."

Robin faces me, holds up her pinkies, and mouths the word "tiny."

"I saw that," says Trevor, the taller one, as he crosses the room to shake my hand. Julian remains by the door.

"Nice string tie!" says Trevor. "Beverly Hillbillies?"

"Yeah," I say.

"Cool as shit," he says. "Rob, you mind if I visit the pharmacy?"

"You know the way," says Robin.

"Can I get anyone anything?" Trevor asks enthusiastically.

Julian and Robin say no. I shake my head, not really understanding the question. Robin disappears into the kitchen, leaving Julian and me to linger uncomfortably. She reemerges quickly with the blender and refills my glass.

"*Grazie, bella signorina*," I say.

Robin sighs theatrically before offering Julian a glass.

"What he said," says Julian upon acceptance.

"Oh, you're a charmer," Robin says facetiously.

But looking at Julian, I'm certain he doesn't require charm. He's got the sort of looks that could inspire girls to tape his likeness to their locker doors. His vampiric eyebrows endow him with a vague dangerousness, but at the same time, he's pretty, with a face that, after a good shave and the application of makeup, could function equally well as a woman's.

Trevor returns to the room and claps his hands as if it's the signal to leave. "More drinks?" he says, observing the fresh margaritas in our hands. He looks distressed. "That's so late eighties. Let's get out there before they start giving tables to the common folk."

Nobody cards me. Nobody makes me pay cover. We walk in ahead of all the people lined up outside. It's the same at every club, and if Trevor has his way, we'll hit them all tonight. We're in our fourth. It's right across the street from Paramount Studios. Trevor says it's called Smalls, but there's no sign. In fact, none of the clubs we've been to tonight have had signs.

"It would be gauche," says the ever-grinning Trevor. "Besides, if the club needs a sign, it's not worth going to. That's a fact of life. Someone write that down."

Everyone—every waitress, bartender, doorman, and valet—knows Trevor, but I'm still not sure what for. Julian, I've learned, is a model. Trevor asks me if I've seen the Soloflex ads in *Esquire*.

"I'm not sure."

"Well, that's him."

That might explain my festering hatred for him. I'm getting introduced to so many people, I've quit trying to remember names. We don't actually move. People just come over to the table or pull up chairs. Some of the hottest girls I've ever seen sit down next to me and ask what I do. They ask before they even ask me my name. Julian seems to keep moving closer to Robin. It's making me uncomfortable, even though I know it shouldn't. Maybe it's because I'm drunk. Trevor keeps buying me tequila shots. He says every Texan he's ever met can really put away tequila, and I don't want to disappoint him. I love Trevor. He and Anderson and Zeb. They're all my best friends. The girl sitting next to me now, a dancer— she's informed me of that twice—is telling me about a party up in the Hills. She wants to know if I want to come. I'm tempted, but Robin intercedes. "We might make it up later," she says.

Trevor returns from yet another trip to the men's room with news. "Kids, I found us a rave."

The pill doesn't look any different from aspirin. I wish Trevor would have just told me it was aspirin; then it would be easy. I know I'm going to be hungover tomorrow; aspirin would make sense. But he told what it was. Julian takes the pill he's offered. So does Robin. Mine just sits there on the cocktail napkin. Robin picks it up and puts it in her mouth, leans over, and kisses me. I feel the pill enter my mouth along with her tongue. We did a series on X earlier this year on *Classroom Direct*. We made it look very bad. Of course we did. We wouldn't want to lose any subscriber schools, would we?

I swallow the pill and continue kissing Robin.

The dancer leaves our table.

The cab drops us off in front of a warehouse. I feel nothing, which is fine with me. Still drunk, maybe, but nothing else, I wander through makeshift stalls where the tattooed and pierced hawk goods and services: smart drinks, body piercing, fortune-telling, holistic healing, and handcrafted rain sticks and kaleidoscopes. The music is deafening. All beat. Snare drums that give you enough time to compose poetry between the initial snap and the end of the reverb. Bass drums that take up physical space inside your stomach. Vivid pink and green amoebas are projected onto giant screens. They swirl and divide. Hundreds of people are dancing. Some with partners, but most without. Trevor's already out there, his head bouncing above the others'. I turn to tell Robin that I'm going to take a cab home, but she's dancing. And that becomes my world. Her hips. Her bare shoulders. The memory of her taste.

The sensation starts at my fingertips. It's like warm, liquid electricity. It spreads, and I move. Every motion on beat. I can function no other way. My lungs expand with air from the mountains. Not the smog-covered hills surrounding us, but from Angel Fire. The pure, cold air I swallowed on Immaculate Conception ski retreats. When the jolt arrives at my heart, no doubt remains. I love Robin Ferris. I close in on her and tell her so.

"Feels good, doesn't it?" she says.

"Oh yeah," I say with enthusiasm, even though I don't know whether she's talking about the drug or being in love. I'm not sure I can separate the two anyway.

Still dancing, Robin turns away from me, but she reaches back and grabs my arms. She wraps them around her, and the two of us move as one. I spot Julian leaning against a wall surrounded by girls. He's not such a bad guy. Trevor approaches and hugs Robin and me, but then he's off again. Robin and I dance. I don't notice songs ending, and I don't get tired. Some guy dancing next to us catches my eye. He cups his hand around my ear.

"I know you, man."

"You do?"

"You're the only cool one, man. The only one on *Classroom News* that's real."

"Thanks."

He gives me a thumbs-up and resumes dancing. God, I'm lucky.

"You star, you," says Robin.

"He didn't know the name of the show. He might be thinking of . . ."

But I don't get to finish. Robin puts her hands around my neck and kisses me. We keep kissing as songs fade into new songs. Barely moving. Small kisses initially. She covers my face with them. I close my eyes, and she presses her lips to my eyelids. I drag my fingernails across her bare shoulders. Robin purrs. Kate likes that too. I love Kate. I miss her. Robin bites my ears, and I smile. I'm trying hard to make this real. I'm Patrick Sheridan. From Doggett, Texas. I drive a Cordoba. I couldn't make the football team. I've got my hand on America's sweetheart's butt.

I don't know how much later it is that Trevor interrupts us, but we've moved on to exploration of each other's throats.

"Get a room!" he laughs.

The ceiling of Robin Ferris's bedroom is painted black with tiny dots of white that represent the stars. They're the first I've seen since I moved to Los Angeles. She's still asleep. I'm naked—I've checked.

We did it. At least I think we did.

The thud of the stack of books and papers landing next to my head scares the shit out of me. I was dozing off at my desk. I haven't been getting enough sleep lately. I've been spending every night at Robin's, and, well, you know . . .

"Jesus, Lydia! What are you doing?"

"Oh, I'm sorry," she says sarcastically, "I thought you worked here."

"What's this stuff?" I ask, glancing down.

"Homework," she says. "We're going to Belfast, Northern Ireland, sometime before the end of the month. I want you up to speed."

"No shit?"

"Prentiss liked the way it sounded—'*Patrick Sheridan* reporting from Ireland.' I thought about telling him it would sound even cuter if we called you Patrick O'Sheridan and dressed you in a leprechaun costume, but I was afraid he'd take me up on it."

"I get to go to Ireland?" I still can't believe my luck.

"Northern Ireland."

"I don't care which part."

"You'd better read your materials, then," Lydia says with some concern.

"No, I know the North is where the fighting is. I just want to go."

"Patrick, it's good to see you finally excited about something again, but there hasn't really been fighting since the cease-fire in '93. We're doing a piece marking a year and a half of peace. It's still not exactly *Brigadoon*. Try not to mention your papist masters in Rome while we're there."

"Check," I say, not entirely sure what she means.

I'd better look this stuff over.

Slow day for mail. I only get three things: my airline ticket back to Doggett for prom, a phone message from Kate (Nicola's scribbled "Call this poor girl back!" in the memo), and another letter from Drew Hartsock.

Patrick,

Poor baby.

People don't give you credit for all the wonderful things you do because you're so handsome. My heart bleeds. Boy, I thought I had it tough. Just as an example—and I know this is nothing compared to the hardship in your life—let me tell you what happened to me the other day.

There's this girl. (There's always a girl.) Let's call
her Bessie, because she's a bit of a cow. But I'm not
so picky. I can't afford to be, and Bessie's smart, and
she was reading a Raymond Carver book once, so
I thought she might have some soul. Big mistake.
I wrote her a note. You do a lot of note-writing
when you're a stutterer, Patrick. My note was just
a suggestion that we get to know each other a
bit better. I said I thought we might have a lot in
common. I put my phone number on it. You know
what she did? She showed all her stupid friends. One
of them took it to the library and made photocopies
of it and handed them out to everyone she knew.

Patrick, do you know what it feels like to have
everyone at school laughing at you? I get calls
every night from girls saying, "Let's get to know
each other better," then laughing their asses off and
hanging up. But, Pat, you know real pain. People
don't give you your due. Let me be the first, then.

Patrick, you deserve everything you get.

Drew

I take a promo photo out of my desk drawer. I sign it, "Drew—
thanks for watching *Classroom Direct*. We value your input. Patrick." I stick it in an envelope and drop it on Nicola's stack of
outgoing mail.

*   *   *

I've got on a tux. This is a first. I'm riding in a limo. First time for that, too. But it feels right. It definitely feels good. I lean over and kiss my date.

"Are you ready?" she says as the limo pulls up to the curb. She squeezes my hand.

"Yes, ma'am," I say.

She pinches my cheek and kisses me again before opening the door.

Flashes illuminate us, and the sound of automatic cameras advancing provides the first background noise. Then voices shout out Robin's name, and she turns to the crowd lined up in front of Mann's Chinese Theater and waves. And smiles. God, she's pretty. A woman I recognize from somewhere on TV sticks a microphone in front of Robin's face and asks her if she's nervous about her first movie role.

"I'm excited," Robin says. "I think people are going to see a side of me that I don't get to reveal in *Prairie Girl*."

We're both X'ing, which is probably a side she doesn't reveal as Prairie Girl. I wonder briefly if the photog is getting a one-shot or a two-shot and whether it's obvious I can't stand still.

"Anything you want to say to your fans?" says the woman with the microphone.

"See the movie. Take an open mind."

I hear the crowd gasp. Behind us, her costar, Rory Kidd, has arrived. He's only the richest seventeen-year-old in the country. He's been starring in movies since he played that little boy who took over for Santa Claus in some Christmas movie ten years ago. Everyone focuses on the limo door—everyone but Robin, who told me Rory Kidd was a weirdo who carried stuffed animals around the set and talked to them in a baby voice. She takes advantage of the moment to kiss me. It's killing me trying to keep my hands off of her. I'm not sure I'm going to be able to stay seated all the way through the film.

Robin has to be on the *Prairie Girl* set so early, I don't know how she does it. I mean, I don't think we went to bed until two, and I'm sure we didn't get to sleep until three, but when the alarm rang at five, she just sprang out of bed. She doesn't make me get up at the same time, so I don't. By the time I wake up, it's ten. I'm already an hour late for class, so I guess I'll blow that off. I let myself out of Robin's apartment and trudge down the hall to my own.

The message light is blinking on my phone. I dial the voice mail access number. It's Anderson.

"Hey, Patrick," he says in a voice strange even for Anderson. "I thought you should know that you were on TV last night. They showed the premiere of that Rory Kidd movie, and in one of the shots you could see you and Robin Ferris mugging down pretty hard. Kate didn't show up to school today. I heard she's upset in a major way."

Chapter Eight
DOGGETT, TEXAS

PAPA PICKS ME UP FROM THE AIRPORT IN LUBBOCK. I don't really know why I'm still flying in. Kate's refused to talk to me all week, but I had the ticket already. There are so many things I want to explain to her—how I still care for her so much, how I was lonely, that maybe we're too young to get so serious—but her parents just tell me they'll let her know I called.

"You want to tell me what happened between you and Kate?" asks Papa as we're pulling into town. He knows something's wrong. Otherwise, Kate would have been at the airport.

"Things," I say, hoping he'll leave it alone.

I get my wish. We drive the next several blocks in silence. But one of the things that makes Papa a good lawyer is he always gets in the last word. "Haven't seen much of her in church."

Even though he says it matter-of-factly, I know the judgment going on in his head.

"So what."

He slams on the brakes. My seat belt prevents me from flying through the windshield.

"You watch your mouth, boy," Papa says. The words come out

calmly, but the veins in his neck are bulging out. "You're not in Los Angeles anymore."

He grinds his old Chevy truck into gear.

"You could call your mother more often. She worries about you."

"Yes, sir."

After dinner I drive to Kate's house. Past the Dairy Queen. Past the high school. Past Immaculate Conception. In less than five minutes I'm pulling into the driveway that I know so well.

I knock on the door before I have time to talk myself out of it. Mr. Mosely answers. He doesn't look happy to see me. "Oh, Patrick," he says. "You shouldn't have come here."

But I'm not paying much attention, because Kate has come down the stairs. She's wearing a formal dress. She looks unbelievable.

"Hello," I say, directing it past Mr. Mosely to Kate.

She freezes when she sees me. She just stands on the bottom step and stares at me with her mouth open. My first thought when I see her in the dress is that she knew I was going to show up. Her expression erases that notion, and a new, uglier one, takes its place. She's going to the prom—just not with me.

"Get out of here," she screams. "Go back to Hollywood."

"Just let me talk to you. Just for a minute, Kate."

But Kate is pounding back up the stairs.

"I'm going to close the door now," says Mr. Mosely.

"Tell her I'm sorry," I say. "Please tell her I'm sorry."

As I'm driving home, I stop at the light in front of the high school. A pickup pulls alongside me, and the driver, a junior on the football team, rolls down his window. Mine's already down.

"Robin Ferris?" he yells. "You are the man."

I break the silence of the Sheridan dinner table with a question. "Where did Grampa grow up? Which part of Ireland?"

"The West Coast," says Papa. He pushes back his chair and lights a Winston. "Why do you ask?"

"I'm getting to go. They're sending me to Ireland."

"Really?"

"Well, Northern Ireland. I doubt I'll get to go anywhere else."

"Northern Ireland," says Mama as she refills my milk glass. "I don't think that's safe."

"Hush, Mother," says Papa. "There's a cease-fire."

"That's why we're going. We're doing a story on eighteen months of peace."

"Knock on wood," says Papa.

His comment makes me recall a dinner we had several years ago. After Grampa died. A bony Irishman came to our house. He gave me a big green sucker shaped like a four-leaf clover. He called me young fella and lad, which is what Grampa always used to call me. After the meal, he pulled a stack of photos from an envelope. I caught a glimpse of a couple before Papa sent me to my room. They were of mangled bodies lined up in rows in the street. I left the kitchen, but I didn't make it upstairs. I hid behind the swinging kitchen door and observed from the crack.

"It's shocking, Mr. Sheridan. Without a doubt. I'm truly sorry to be showing you these."

"Why are you showing them to me?" my father responded.

"The people in the States have to know what's happening to our Catholic brothers and sisters in Derry and Belfast—all over Ulster. We're a defenseless people, Mr. Sheridan. The Unionists have the Brits doing their dirty work for them. All we have are some lads ready to die if need be. But they can't do it with pea-shooters. Which is, nearly, all they got."

From the crack in the doorway, I watched my father's face darken.

"Peashooters didn't kill those women in London last month."

"Regrettable. Truly regrettable," says the Irishman, his head shaking contritely. "But in every war there *are* civilian casualties. It's with the help of Irish American Catholics like yourself—with financial means—that we can ensure peace. The Brits, they won't talk to a bunch of unarmed, working-class papists. You know that. If you could see the conditions I'm talking about. The poverty, the unemployment, the . . ."

But Papa's already standing up.

"Call it what you want, Mr. Ryan. I'm a lawyer, I call it murder. Now if you'll kindly leave my house."

"I'm sorry you feel that way," says the man. He quickly gathers his materials to leave. "There are some true patriots, some brave young people back home who are trying to make things better."

"That's one thing we agree on," says my father, "but I don't believe you know who they are."

Papa never talked to me about that night. After reading the materials Lydia gave me, I finally think I understand. Mama clears Papa's plate away.

"Can I see Grampa's stuff?"

"It's up in the attic," says Papa. "Be my guest."

I held out some hope that Kate would be in church, but I'm not surprised when she doesn't show up. Father Madigan mentions my return to Doggett at the end of the sermon. Mama squeezes my hand when he does. People turn to look at me, everyone but the Moselys, whom I'm focused on. I attempt to smile, but I'm afraid it doesn't come out right. I'm glad I'm flying home this afternoon. Home? Jesus, I'm not really calling L.A. home, am I?

After the service, Father Madigan posts himself by the church doors. I shake his hand as I'm exiting. He asks me if I'm in need of confession. I tell him that I've just gone in Los Angeles. I can't believe I'm lying to my priest. We Sheridans take the longest to leave the church, as usual, because Papa likes to chat with everyone. When we finally get to the car, Kate's standing next to it.

"Hello, Mr. and Mrs. Sheridan."

"Well hello, Kate," says Mama. "It's been too long."

"Can I talk to Patrick?" Kate says.

"Y'all go ahead," I say. "I'll walk."

My parents get in Mama's Lincoln and drive away. I can feel my heart pounding. I'm not prepared for this. I don't know what I want to say. Kate takes the pressure off by starting. "Did you have sex with her?"

"Yeah," I say.

"Are you still having sex with her?"

"I can stop. If I can just have you, I'll stop."

"You already had me—I was your girlfriend, remember?—it didn't stop you then."

"I'm sorry. I was just so lonely."

"I was lonely, Patrick. You're the one who chose to leave me and go work for that stupid television show. You have no right to be lonely."

"I still love you," I say.

"Well, I feel sorry for you, then," says Kate. "But I don't really think you do. I was so stupid. When I didn't get calls, when you didn't write as often, when you plain forgot our two-year anniversary—I just told myself you were busy. Do you know what I felt like when I saw you on television with your tongue down Robin Ferris's throat?"

I don't say anything.

"That's a stupid question," says Kate. "Of course you don't."

Father Madigan appears across the parking lot. I don't want to have this conversation here. "Let's walk," I say. I almost reach out for Kate's hand. It's practically reflex, but I catch myself in time.

"You know what?" I say. "You may not believe this, but it wasn't any fun. The first time, that is. I felt like I wasn't even there—"

"Patrick, come on."

"Let me finish. What I mean is—it was like I was orbiting. It's the way I feel all the time now. Like I can't really touch anything or anyone and nothing touches me. I just circle and never land." I stop walking and face Kate. "Sex—losing it, but not with you—it just proved that you can be as close together as two people can possibly be physically, and still feel . . . I don't know . . . like a ghost."

Kate looks down at her shoes. I think she's considering slapping me, but she doesn't. "Yeah, I do know what you mean," she says.

I'm surprised by this. "You do?"

"Yeah," she says, "I do."

I cover my face with my hands, anticipating the answer to my next question. "Did you keep the reservation at the Holiday Inn?"

I'm shaking as I ask it. Kate looks away but nods slowly.

"Are you still a virgin?"

This time she shakes her head.

"Oh, God."

A million ways of hurting myself flash through my head. "I thought you said you weren't in love with Blaine."

She turns back and faces me. Tears are running down her cheeks. "I didn't go with Blaine."

"Who, then?" I demand.

She puts her fingers on my chest, but I slap her hands away.

"Answer my fucking question. I want to know who."

The steeliness that I've always admired in Kate returns to her eyes.

"I went with Zeb," she says.

* * *

The condom is sitting in the middle of the kitchen table. Mama's pacing around the room. She keeps alternating between the phrases "Your father's gone out looking for you" and "This isn't how we raised you."

It's been hours since I left them in the church parking lot. I've filled my day with various masochistic missions. I parked for an hour in front of Zeb's house until he finally came outside. Then I peeled out. I must have averaged a hundred miles an hour on my way to Lubbock. I pretended to be Kate Mosely's brother at the Holiday Inn. I said she had left a ring in the room and that I was there to look for it. A maid let me in. The bed was already made. I scanned the room. Detail checked it. Burned every last article into my brain. All from the doorway.

"I don't see it," I told the maid. Then I walked out.

I called Carlina Knott, this girl I dated at the beginning of my sophomore year, and asked her if she wanted to go get something to eat, maybe grab a milk shake. She said yeah, but I blew it off and came home to find this scene.

"What were you doing in my stuff?" I ask Mama.

Her face gets red. She starts wagging her finger at me. "You don't have 'stuff,' smart-mouth," she says. "You have things we gave you. I was doing your laundry. I was being your mother."

"I didn't ask you to," I say.

"You get up to your room," shouts Mama.

"Glad to," I say.

I climb the stairs, enter my room, and start throwing all my clothes back in my suitcase. When I'm done, I carry it downstairs and through the kitchen where Mama is smoking one of Papa's cigarettes. She looks up when she sees me. "You're not leaving this house until your father gets home," she says, "and you'll be lucky if we let you go then."

"I'm getting the fuck out of here," I say. I pick the condom off the table, stick it in my pocket, and walk out the back door. Forty minutes later I park the Cordoba in the short-term parking at the Lubbock airport and head up to catch my plane.

Chapter Nine
LOS ANGELES, CALIFORNIA

I'M GLAD THE MISSISSIPPI IS FLOODING, OVERFLOWING its banks and wiping out cornfields in Iowa and burying schools in Missouri in blankets of sludge. It gets me out of Los Angeles for a few days, and it keeps my mind off of everything else.

Yesterday I was outside of Des Moines with Billy Trundle interviewing some kid whose family farm was now five miles downriver. We couldn't get a usable bite from him because he was more interested in whether or not Nan Spencer was single. Now those are priorities.

Billy has to crash the story, so as soon as we're back in Los Angeles, he heads for an editing bay. I could go back to Sunset Villas, but I think too much there. I walk into the newsroom, where a few of the staff members are watching satellite coverage of a bank robbery that's turned into a hostage situation.

I stay at the office until past ten, then I take a taxi to Sunset Villas. I stay in the shower long enough for the hot water to run out. I let it get colder and colder, waiting for it to become unbearable, but it never does. Eventually I get out and brush my teeth. I'm standing there naked in front of my "star" mirror holding my

Accutane capsule. I spit the toothpaste out at my reflection and toss the pill in the toilet.

I haven't checked my mailbox at work since I got back from Doggett. This morning when I walk in, Nicola orders me to clean it out.

"You're going to need a crowbar to do it."

I ask her for her trash can, which I set below my box. I pull everything out at once, letting it fall to the receptacle below.

"That's one way to do it," she says.

In the pile of letters that spilled out I spot a copy of *Sassy* someone must have stuffed in there. A page has been marked with a Post-it note. I flip the magazine open to find an article on the fashion of Robin Ferris. There are two pictures of her with guys. The caption says, "Whether she's out clubbing with former beau, model Julian Worthy, or vamping it up for a Hollywood premiere with current flame, news hunk Patrick Sheridan, the statuesque actress knows quality when she squeezes it."

Great.

"You don't have to wear that, you know," Nicola says.

"Hunh?"

"The hat. You don't have to wear it or the sunglasses. The cameras aren't rolling. The lights aren't on."

"I thought you were a fan of my Texasness, my general Texacity," I say, a little surprised by Nicola's comment.

"I was a fan," she says, "of your sincerity."

*   *   *

Robin's been gone since the day I left for Texas. She's been out promoting her movie. It's funny, but we haven't called each other once. Funny because I don't think much about it. I don't even know where she's supposed to be on any given day of the week. I've seen her a few times doing talk shows on the monitors in the newsroom.

So I'm surprised when the phone rings at three A.M. and it's Robin. "Come over," she says.

"Over where?" I say groggily.

"I'm home."

"Vermont?"

"Across the hall, sleepyhead. Lonely. Cold. Horny."

I allow a pause. "Who is this?" I say.

"Oh, you are so dead," she says, but I'm already throwing on some shorts for the trip down the hall. Robin's door has been left cracked open, and the lights are off. I climb the stairs to her loft in the dark.

When we make love I feel human for the first time in weeks. As I'm falling asleep with her wrapped around me, I consider telling her everything that's happened since she's been gone. About Kate and Zeb. About my parents. But I don't. There are people who are great talkers and people who are great listeners. Robin only does one of those well, and I'm not especially good at either.

I'm sitting up in bed when Robin returns from the shower wrapped in a towel. Though she tries to hide it, I see the look that I recognize so well. It's the same one I used to get from my girlfriends at pep rallies. The one that lets me know my days are numbered.

It's my face. She hasn't seen it until now. A week and a half without the bacteria-loathing assassins of Accutane ridding my pores of grease has left trails of ripening whiteheads across my cheeks.

"Come back to bed," I say, testing my theory.

"Patrick, I've got things to do, and don't you have tutoring or something?"

"So?" I say. I get up. Naked. And I walk toward her. She's still wearing only her towel. I know by the confused look on her face what's running through her brain. It's the process of rationalization operating at full tilt. I can practically hear the synapses crackling. She's wondering how she can justify—to herself, not me—wanting me last night and being repulsed by me this morning. Logic is patiently explaining to her it's my face, but she's not allowing herself to accept that. She's telling herself she's not that shallow.

But she is. Everyone is.

She's in my arms. I'm enjoying this. I'm even turned on by it. Not the touching. Not her hesitant kisses. But making her see the ugly truth about herself. We're all usually so able to hide from it.

I guide her back onto the bed. As we're having sex, I know it's for the last time. I'll settle down for a set of random excuses while she figures out what it is about me that's always bothered her. Maybe it's my lack of ambition. Maybe it's that I have no sense of humor. It's got to be something.

It just won't be my face.

*   *   *

It's the noon meeting, and Lydia is on fire. We've just learned that Shaquille O'Neal has been booked to guest anchor the show on Thursday. But, as Lydia points out, he's also a spokesperson for Pepsi, which just happens to be one of our biggest sponsors.

"Prentiss, this is going too far. You do this, and we lose whatever credibility we might still have."

"Really?" Prentiss responds. "With whom? Do you think our audience gives a rat's ass whether Shaq drinks Pepsi?"

"Of course they do. That's why Pepsi pays him so much."

"Don't play games with me, Lydia. You know what I'm trying to say. My point is, they—our audience—don't make the connection between who our advertisers are and who we have guest anchor. On top of that, Pepsi isn't pitching him to us— his agent is. The agent thinks it would be good for his profile. Young people love Shaq. Shaq loves young people. That sort of thing."

"Who are you trying to convince here, Prentiss? Let's call it what it is. We're Pepsi's concubine. The offer may have come from his agent, but it's an offer we can't refuse. Maybe the kids out there won't put two and two together, but you're always underestimating them; some of them will. Either way, our peers will see it. Some of us actually go out in the field and work with these people. How do we defend this move?"

"I'm sorry if working here embarrasses you in front of your peers, Lydia—"

"Stop it. What embarrasses me is that we do some good work

here, but no one gives us credit for it because we treat our credibility with such contempt."

There's murmuring around the meeting room, but no one dares jump into the middle of this. I scan the faces of the anchors, producers, and assorted other staff members, assigning them to categories: *Would dance on Prentiss Scott's grave but too afraid to speak up. Just here until picked up by* Entertainment Tonight. *Wonders why we all can't just get along. Thinks it would be cool to meet Shaq.* I look at Billy Trundle. He doesn't fit any of the categories. He would need his own: *Used to give a shit, but that was a long, long time ago.*

"Well, we've got a couple students here. Let's ask them what they think." Shayla and I catch each other's eyes when Prentiss decides on this course of action. The two of us have talked about how much we hate these moments. "Do you think students consider whether our guest anchors are somehow"—Prentiss makes quote signs with his fingers—"*connected* to our advertisers. Shayla?"

"No one in my school would think about that stuff," she says without looking up.

"Mmmhhmm." Prentiss nods earnestly like this means something to him. "And, Patrick, what would the students of Doggett think?"

The mention of my school reminds me of Kate.

"The smart ones would catch it," I say, "but they're probably not watching."

The murmuring stops, and everyone in the room starts looking at me. I see a sly grin creep across Lydia's mouth. She winks at me, and I wonder if it's the first time I've seen Lydia smile. Connie is the first to speak.

"Maybe if we could get the anchors to act a little more professional, maybe show up on time, become familiar with the news they read . . ."

Earl Woodbie jumps in. "'Professional'? Am I hearing this from the same person who screams—*screams*—at the P.A.s to get her *fucking* coffee?"

I'm not sure where that exchange leads, because our PR person Vivienne, who is responsible for booking the guest anchors, comes after me. "Patrick, since you watched *Classroom Direct* before you came out here, did that make you one of the dumb ones?"

"Yeah," I say.

Vivienne storms out. By now, the room has erupted into a half-dozen confrontations.

"Patrick, let me see you in my office," says Prentiss as he gathers his things to exit. I follow him, completely resolved to being fired.

But he doesn't fire me. Instead, he sits on the couch, leans toward me, and, with a concerned expression on his face, asks me what's going on in my life.

"Nothing," I say.

"You're not getting into drugs, are you?"

"No."

"I've had some disturbing reports from Kim that you're not

showing up to class, not turning in any of your work."

"I'll get it done. It's just so easy. It's stuff I've already had. I do fine on the tests."

"She says you're not doing nearly as well as you used to."

I sit there staring out through the smog at where the Hollywood sign should be. Never mind the sign. I can't see the Hills.

"We're still counting on you, Patrick."

I wonder who else he's including in the "we." As far as I can tell, no one counts on me anymore.

Prentiss stands, which I guess is my cue to get out of his office, but as I'm walking out he gets in a last word.

"Let's see if we can't lay off the sweets."

"Hunh?"

He points to his cheeks.

"There's only so much we can do with makeup, Patrick. Only so much."

I guess in the back of my mind, I've been expecting a phone call from Papa. I even thought there was a chance he would just show up and drag me back home by the hair. The package sitting in front of my door when I get home from work tonight cures me of that romantic notion. I know what's inside even before I drag the box into my living room and cut it open.

Tearing back the cardboard, I find what I anticipate— everything I own.

Mama's even taken the unsubtle step of packing my Bible and my pictures of Kate on top. As I dig down, I find all the framed pictures of me that used to grace the walls of the house. Other than that, there's lots of clothes. Things I wouldn't be caught dead in anymore. Medals from journalism competitions. At the bottom there's an envelope. Inside it are my Social Security card and my birth certificate. There's no note. It's not until I open this envelope that I start crying. It means it's permanent. I'm on my own.

I must lie there for an hour with my arm draped over my eyes, sobbing. How did I end up like this? When did I start hating myself? I just want to go home. There's nothing here I want or need. I reach for the phone and dial my parents' number. Mama answers. I try to say something, but I just start bawling into the receiver like a little kid. I hear a "Patrick? Patrick? Is that you?" Finally I manage a tortured, "Mama."

I'm met with silence. I sniffle, and I hear her say my name. That's the last word, though, from Mama. I make out Papa's voice in the background.

"Is that him?" he says. Then the line goes dead.

For a few minutes I just sit there stunned. Then I feel myself getting cold. Even angry. I wonder if this is how it happened with Bridget. I wonder what kind of parents are so willing to give up on their kids and how such devout churchgoers can know so little about forgiveness. With Papa, it's pride. With Mama, it's weakness. It stands to reason that I'm a product of that.

The light on my telephone is blinking. I play the voice mail and listen to Robin explain why she can't meet me at Chan Dara, this Thai place where we'd agreed to meet after she got back to town. I don't even pay attention to the reason. My mind is still in Doggett.

I decide I've got to know. I've got to know what happened between my parents and my sister. What's kept them from speaking for all these years. Her last name is Rathmore. She lives in Reseda. I call information, and they give me a phone number, but that not what I want.

"Do you have an address?"

And I'm given that as well.

I call the cab company. I go stand outside. It's warm during the day in California, but the nights are always cool. I decide that's something I miss about Texas—warm nights, on the porch, iced tea . . . with Kate. I bring my hand up to my face and feel the bumps. My security.

A little boy answers the door. My nephew.

"Who are you?" he says.

"My name is Patrick. Is your mother home?"

He pivots and yells, "Mom!"

A moment later, Bridget rounds a corner and sees me. She looks every bit as surprised to see me as I did the first time I found her at my door. At first she doesn't say anything. Then I guess she notices the tears in my eyes.

"Hey, kiddo," she says. "Come inside."

She leads me into a dining room and pulls out a chair. A stack of watercolor paintings are spread out on the giant table.

"Grading," she says before disappearing into the kitchen. She comes back out holding two cans of Coke. She sets one down in front of me and takes a seat across the table. "Tell me about it," she says.

And so I do. I tell her everything. I tell her like the journalist I used to be. I give her the facts without comment, without subjectivity. It's the only way I can keep from bawling my head off. The last thing I tell her about is Mama finding the condom, about the way I left Doggett, about the package I found at my apartment, and about my brief phone call home. She leans across the table and takes my hand.

"So what do I do now?" I say. "There's no one better at holding a grudge than Mama and Papa. Look at what they did to you."

Bridget looks down at our hands.

"Is anyone ever going to tell me what happened?" I ask.

As I ask the question I hear the front door open. A man enters wearing running shorts and a T-shirt. He's covered in sweat and breathing hard. He looks at me, but he's unable to catch his breath.

"Honey," she says, "this is Patrick. Patrick, this is Charley."

I wipe my eyes with my sleeve and offer a hand, but he's already out of the room.

"Patrick," Bridget says, her voice sounding hollow and resigned as she keeps her eye on the hallway her husband has escaped down. "I think it's time you know something."

"I'm sorry if this is a bad time."

"No. That's fine. You need to hear this. It might help you understand Roman and Marge—sorry, Mama and Papa—better. You might understand why finding a condom in your pocket made them fly off the handle. You see, Patrick, my theory is that when you have parents as strict as ours, you end up either completely accepting it or going just the opposite way, and rejecting it. From what it sounds like, you were buying into all of it, which is great. But by the time I started high school, I didn't believe a lick of it. I didn't believe in their God. I didn't believe in their morality. I hated the way Papa treated Mama, and I thought both of them were hypocrites. Mama was such a gossip back then, and Papa, well, I'll get to him in a minute. I did my best to make their lives miserable. I didn't come home some nights. I was drinking in junior high. I made it a mission to violate every last "rule of the house." By the time I was sixteen, I had violated the big one. I was pregnant. I decided right away that I was going to get an abortion, but the doctor I went to golfed with Papa, and the concept of doctor-patient confidentiality hadn't quite reached Doggett, Texas. One day I get home from school, and I'm kidnapped, literally kidnapped, by my own parents. They take me to a home for unwed mothers in Austin.

"They told everyone back home that I was living with Aunt Chloe in Austin because of the great art program some school had, and I was supposed to live that lie, but the longer I was pregnant, the less sure I was that I wanted to put the baby up for adoption. I thought I wanted to keep it, but remember, if I came home with a baby, everyone would know. All of Mama's gossip circle. All of Papa's clients.

"I didn't know what to do. After I had the baby, and they found out who the father was, Roman said there was no way I could come home with them. I knew I couldn't raise a child on my own, but I couldn't bear to live with them either. I never came home, and they never called, but they knew how to get even. They adopted you."

Neither of us says anything for a moment. She squeezes my hand tightly.

"So can you understand what must have been going on in their heads when they found out that you've been having sex? Do you know how much that must scare them?"

But I don't care about any of that. I want her to back up. I want to make sure I heard her correctly. "So they're really my grandparents?"

Bridget nods.

"And you're my . . ."

"Mother," she says.

At this point I can actually feel whatever connections I have binding me to other people in my life unraveling. I'm sitting here with my mother, and I've never felt as lost in my life. I was never one of those adopted kids who was dying to know who their parents were. I always thought I would be disappointed. Without knowing any of the facts, I was free to imagine them however I wanted: a country-western star and a lonely Lubbock waitress, two Pulitzer Prize winners unable to take time from their careers to raise a child. Something like that.

"Who was my father?" I ask, remembering her earlier comment about my parents' outrage, and no longer sure I really want to know.

"Peter Garcia, valedictorian of Doggett High class of 1982. The last I heard he was working as a lobbyist in D.C."

"So I'm half Mexican?"

"A quarter. Peter was half, but that was too much for Roman. He couldn't bear the thought of his daughter giving birth to a mixed-race child."

"But they adopted me."

"But that's different, Patrick. The way things worked out, they look like a couple of fine Christians adopting an unwanted mixed-race child. It's different from taking care of their daughter's Mexican bastard."

"You said you never came home, but I can remember you. Barely, but I can."

"I stayed in touch with Grampa. You're so lucky you got to know him, Patrick. He was the best. He would let me know when he was going to have you for a few days. I would hitchhike out to see you. Or, if I had enough money, fly. One day, after you learned to talk, you told Mama and Papa about playing with me. They wouldn't let you stay with Grampa after that. I didn't get to see you again, except in the pictures Grampa would send me, until I saw you on TV."

"So does your husband know who I am?"

"I told him what happened before we got married. It really upset him, Patrick. I don't know if you'll understand this, now, but he wanted our children to be the first for both of us. He accepted the news, but it wasn't easy for him, and I don't think he ever planned on you appearing in the living room. I hadn't told him about you living here in town, or me meeting with you."

"I'll leave," I say, and I stand up.

"Please don't," she says.

Just then a little girl comes into the room crying and holding her elbow.

"Mommy, Shane pushed me," she whimpers.

"Ooh, let me see, baby," she says, taking her hand and walking her into the kitchen.

I slip out the door while my mother tends to my half sister.

I work at filling my head, filling my time. The first thing I do is clean my apartment. Somewhere in the excavation, I uncover my textbooks. I turn the ringer off on my phone and the volume off on my answering machine, then watch as the message light blinks in lengthening intervals, but I never push the play button. I begin washing my face again, but I refuse to take any Accutane. I don't say a word at work, and I leave as soon as I've clocked my required hours. At night, I complete assignments for Kim. In three days I turn in four papers and sixteen workbook pages. The papers are uninspired. In my *A Tale of Two Cities* essay, I describe the novel as "a fable . . . drowned in hopeless romanticism totally disconnected from any hard truths of the real world." Lydia would tell me my papers lack voice, but I don't really care. The work keeps me from thinking, and when I think, I begin fantasizing about tall buildings. Climbing the stairs. Standing on rooftops. Crashing back to earth.

I come home one day but notice Bridget's car in the apartment parking lot. I spend the next four hours at a Denny's poring through the packets of information Lydia's been providing me on Ireland. One of the pamphlets talks about the number of people who have invaded the island starting with the Vikings, who founded most of the major ports: Dublin, Cork, Waterford. One of the groups that raided the coasts of Ireland were Spanish pirates who later settled there. Their dark-haired, fair-eyed offspring became what the rest of the population referred to as the Black Irish, renowned for their romantic, passionate, and drunken nature. "In effect, more Irish than their fair-skinned, redheaded countrymen," the article said. Wouldn't Papa love to hear that?

When I come back to the apartment I find a pizza coupon taped to my door. On the back of it, Bridget's written a note.

> Patrick,
>
> There must be a million questions you want to ask me. I told you those things because I wanted us to be closer, not to drive you away or turn you against Mama and Papa. Please call me. I don't expect to step in as your mother, but I do want to be your sister again.
>
> Love,
> Bridget

I pick up the phone and dial. A woman answers. I tell her I want the four-toppings-for-the-price-of-one special.

At ten o'clock, the day after the Shaquille O'Neal episode, Prentiss fired Lydia. Maybe she gave him good reason, but the guy just looked so damned happy all morning that I keyed his Jaguar in the parking lot on the way back from lunch anyway.

Lydia, as the news producer with no segment in yesterday's show, was responsible for writing intros and tags to the stories as well as the end-of-show happy talk. I got the envied spot of coanchoring with O'Neal, thereby virtually assuring that Shayla would never speak to me again. The show actually went smoothly, even though I saw more staff members down on the set than usual—all of them pretending they had things to do. Shaq didn't seem to mind. He signed autographs and joked around with everyone. He was even better than most at reading off the teleprompter for the first time. During a break he asked me where I was from. I told him, and he said he went to high school in Texas too, but I already knew that.

I'm watching as Lydia throws stuff from her desk into a box, explaining to me what happened. She says the problem didn't come to the surface until this morning when Prentiss received calls from Pepsi representatives who had just seen the show. They threatened to pull their forty million dollars in annual advertising because Lydia had managed to work in old Coca-Cola slogans throughout the show. In the intro to our drug story, Shaq read the line, "But if there is a drug making a comeback, coke is it." As the tag of the piece on a successful railroad workers' strike, she had him quote one jubilant— and notably anonymous—striker as saying, "You can't beat the feeling." As Lydia is explaining this to me, I recall the end of the show.

Shaq: PATRICK, THANKS FOR SHOWING
ME HOW TO READ THE NEWS.

Patrick: NO PROBLEM, SHAQ. NOW HOW
ABOUT YOU TEACHING ME TO RAP?
Shaq: PATRICK, I'D LIKE TO TEACH THE
WORLD TO RAP, BUT THERE ARE SOME
THINGS EVEN KAZAAM CAN'T DO.

It hadn't seemed exactly Lydia's style to me. Now I understand why.

She seems strangely calm as she fills the box with her personal mementos. I keep throwing in *Classroom Direct* office supplies, but she keeps taking them out.

"Did you try telling him it was just coincidence that it happened that way?" I ask, but Lydia just looks at me like I'm crazy.

"Patrick, don't look so worried about me. My contract was going to expire after this season. That's three weeks from now. Do you really think Prentiss was going to keep me on here? This way I'm actually getting severance pay. More importantly, I may be able to look myself in the eye each day."

"What are you going to do?"

"My editor at the *Post* said I was welcome back anytime. I may call her up and remind her of that promise."

"The noon meetings aren't going to be the same without you here."

"I don't know about that," she says, then she pats me on the knee.

Cal Sherman and Prentiss enter the talent office an hour later.

"All set for your trip?" Prentiss asks.

"What?"

"Are you packed for Ireland?"

"I'm still going?" I ask, glancing nervously at Cal.

"We'd have to eat the cost of the tickets and the hotels, otherwise. They're already booked."

"Who's producing it?" I ask.

"Cal here is. Now listen, all we want on this is something light about the lifestyle of teenagers growing up in a war zone."

"It's not a war zone," I tell him. "It's not even really a war in their minds. Besides, if they're teenagers in school now, they probably weren't teenagers before the cease-fire."

"Just find out what it's like to be a teenager in Belfast," Prentiss says.

"Find out if they like blue jeans and rock and roll?" I say.

Prentiss can't tell if I'm serious. "Something like that."

Cal and I share a cab to LAX. Cal knows that I can just sign vouchers. He has to go through the hassle of expense reporting it. Riding with me saves him the headache.

"What airline?" says the taxi driver as we near the airport.

"Delta," I say. "It's terminal five."

We pull up alongside the curbside baggage check, and the driver hoists my bag out of the trunk. Cal shakes his head as he watches.

"Jesus, Patrick, it's five days—not a lifetime. Nan packs less than that."

Ignoring him, I breathe in a lungful of Los Angeles air before stepping inside.

Chapter Ten
BELFAST, NORTHERN IRELAND

NONE OF MY READING PREPARES ME FOR MY WALK down Shankill Road—for the spookiness of it. I feel like every eye is watching us as we walk through the Protestant neighborhood of East Belfast with a camera crew trailing us. Giant murals painted on the sides of tenement houses depict black-hooded, machine-gun-brandishing men in paramilitary outfits. I know from my research that the giant red hands painted on walls signify not only Northern Ireland's separation from the Republic of Ireland, but the perceived heroism of a Protestant who cut off his own hand to show his loyalty to the British government—the government that most Protestants here are loyal to. The curbs are painted in alternating red, white, and blue bands of the British Union Jack. We're shooting B-roll for the first of three pieces that we'll run over the course of the week. We stop and shoot a mural that commemorates the three hundredth anniversary of the Protestant William of Orange's defeat of the Catholic Charles I. Beside it is a vow to die before submitting to the rule of the Irish.

Our crew is from Belfast. They normally work for the BBC, and they're anxious to give us pointers. They tell us that there are three questions you never ask in Belfast: a person's surname, the neighborhood where they live, or what school they attended.

"Why?" asks Cal, embarrassing me.

"Any one of those questions will give away a person's religion here," answers Mark, the cameraman. "For example, Patrick Sheridan—it's a Catholic name, no question about that. Same with O'Reilly, Fitzpatrick, McGuinness. If your name is Carson or Cook or Miller, you're Proddy. Another thing, here in the Shankill, you don't wear crucifixes or medallions of saints. Just use your head."

"I thought things had really changed since the cease-fire," I say, still overwhelmed by the naked hatred surrounding me.

"Aye. Night and day," says the soundman, Ciarán.

"I'd hate to see night, then," says Cal.

"You can go out on the street at night. You can go into a pub," Mark adds. "There's a joke going around about being in a pub and saying to your mate, 'Who does that wee package at the end of the bar belong to?' It's dark humor, to be sure, but at least people are laughing about it."

Cal looks confused.

"A bomb," I tell him.

The nights are long in Belfast in the summer. It doesn't get dark until nearly ten, so we keep shooting. Our trip down Falls Road, or "The Falls," as the crew calls it, makes the surrealism complete. I never imagined the two neighborhoods existing right next to each other. They're separated by long spiked fences called The Peace Line.

"This is where we should shoot the remote," I tell Cal as we wander up to the fence.

"I thought we'd do it in front of the Europa," he answers. "It is the most bombed hotel in Europe, you know. Clinton stayed there. It's got significance, and the added bonus that nobody's likely to shoot us there."

"The last thing anybody wants to do here is shoot at Americans," Ciarán tells him. "If the IRA actually killed an American, all those dollars from Boston would disappear."

"We ought to go live from the neighborhoods where The Troubles flare up," I argue. "Where teenagers actually live, not where rich tourists stay when they're in town on business."

The best I get out of Cal is an "I'll think about it."

The murals in the Catholic section are every bit as extravagant, but for the most part, they paint themselves as victims rather than soldiers. In one, a line of British soldiers are pointing machine guns at peaceful Catholic protesters. Another shows starving Catholics beside the slogan "There Was No Famine."

I don't get it. My reading dealt extensively with the famine. Nearly half the population of the country either died of starvation or emigrated, primarily to America. I ask our crew about it.

"If you grow up around here," says Ciarán, "you learn completely different histories in the Protestant schools and in the Catholic schools. In Catholic schools, they teach you that there was plenty of food to go around, but that the Protestant British landowners actually exported the food to Britain, where they could get better prices for it. There's still a good deal of hatred left over from that."

The houses and neighborhoods are in shambles. Litter fills the streets. We're out of the car and walking when what looks like a miniature tank passes us on the street.

"Shoot that," Cal commands, but the crew doesn't respond. "Okay, tape it. Aim the camera and press record. Jesus, will you do your job."

"If you take pictures of any of the military or police movements, they'll take your camera."

Strangely, the area reminds me of sections of Los Angeles that I've cabbed through. "Are drugs a problem here?" I ask.

"They're actually more of a problem since the cease-fire because security at the borders isn't quite what it used to be, but it's still not nearly as bad as in the South or in Britain. The paramilitaries take care of that."

"How?" I ask.

"They kneecap or execute anyone they catch dealing drugs in their neighborhoods."

"Kneecap?" I ask.

"Shoot your kneecap off."

"Oh."

When *Classroom Direct* does what it calls a live feed, the description is only partially accurate. The feed is actually taped, but because we're renting mega-expensive satellite time, we try to get it right on the first or second take. That's as live as it gets for us. There's really no legitimate reason to do a remote from here. It might make sense if there was some sort of breaking news that we were on top of, but this is a feature story about a Protestant girl and her Catholic boyfriend, who live on opposite sides of The Peace Line. The decision to do the remote was made in L.A., and, as usual, it's all about appearances. Students back in classrooms across America will see the wind whipping my hair around. I'll speak with some false urgency, and miraculously we'll look."

It's eight hours later in Belfast than in Los Angeles, so it's two A.M. before we're ready to shoot from The Peace Line. Our crew picked us up at the hotel in the satellite truck. It's weird how, as you drive through Belfast, so much of the city seems like any other, but then you'll make a turn and end up in front of a police station that looks like a military bunker with fifteen-foot-high steel walls, barbed wire, and machine-gun turrets. Or you'll get passed by an armored vehicle. Or you'll see the names of "martyrs" painted on the walls of buildings.

And everyone we've talked to says how much better things are.

After Ciarán wires me up, Cal approaches. He's got some sort of vest in his hands. "I want you to wear this for the remote," he says, handing me the garment. I realize, based on the weight of it when I take it from his hands, what it is. It's a bulletproof flak jacket.

"Why?" I say.

"It'll be safer."

"Safer? How?"

"We just shouldn't take any chances, Patrick," Cal says, but I know what this is really about. He wants, or Prentiss wants, an illusion of danger.

"So why aren't you wearing one? Why isn't our crew wearing one? There is a cease-fire, remember? Haven't you heard all the people we've talked to today complain about how they think all Americans perceive this place as being a war zone?"

"Look around you, Dorothy," says Cal, gesturing to the fence and the murals. "We're not in Kansas anymore."

"Cal, don't treat me like I'm stupid. I know what you want here."

"If you're that bright, Patrick, why don't you just act like a professional and do it. Jesus, when did you become a producer?"

Ciarán tells us we've got two minutes before our satellite time opens up. I'm holding the jacket, wondering what Lydia would do in this situation. I stand here frozen.

"Ninety seconds," says Mark.

I put the jacket on. Before I know it, I've got Connie in my ear, talking to me from Los Angeles. "You all set?" she asks.

"Ready as I'll ever be," I say.

Because it's a remote, I don't have a eleprompter. I've had to memorize what I'm going to say. For fourteen minutes, I manage to screw it up. I forget my lines. I trip as I walk down The Peace Line. I turn the wrong way. I mispronounce words. Connie's voice gets edgier and edgier as she talks to me.

"Patrick, we have time for one more take before we lose the satellite. Do you realize how much this costs? If you don't get it here, we've pissed all this money away."

"I'll nail it this time," I say.

"Tape's rolling," she says.

This time I play it for all it's worth, changing a few words and clutching my bulletproof vest like a security blanket.

"*Belfast, a city torn in two, divided into warring factions. The IRA, the UVF, and countless other paramilitary groups—they've sworn to fight to the last man. They're headquartered just a few blocks on either side of this spot optimistically called The Peace Line. For nearly eighteen months an uneasy cease-fire has been in effect, but for two teenagers—one Catholic, one Protestant—danger is still a constant. They've never seen each other's houses. They meet in 'safe' areas of the city. Today you'll hear their story, but I'll be back all week with reports about life in this city of violence.*"

There's a pause before I get any reaction. Then I hear Connie's voice in my ear. "That's a keeper."

Mark and Ciarán are noticeably silent as they break down the equipment and unwire me.

"'City of violence'?" Cal says. "That wasn't in there."

"Whoops," I say flatly.

The wake-up call comes at five A.M., but I'm not sleeping. I packed when I got back to the room, and even though I'm dead tired, I've just been lying here thinking, unable to sleep. I guess I've known that this was what I was going to do from the moment Lydia got fired. Was that the last straw? Was tonight's remote? Now I'm trying to weigh everything out. If I go through with this, I'll lose my job. I'll piss a bunch of people off. I may cause an international incident. And what about my family?

What about my family?

I decide there's only one member of it who really concerns me. That's the one I'll go see.

I shower and make it down to the lobby by 5:20. Behind the front desk is a woman sipping coffee and reading a newspaper.

"Can I leave a message for someone?" I ask.

"Would you like me to ring the room for you?" she asks.

"No, he's sleeping. I'd rather leave a message."

She slides me a pink notepad, the same kind we have back in America. I jot down the message for Cal.

> Cal,
>
>   A group of IRA or UVF terrorists—I'm still having trouble with the accent—came to my room last night. They said they were "recruiting" me, whatever that means. Anyway, good thing I have this jacket. (I was actually wearing it to sleep in!) They were nice enough to let me stop and write this note, but I can't keep them waiting.
>
>   Cheers,
>   Patrick

I fold the note and hand it back to the receptionist, then I reshoulder my pack and head out to the street. I hail one of the big black taxis. The red poppies displayed in the window let me know this one's for Protestants. Ciarán told us it doesn't matter if you're an American, so I climb in.

"Where would you be going?" the driver asks.

"Train station," I say.

"Here from the States, are you?"

"Yeah."

"Anxious to get home?"

"No," I say. "Not really."

Upon arrival at the station, I try to draw out all my money from a cash machine. All three thousand dollars. The money is in my account, but the machine won't give me more than three hundred dollars in pounds sterling. I remember something about having a daily limit on what I can withdraw. Two hundred pounds. I'll be lucky to make it two weeks on that. Since all anyone who wants to find me will have to do is track me by my cash card, I'm screwed, but there's nothing I can do. I take the money and walk up to the counter.

"Could I get the first train to Limerick?" I ask.

"Return?" says the man behind the glass.

"One way," I say.

I'm able to sleep for most of the train ride. I wake up once, and it happens to be where we cross the border from Northern Ireland into Ireland. Of course, in Northern Ireland, they call their neighbor "The Republic" or "The South." In any case, it's the part of the island that's been independent from England since 1922. From the window on the train, I can see an old border checkpoint. According to Lydia's notes, they used to stop and search every car. They'd have lip-readers staring through windows with telescopes, and they'd use mirrors on long poles to search underneath cars.

The British established the checkpoints to prevent weapons coming up into the North and to stop terrorists from escaping into the South. Now they're deserted, and the grim exterior of the one above me—all green steel and barbed wire—makes me feel like I've accomplished little so far by running away. I might as well be in Los Angeles.

I have to switch trains and stations in Dublin, but I'm in such a stupor that I don't pay much attention to the cab ride. Once I'm on the train, I stretch out across two seats, and the next time I open my eyes, I'm in Limerick, one of the few places that qualifies as a city in Ireland. The train station and bus station are in the same building. I walk up to the ticket counter and ask to get on the next bus heading to Kilbeg, but I'm told the next bus doesn't leave until the following day. I sit down in one of the waiting areas and open the *Let's Go* guide to Ireland Lydia loaned me. I look up Limerick and learn its nickname within the country is Stab City. They recommend not wandering around the city alone after dark. Under the "Getting Around" heading, the book talks about bicycling, hiking, renting cars, trains, and buses, but it also mentions that Ireland is perhaps the safest country in the world to hitchhike. I consider my funds and my desire to make it to Kilbeg before dark. I go back up to the information counter and ask the directions to the highway heading south along the coast. Then I begin my hike.

As soon as I'm out of the station, I'm nearly mowed down. I forgot they drive on the left, and I look the wrong way before venturing off the sidewalk. The driver honks, and I can see why. The car might have taken more damage than me. I'm struck by how small they all are. With a running start, I feel confident I could actually knock over one of these little Nissan Micras, Toyota Starlets, or Daihatsu Dominos zipping down the street. A Ford Escort drives by, hogging the road like Mama's Lincoln back home. I'm able to find the coast road without too much difficulty, and a half hour later I decide I've put enough civilization behind me. I set down my bag and stick out my thumb. The fourth car to come along stops.

"How far are you going?" asks the driver, a man of sixty or so.

"Kilbeg," I say.

"I'll get ye nearly there," he says with the thickest accent I've heard in Ireland so far.

I throw my bag in the back and take a seat next to him. It feels weird at first, sitting where the driver should be. I keep feeling like I should be the one shifting, especially when I watch the tricky way he's doing it. Apparently there's something wrong with his left arm, because he actually reaches across his body with his right hand when he shifts. We travel in silence for a few minutes. As we come out of a bend in the road, the Atlantic Ocean appears in front of me. From then on, it's a constant on the right side of the car. I've never seen the ocean before, and I can't keep from staring. I lived in Los Angeles for four months and never made it to the beach. Somehow, though, I think it would have been less impressive than this. There are no million-dollar sea-view mansions. Just lots of sheep corralled in rock fences that lead to the edges of cliffs overlooking the ocean.

"Where're ye from?" asks the man.

"Texas," I answer, guessing he can already tell I'm American.

"Gotcher all well."

"I'm sorry."

"Gotcher *all* well," he says again, this time louder.

"Uh, what?"

"Your *all* well. *All. All. All.*"

"Oh, um, no. I don't have an oil well."

This news seems to disappoint him.

"What are you doing over here? On holiday?"

"Yeah," I say. "Just traveling."

"What did you wanna see in Kilbeg? Most Americans go straight up to Killarney or Dingle or they want to kiss the Blarney Stone. It's nothing but a rock, you know."

"My grandfather came to America from Kilbeg."

"Searching for your roots, are you?"

"Sort of," I say.

The old man again uses his opposite hand to downshift as we enter a town. I glance over at him and I realize how small he is. The bulky corduroy jacket he's wearing gives him the illusion of being normal-sized, but his wrists and neck are like Tinkertoys poking out of the coat. We travel the next few miles without speaking, which is fine with me.

"Are you a student?" he asks eventually.

"Yeah."

"What is it that you're studying?"

"I want to write someday," I say, realizing I'm giving this answer just to fill the space. "For a newspaper."

"Been doing some writing meself," he says. I get the feeling that he wants me to ask about this, but I don't. After a while he continues unprompted. "Letters, mostly. To politicians and newspapers. Can't get the newspapers to print them. Can't get the politicians to lift a finger."

Now I feel like I'm obligated to ask. "What are you writing them about?"

"About me arm," he says, ". . . about me arm."

The old man launches into a story. He says the Irish government experimented on polio victims in the 1930s, and that he and a few thousand others were given an untested vaccine. The survivors, he says, all ended up with withered limbs.

"And we've never received a penny," he says. "Not even an apology. They'd rather we'd just die off, so we'd quit making so much noise."

As he's speaking, I become fixated on his teeth. His gums have worn away and turned black. I don't think he has any molars remaining in his mouth.

"I'm a farmer. I don't have that much to me name. I don't work me own farm. I work for a man who owns a farm, but it's not fit work for a man in me condition. They should have at least given me a job I'd be better suited for. Maybe a postman. I could do that, you know."

I've been watching the road signs as we've traveled. They're in both Irish and English and they give the distances in kilometers. Kilbeg has been getting closer and closer. The old man said he would get me nearly there, but, if I'm not mistaken, it's the town we're entering now. The old man pulls up in front of a pub and parks.

"Do ye still have cowboys in Texas?" he asks.

I have to think about that for a second before answering. "Some," I say.

"When I was a lad, I used to love John Wayne movies. I always thought that I'd like to be a cowboy. Ride a horse into the sunset."

The old man isn't looking at me when he says this. He's staring west toward the ocean. The sun is just beginning to redden where it touches down on the water.

"It's not all it's cracked up to be," I say.

Chapter Eleven
KILBEG, IRELAND

IT TAKES ME TEN MINUTES TO INVENTORY KILBEG'S one road, two pubs, two grocery stores, tourist center, and hostel doubling as a bicycle rental shop. The imposing Catholic church looks like it could hold three times the town's potential population. The sun has, by now, nearly disappeared. The final rays of light reflect against a dozen brightly painted fishing boats in the harbor. So far I haven't seen a single citizen of the town. I wander up the road about fifty yards and find a gas station. Several disassembled cars clutter up the dirt parking lot. Upon further investigation, the gas station turns out to be Kilbeg's third pub. Oil drums are stacked next to the door, partially obscuring a sign that reads TIGH TÁBHAIRNE. I'm drawn in by a small placard on the door frame that uses tiny U.S. flags as a border. It says AMERICAN ALSO SPOKEN.

Tigh Tábhairne is empty inside. There's not even anyone behind the bar. It's easy to see why the place is deserted. It's a dump. The ashtrays on the tables and the bar are overflowing. Last night's—at least I hope they were last night's—glasses are scattered around the room. There aren't two pieces of furniture in the place that match. The assorted stools and folding chairs look like they were pulled from rummage sales. I swear, on one padded stool, the butt cheek indentions are an inch deep. The pub also smells more like a garage than any place you'd want to consume refreshments. What little decoration the place offers is limited to unframed curling photographs of men holding fish or men holding fiddles. A 1975 calendar featuring mischievous bear cubs tangled up in a distressed fisherman's line hangs from an eave above the bar. A dozen or so postcards are tacked up next to it. I take one down that has a picture of topless women sunbathing and the word "*España!*" on the front. I flip it over, but I can't read the message. I don't even recognize the language, so I guess it's Irish. As I'm tacking it back up, I notice something behind the bar that just about makes me gag. Three disembodied pigs' heads are staring up at me from the floor.

I drop the postcard and the tack I'd been holding in my hand. I bend down to pick them up, and when I return to an upright position, there's a scraggly bearded man standing on the other side of the bar. My sudden appearance scares him almost as badly as his scares me.

"Jesus Christ!" he shouts.

I drop the postcard and tack again. "Sorry," I say. I bend down again to pick the articles up.

"What, for fuck's sake, are you doing down there," he says. He leans over the bar and sees what I'm picking up. This starts him laughing. It's this laugh that makes me like him before I even know his name. It's an easy laugh. Well-practiced. Clearly often used.

"This fell down," I say.

"You don't say? Damndest thing. I may have to get my money back for those tacks. Made in America, don't you know."

Two glasses have appeared on the bar, and the man is either pouring himself two whiskeys or each of us one. He pushes the second glass toward me. "Cheers," he says, lifting the glass.

"Cheers," I say, surreptitiously examining my glass. He downs his in an instant. I take a sip from mine and try not to flinch too obviously.

"You're a couple weeks early, aren't you?"

"What?"

"America's not supposed to get here for a couple weeks."

"I wanted to beat the rush." I make an obvious visual sweep of the room. "Looks like I did."

This makes him laugh. "Haven't you heard about the rule of barbershops, lad?"

"Uh, no."

"Let's say you go into a town, and you find out that there are two barbershops." He catches me staring at the pigs' heads. "You following me? What are you, a salon man?"

"I'm with you. Two barbershops."

"Okay. You want to get your hair cut. You go into the first shop, and there's a whole crowd of people inside. The floor is clean. The mirrors sparkle. The barber himself is neatly trimmed. Then you go to the other barbershop. Only one gent in the place. Poxy haircut. He's sitting in the chair. The floor is covered with hair. Which one do you go to?"

"This is a trick question, isn't it?"

"Answer's simple."

"I think I'd go to the clean one."

"Of course you would. You're an American. Never mind that the two barbers cut each other's hair. Never mind that the reason the floor's covered in hair is because that's where everyone gets their hair cut. Second barber doesn't have time to spit-shine his mirror. He's cutting hair, for fuck's sake."

I see what he's getting at, but to me there's a big difference between a pub and a barbershop.

"Name's Eamonn," he says, holding his hand out across the bar.

"Amen? A, M, E, N?"

He shakes his head, a bit disgruntled.

"No. Eamonn. E, A, M, O, N, N. Just like it sounds."

"Patrick," I say as we shake hands.

"Patrick, huh? Back visiting the old country?"

I take another sip of my whiskey, but before I have a chance to answer, Eamonn spots something out of the dirty window that makes him panic.

"That drink's on the house, lad, but I need you to do me a favor."

"What?"

I already thought the drink was on the house.

"Come back here behind the bar. Give the man coming in anything he wants. Just tell him I've gone into Dingle for a couple hours."

With that, Eamonn ducks out the back door even before I agree to do it. I glance out the window in time to see an older man approaching the pub. He's carrying something large and silvery across his shoulders. There's an apron hanging from a nail. What the hell. I put it on and step behind the bar.

"Howdy," I say to the man when he walks through the door.

"Evenin'," he says. "Where's Eamonn?"

"Gone to Dingle." I realize now that it's a huge, unwrapped fish the man has with him.

"Be a good lad and put this in the freezer for me."

The old man plunks the fish down on the counter. Now that I'm behind the bar, I notice the Deepfreeze. I also find out that the shelves facing me come stocked with 7-Eleven necessities: tea, coffee, bread, Kit Kats. There's also a glass-doored refrigerator with cream, milk, sodas. I grab ahold of the fish and swing it into the freezer.

"You the new barman?" the old man asks. His accent is so thick, it's tough to understand him.

"Just filling in," I say.

"Since you're back there, you might as well give me a pint."

"A pint of what?" I ask. There must be six taps in front of me.

"*Jesus!* A pint, lad."

I stare at him blankly.

"Guinness." He sighs.

I take the cleanest glass I can find down from a shelf behind me, put it under the spout, and pull the tap toward me. A black foamy liquid spews out. When the glass is full, I set it on top of the bar in front of the man. He looks at me like I just arrived from the moon with an arm growing out of my head or something.

"Is that one for the Bishop, lad?"

I shake my head.

"Then why's the collar so big?" The fisherman shakes his head. "Have you never drawn a Guinness, lad?"

"That's my first," I say.

"Well, it looks like it; don't it, now?"

The pint is roughly two-thirds thick black liquid and one-third white head. Some sort of chemical reaction seems to be taking place in the body of the beer, with flecks of beer matter diving toward the inky depths of the glass.

"If you're going to be the new barman, I'd better teach you a thing or two."

With that, the old man joins me on the working side of the bar. He smells like fish. Or maybe that's me now. He takes down a new glass, tilts it to a twenty-five-degree angle, brings it right up next to the spout, and pulls the Guinness lever forward. He only fills it a little more than three-quarters. He sets it on the bar. It looks only slightly less foamy than the one I drew.

"So that's it?" I ask. "You just don't fill it as far?"

The old man shakes his head and makes a *tisking* sound.

"Patience, lad. Patience. Americans—always in a hurry."

So we wait. The beer flakes settle again. When the head is less than half an inch deep, the old man puts it back under the spout and tops it off. The head now rises slightly above the rim of the glass.

"That, lad, is how you do it."

Over the next forty-five minutes, I learn why Eamonn high-tailed it out of the bar. The old man—Noel, it turns out ("Born on

Christmas Eve, I was")—talks nonstop, which wouldn't be so bad, but the subject doesn't vary from the maintenance of his boat. I thought the Irish were supposed to be great storytellers. I nod along while he goes on about the advantages of nylon netting and the "clackity" sound his engine's been making for a fortnight. He takes a break from his discourse on the shortcomings of boats built after 1955 to point out the creamy white rings spaced out on the inside of his beer glass. "One for each drink ye take—that's the rule," he says.

I can't believe Eamonn has left me here this long. I start picking glasses and ashtrays off tables. I rinse them out in the steel sink behind the bar. Noel's words have been relegated to the consideration level I normally give the music they play at the Sears in Lubbock. After a while, I get to try my hand at pouring another pint. This time I'm more successful. Noel looks satisfied with the results.

"So does anyone come here?" I ask when Noel's forced to take a breath.

He looks around as if he hadn't noticed that he was the only one in the pub.

"You expecting somebody?"

"Not really."

"Well, you should be. The match'll be over soon."

"The match?"

"Football—Kerry and Cork. Everyone's over at Mulligan's. They've got a big screen over there."

Having answered my question, Noel returns to his one-man defense of oak decking.

Thirty minutes later the pub is swarming with locals casually ordering pints and shots from me like I've been a fixture behind the bar my entire life. Noel remains in his seat and helps me out by translating the orders spoken in Irish, explaining how the cash register works, deciphering the Republic's currency for me, and regaling me with data about the tricky spring winds within the harbor. Twice during the onslaught, men hand me fish. Noel points to their tabs, and I make a slash for each Guinness they request thereafter. I'm having fun, but I'm beginning to worry about where I'll be sleeping tonight, when I hear Eamonn's distinctive laugh resounding from a table in the back corner. The bastard is sitting there with a pint, engaged in a spirited discussion with three other men. I walk out from behind the bar and approach his table.

"No one's tipping," I say.

"You're a barman, not a showgirl," he replies cheerfully.

"I need to walk down to the hostel to see if I can get a bed," I say.

"Hostel's not open for another week. I told you—you're early."

Eamonn turns his attention back to the table and interjects something about Liverpool paying too much for a gutless midfielder. The four men all seem to agree on that point. Eamonn takes advantage of the head-nodding to introduce me.

"Lads, meet my new barman, Patrick."

I shake hands with Tom, Ray, and Alan.

"What does a barman get paid around here?" I ask.

"No flies on your man, there," says Tom.

"Room and board," says Eamonn.

"Deal," I say.

Eamonn smiles. "Hope you like fish," he says.

*   *   *

I wake to the smell of sausage and, in the moment before I open my eyes, I'm sure that I'm back in Doggett. Then I'm pounced on by a six-year-old in Power Ranger pajamas.

"Get up, sleepyhead," she says in a singsong accent.

And I remember I'm a few thousand miles away from home.

I pull myself out of the foldout bed in Eamonn's living room. Out of the front window I can see the back door of Tigh Tábhairne about seventy-five yards away. Eamonn's frying when I stumble into the kitchen.

"How do you like your eggs?" he asks.

"Scrambled."

"You and Maeve," he says, looking amused.

"How do you say the name of the pub?" I ask. "I should probably know."

"Tee TARNya," he says. "But it's not really a name."

"What does it mean?"

"Literally, home of the tavern. I just painted Tábhairne on the door so people would know they could get a pint inside. Then we got a great laugh when an American guidebook listed us as the Tábhairne Pub. It was like calling us the Market Market. The name stuck. They said we were the place to go in Kilbeg for 'authentic local charm.'" Eamonn pokes at the eggs. "What bollocks."

Over breakfast, I meet the family: Eamonn's wife, Maria, and his daughters, eleven-year-old Yvonne and Maeve the Power Ranger. Both girls stare at me throughout the meal despite Maria's frequent chiding.

"You talk funny," Maeve finally blurts out.

"You look funny," I say while reaching over and tickling her stomach. She giggles.

"So how long were you planning on staying in Kilbeg?" Eamonn asks after the plates have been cleared.

"I don't know," I say. "Awhile, I guess."

The answer must satisfy him, because after that he gives me my work schedule. He says I can have Sundays and Mondays off, but other than that, he expects me to run the pub from opening at eleven until closing at half eleven.

"Half eleven?" I ask.

Eamonn shakes his head. "Eleven thirty," he says in a bad American accent. "You can eat and drink anything you want at the pub, and we'll always have breakfast here in the morning."

Maria leads Yvonne and Maeve out the front door. The girls are wearing matching school uniforms made up of blue skirts and white blouses. Maeve waves good-bye to me as she exits. I wink back at her.

"Looks like you've got a fan," Eamonn says.

By my fourth night at the pub, I know what almost everyone orders. I've even gotten used to people calling me Paddy. Tourists have begun passing through Kilbeg, usually on their way to Dingle or Killarney. They stop and fill their rental cars with "petrol" and try to get directions from Eamonn, who suddenly transforms into what my mother would remember as a "real character."

"Dingle? Hmm . . . ," he'll say, scratching his beard. "Had me shoes shined in Dingle once. Let's see. How did I get there?"

Then he'll digress into an adventure that has absolutely nothing to do with the directions, but does feature leprechauns, sheep, Guinness, and the luck o' the Irish. It doesn't matter where the tourists say they're from—Cleveland, Perth, Brixton—Eamonn has a cousin, Danny, living there who they ought to look up when they get home.

Eamonn sells a lot of maps.

"You love doing that," I told Eamonn once when he handed me the cash to put in the register.

"I'm not the one who gave them passports," he said, a grin spreading across his face.

Tonight I'm getting to see my first trad session. Musicians drink free on Thursday nights, and Tigh Tábhairne attracts some of the best from a fifty-mile radius every week. The pub is packed, and I'm running behind. I start prepouring pints of Guinness so that they can settle and I can just top them off when someone orders one. That's before Eamonn notices what I'm doing.

"What are you thinking, boy? This isn't McDonaldland. Wait until someone orders one."

So from then on, I do. Eamonn hops around the bar when he sees too many people waving money at me. When he's not helping out, he's sitting on the session playing the bodhrán, a handheld drum made of goatskin that he thumps with a little stick. Other musicians play fiddles, pipes, tin whistles, guitars, and mandolins. The music is alternately hyperfestive or melancholy, taking me from one emotional extreme to another, but I like it. In some ways it reminds me of country music.

About half nine, two of our local sheep farmers, Gilly and Sean, make their way through the door. I take down a bottle of the brand of cheap whiskey, McMurtrey's, they always order.

"Don't be pouring us no glasses, Paddy!" Gilly slurs. "Just hand me the bottle."

He takes the whiskey from my hand and pours its entire contents into the cup of a large trophy that Sean has hoisted onto the bar.

"Grand champion!" says Gilly.

"Finest sheep in County Kerry," adds Sean.

Gilly lifts the trophy to his lips and drinks the whiskey, then passes it to Sean. The trophy then begins a journey around the pub. Almost everyone takes a gulp or two from the cup. It seems to take an especially long time to pass through the assembled musicians. Eamonn's mate Tom takes a remarkably long swig before bringing the trophy up to me.

"Are you with us tonight?" he asks.

I look around the pub, taking note of the people with whom I'll be hygienically linked. Then I kill what remains of the first bottle of whiskey.

"Fair play to ye, then," he says.

Sean gives me another tenner for more whiskey, empties it into the cup, and sends it on its way once again. About that time, Gilly breaks into song. The musicians stop playing, and his voice cuts through the din of the crowd. He sings in Irish, so I have no idea what the song is about, but it's clearly sad. He reaches a chorus, and three or four of the older guys join in. Ray, the fiddle player, provides a swelling orchestral touch. A tear runs down Gilly's cheek. For the two or three minutes that the song lasts, everyone is silent. I don't serve a single pint.

And that's how things continue for the next couple hours. Gilly's Grand Champion Sheep trophy continues making its way around the pub. The musicians play tune after tune, pausing now and then for the odd a cappella, tear-inducing Irish standard warbled by one of the fishermen or farmers who've bellied up to the bar. After my third or fourth turn with the trophy, I start teetering a bit as I pace from one end of the bar to the other. It's the first night that I've worked that we've had almost as many women as men in the pub. There's also a table of locals who look about my age. The drinking age in Ireland is eighteen, but Eamonn said most of the younger crowd hangs out at Mulligan's for the pool table and the disco nights every Saturday.

I'm afraid that Eamonn's going to notice me stumbling when I walk out to his table to tell him it's closing time. Instead, he makes me tilt back the trophy, which has once again come to rest in front of the musicians. After I've completed this task, I've forgotten what I came out to tell him. He makes me drink again. Then I remember.

"Closing time," I inform him.

"Is it, now?" he says.

Eamonn bounces up, looking inexplicably peppy considering the amount of alcohol I've seen him consume tonight. He navigates his way to the door, fishes a key out of his pocket, and locks the door.

"Uh-oh," says Tom, who's sitting next to me.

"What's that mean?" I ask.

"Lock-in. These nights get ugly. No one else can come in, but everyone who's already here can stay as long as they want."

"He won't get in trouble for that?"

"I don't think he cares," Tom says just before Eamonn begins yelling for everyone's attention.

"Have yis heard of the karaoke machine they'll be getting over at O'Donoghue's?" he shouts.

The intoxicated clientele mumble or boo in response. O'Donoghue's, I've been told, is the pub in town that no self-respecting Kilbeggian will step foot into except for a sandwich at lunch, and never, in any case, during the tourist-saturated summer months.

"Well, we don't have a machine, but we can play along as well as anyone. Who's going to be the first to take part in Tigh Tábhairne's first-ever traditional karaoke night?"

He looks around the room, but no one seems ready to participate.

"Ah, to hell with yis."

With that, Eamonn launches into a version of the Rolling Stones song "(I Can't Get No) Satisfaction."

It takes them a verse or two to find it, but soon enough, the violin and pipe players are laying down the famous guitar riff that repeats throughout the song. Everyone in the pub joins in on the hey, hey, heys. Even Gilly. Tom handles the drum solo on Eamonn's bodhrán. It's not tough finding volunteers for the next song once Eamonn concludes. Tom jumps up next and breaks into an Elvis song. I'm back at my post behind the bar. The orders haven't slowed, but I'm finding standing a bit challenging. Eamonn must see me lurching around back here, because he joins me and starts handling orders.

"You sit down for a while, lad. I don't pay you for lock-ins anyway." He hands me a shot glass full of brown syrupy liquid. "This'll help clear you up. Off you go now."

I take the small glass out onto the floor and pull up a stool next to Tom, who's finishing with "Hound Dog" with a hip-swiveling flourish. One of the older guys is up doing a song. I don't know what it is, but everyone is singing the last line of the chorus, "There's whiskey in the jar!" I force down the concoction provided by Eamonn, but it seems just to accelerate my spiral downward. I think I'm out of it for a couple songs. The next thing I know, one of the girls my age is singing "Nothing Compares 2 U." She's really good. The song even sounds better with a pennywhistle. The singer looks like the girls in the Irish tourism brochures—redheaded, pretty, and plain at the same time. As I'm listening to her sing about her broken heart, I feel all right. I join in with all the other under-twenties for the chorus.

When the song is over, Tom kicks my leg under the table.

"Your turn, lad."

"What?"

Then he shouts out, "Who wants to hear Paddy sing one?"

The suggestion is met mostly with cheering, though a few heckles are mixed in. I do it anyway. I'm too drunk to care how big a fool I make out of myself. I can only think of one song that

I know all the words to. When Zeb first got a CD player in his truck, he only had one CD, so it was all Anderson and I heard when we rode anywhere with him. George Strait, *Ocean Front Property.* So I do it. I take a breath and break into "All My Exes Live in Texas."

I almost give up midway through the first verse. The room has grown too quiet, and the musicians aren't filling in behind me like they have with everyone else. Then Ray saves me with a little country lick on the fiddle. By the time I hit the chorus, I have some backing music. Eamonn shouts out "Yeehaw" from behind the bar. The next time I make it to the chorus, a few of the brave join in—Tom louder than the rest. The girl who sang the Sinead O'Connor song unexpectedly sings a harmony line. I close my eyes and belt out the third verse with as much gusto as I can muster. When I hit the final chorus, all of Tigh Tábhairne is with me.

I wake, once again, with Maeve's knees on my chest. This time, though, she's trying to suffocate me with a pillow. The way I'm feeling, I consider putting up no resistance, but the pillow's forcing me to smell my own breath, and that's something I simply can't tolerate.

"Someone's here for you." She giggles when I finally wrestle the pillow off my face.

The first thing I think is that *Classroom Direct* has tracked me down. That would mean Mama, Papa, or Bridget must have helped out. They're the only ones who would even be able to guess where I am. Oh, well. Five days. Five great days. At least I don't have to worry about moving back to Los Angeles now.

But that's not who it is. At first I don't recognize any of the three people at the door, but when I hear one of them humming George Strait, it snaps into place. It's the girl who sang last night and two of the guys who were with her. The girl speaks. "We're going swimming. Do you want to come with us?"

My head aches. I don't have anything to swim in. I don't know these people.

"Yeah," I hear myself saying anyway.

I brush my teeth, borrow some shorts from Eamonn, and the four of us—Mary, Donal, Kevin, and myself—hit the road. When I arrived in Kilbeg last week, the sun was setting, and I didn't get the same view as this morning. We're driving along the edge of cliffs with the ocean below us. Just off the coast are the Blasket Islands. Mary points out The Dead Man, an island shaped like a floating corpse just a couple miles offshore. Above us are a series of round huts built completely out of large stones. Donal, our driver, tells me that monks used to live in them 1,500 years ago. I tell him that in Texas, if your house is more than a hundred years old, they put a historical marker on it. This makes all three of them laugh. I guess they think I'm joking.

"What made you ask me if I wanted to come along today?" I ask.

Mary shrugs. "We thought we could talk you into doing 'Your Cheatin' Heart.'"

"Think again," I say.

"What are you doing in Kilbeg anyway? On holiday?" Kevin, a muscular blond, asks.

"No," I say. "I'm a runaway reporter for an American television news show hiding out in rural Ireland in order to escape my corporate masters."

The three of them really crack up at that.

"No, really," Mary says.

"I'm just on holiday," I say.

"Well, we missed you at Mass this morning," she says.

"*You* missed him at Mass, Mary," unibrowed Donal says. "Kevin and I were still in bed."

"You'll all burn in hell," she says matter-of-factly. "Send me a postcard."

Donal pulls down a road leading toward the ocean, and I realize stupidly for the first time: That's where we'll be swimming. I've done plenty of swimming in my lifetime. Zeb's pool, mainly. Nothing like this. We park and begin walking down a path toward the water. A sign clearly states DANGEROUS CURRENTS—NO SWIMMING in both English and Irish, but this doesn't seem to dissuade the rest of my party. Perhaps they learn to read later here than back in the States.

"Uh . . . ," I begin.

"Don't worry. It's safe. We know where to go," says Mary.

It may be safe, but it's way too damn cold. I realize this immediately when my big toe touches the wet sand. Back home, I like to wait until it's at least ninety degrees to take out my swim trunks. I doubt it's even seventy here today. Donal and Kevin have already shucked their T-shirts and are out there throwing themselves into six-foot-high breakers. I'm standing up to my ankles in the freezing water feeling pretty self-conscious about my hardening nipples, but I can't find it in myself to move further into the surf. Mary strolls up next to me.

"Cures hangovers," she says.

With that, I give a scream and go charging out until the force of the water makes me stumble and dive into one of the breakers. At the moment the water engulfs me, I feel as wide awake as I've ever felt in my life.

We splash around for thirty minutes or so. I can't say I ever really get used to the frigid water, but it's fun anyway. The beach is enclosed by a little inlet. We're surrounded by cliffs and hills topped with the greenest fields I've ever seen. No one else is out here. Mary was right; my hangover is gone.

We don't go straight home after our swim. We drive to Mulligan's for a televised hurling match. I'm a bit surprised to see Eamonn in there. Today's his day to run Tigh Tábhairne, after all. Maybe there's some confused South African tourist manning it this afternoon who's shaking his head and saying to himself, "But I just wanted to know the way to Killarney." Mulligan's ambience lacks the charm—in my admittedly biased opinion—of Tigh Tábhairne. It's all shiny. There's a brass rail in front of the bar. Everything matches: the curtains, the chairs and tables, the aprons the two barmen are wearing. Jesus.

Still, the place is hopping. I recognize most of the people in here. I'm afraid most of them witnessed the debut of my singing career last night. The number of *Paddys! Come here, lads*, followed by guffaws, confirms this for me. Once the match starts, people quit paying much attention to me.

"Don't worry about them," says Donal. "If they take the piss out of you, it means they like you."

I'm not particularly interested in who wins the Wexford-Galway contest, but the sport, which involves a lot of men on a field swinging clubs at a little ball, keeps my attention. I'm sure if I turn away for a moment, I'll miss a decapitation.

At halftime, we get commentary from some legendary hurling star before they cut to a newsbreak. The next thing I know, up on the screen there's video of me filing my report from Belfast. Even though I can feel everyone turning toward me, I listen to the anchor read the copy.

"American teenager Patrick Sheridan is still missing, six days after his disappearance from a Belfast hotel. Sheridan, a reporter for the U.S. news show Classroom Direct, was in Northern Ireland reporting on the progress of the peace process. U.S. State Department officials are asking anyone who might have any knowledge of his whereabouts to contact the U.S. embassies in Dublin or London."

Donal has a sandwich poised by his mouth for the duration of the report. It just stays there. Kevin punches me in the shoulder. Mary is staring at me. So is everyone else in Mulligan's. The next voice I hear is Eamonn's.

"What did you say your surname was, Paddy?" he shouts.

"Garcia," I say.

"Well then," says Eamonn as he returns his attention to the television, "I guess I still have me a barman."

For the next few days, I operate under the constant assumption that the State Department will arrive at the pub with handcuffs to drag me back home, but weeks pass uneventfully. Well, there is one close call when an American couple comes in. I can tell they're American before they even open their mouths; they're dressed in bright green sweaters with shamrocks on them. I pour them their Baileys & coffees without speaking, but they whisper fervently to each other when my back is turned.

"Have you heard about that American kid who's missing?" the man asks me.

Eamonn is reading a newspaper at a table when this happens, and as I turn to answer, I can see him staring at me wide-eyed.

"There's a Yank missing, is there now?" I say in what I hope is a convincing Irish brogue.

"You look a lot like him."

"Ye hear that, Dad?" I say, hoping Eamonn will take the ball from here.

"Like I told you, boy. It's a small world out there," he says.

The act seems to pacify the tourists, who leave shortly thereafter, but it sure doesn't make Eamonn happy.

"Dad? Dad? Like I look old enough to be your old fella. Besides, look at your hair. Look at mine!" He held a strand of his wild ginger locks in front of him.

"Guess I take after me ma," I say.

"And stop that nonsense too. You sound like an eejit."

The population of Kilbeg has probably doubled with the arrival of summer and the accompanying tourists. According to the locals, we get the best sort of tourists. ("Which is a bit like saying we get the best sort of infectious diseases," Eamonn likes to add.) The foreigners who come to Kilbeg are off the beaten tour bus and hotel path. Lots of them are cyclists and backpackers exploring the coastline and hills of Slea Head, the westernmost point in Ireland. Eamonn likes to claim that Tigh Tábhairne offers the last pint of Guinness before one hits Boston. Every now and then, a regular will point out that O'Donoghue's is at least a few yards farther west than Tábhairne's, forcing Eamonn to modify his story a bit.

"The last decent pint, then."

I've been spending my days off with Mary, Donal, and Kevin. The lads will be heading to college in Galway in the fall. Mary will be going to school in Cork. They've wanted me to tell them all about the television show I worked for and why I ran away, but I think they sensed that I wasn't comfortable talking about it. At least Mary sensed it, and she's done a good job of changing topics when it's come up again. I don't say anything about my family tree or why I came to Kilbeg. One night after the pub closed, I walked Mary home and, somewhere along the way, I told her some of the things that led me to Kilbeg: about my job, my family, my walk down Sunset Boulevard. I've gone to Mass a couple times with her. After the second time, she took me out to the cemetery behind the church and showed me where her family was buried. Nearby I spotted a tombstone for Bridget Sheridan bearing the dates 1865 to 1938. I remember that my sister . . . mother . . . whatever, was named for her great-grandmother.

It's interesting to me how, even though Mary is pretty enough,

I'm content having her as a friend. Part of it may be my recent luck with girls, but I think it's mainly something else. I need a friend more than I need a girlfriend, and Mary is a constant source of wonder for me. She still believes in things: God, her parents, the future . . . everlasting love. After I told her about my experiences in Belfast, she actually told me that she thought Catholics and Protestants would live peacefully in completely nonsegregated neighborhoods and towns in her lifetime.

"You haven't been there. You haven't seen what it's like. They hate each other," I tell her.

"They said there would never be peace either. Look around you, Patrick. Great things happen all the time. Things no one thought would ever happen. The Berlin Wall came down. There's majority rule in South Africa . . ."

"Hundreds of prodemocracy students got machine-gunned to death in Tiananmen Square," I interject.

"I think I'll see a democratic China too," she says.

"Jesus, Mary!"

But I guess I'm glad someone thinks that way.

Mary's in love; maybe that's why she has such a rosy outlook on the world. Her love is the best kind, unrequited.

"Less messy that way," I tell her.

I'm in Donal's car on a weekend road trip to Killarney when I get the inside scoop on Mary's love life. I use an empty Fanta Orange bottle that's been rolling around the floor of the car as a microphone, and I begin interviewing her. I use my reporter voice.

"Mary Callahan, I've learned from well-placed sources—"

"Well-placed—that's us," interjects Kevin.

"That you are seriously jonesing for some old man in Dublin."

"Jonesing?"

"Enamored of, hot for, possessing a desire to churn torso butter with."

"You're sick," says Donal.

"He's not old," says Mary. "Peter's twenty, and he goes to school at Trinity. He's a poet."

"Professionally?" I ask.

"He won the schoolwide poetry contest when we were in fifth year," Donal says dismissively.

"And he's studying literature at school," Mary notes.

"And he walks on water," adds Donal.

"And cures lepers," Kevin tacks on.

This starts the two of them chortling.

"You know, they say Jesus was Irish," Mary says in an attempt to change the subject.

"They do?"

"Well, he didn't leave home until he was thirty. He was always hanging out with the lads, and he thought his mother was a virgin."

"Mine is," says Kevin.

"So's mine," asserts Donal.

I decide not to let Mary get off that easy. I stick the microphone bottle back in her face.

"Will we get to meet St. Peter anytime soon?"

"His mother told my mother at church that he was coming home for a month this summer," Mary answers.

"You mean he didn't call and tell you?"

Mary pushes the bottle away from her mouth and looks out the window, making me feel like a dick.

"How about that Liverpool squad?" Donal says.

"None finer," says Kevin.

The trip to Killarney was Kevin's idea. There are six movie screens in the town, and Kevin needs a fix. He wants to be a cinematographer someday. We could have gone to Limerick, but the three of them thought I should see Killarney.

"It's like Ireland, but more so," according to Donal.

"It's like an Irish theme park," Kevin notes. "Ireland Land, where jolly and superstitious folk actually say things like 'Begorra'—whatever that means—while they're taking your money. Even the drunks in Killarney are required to act lovable."

The thing I'm struck by first as we enter the town is the number of buses. It seems like every other vehicle is forty feet long. Where they're parked, throngs of Geritol-powered tourists dressed in colorful polyester mill about aimlessly. The McDonald's and Burger King on the main road feature "authentic" Irish village facades. We pass one-hour photo shops and stores where they'll gladly ship Aran Islands hand-knitted sweaters, Waterford crystal, or Claddagh rings VAT-free back to the States. The theater is next to a business that guarantees it can, for a nominal fee of forty pounds, trace my Irish ancestry in the time it takes me to watch the movie.

"Go in and tell them your last name is Garcia," says Donal, "and if you've got the forty pounds, they'll still find a great-grandcousin who personally shot at Oliver Cromwell somewhere in the Burren."

I'm outvoted at the theater, which means I end up seeing Robin's movie for the second time. It helps that I don't remember much from the first screening. It's weird watching her. I didn't notice the first time how bogus her Texas accent sounded or how she uses this noise—this humming sound—when she's pleased. It's a sound she used with me. A lot. So was she not acting in the movie, or was she acting with me? I don't know. I guess I don't care.

"Mail for you there," says Eamonn.

I'm behind the bar. The pub's deserted except for Eamonn and a man in a suit who has Eamonn's otherwise undivided attention.

How can I have mail?

I check the basket next to the cash register where Eamonn throws everything. The postmark on the letter is from Los Angeles. It's addressed to Patrick Sheridan c/o the Kilbeg Postmaster—that's it.

It's from my mom, Bridget.

> Patrick,
> I don't know if this will get to you, but I'm guessing that you'll visit Grampa's hometown. If you're holding it in your hands right now, say the word, and I'll send you money for a plane ticket home. Everyone is so worried about you. I've talked to Mama and Papa on the phone. I wish I could say it went well, but when they found out that I told you I was your birth mother, they

242 • ROB THOMAS

blamed me for your running away. I don't know
if this matters to you, but they say that if you
apologize for everything and come back and go to
St. Mary's, all will be forgiven. Your call.

Please call collect or write.

Love,

Bridget

It's comforting to know there are some things you can count on.

When Eamonn goes out to petrol up someone's car, the man in the suit he's been sitting with approaches the bar. There's something about his walk that makes me think he's American—he walks like he owns the place—but his accent is Irish.

"Guinness," he says.

"Coming right up," I say. It's my own little joke.

"American, huh?" he says, but I'm busy pouring. "Quite a nice village, don't you think."

"Lovely," I say.

"A few brochures, some positive word of mouth, a pound or two to the guidebook writers, and this could be quite a hot spot." I slide him his beer. "What we need is a hook. Dingle's got that friendly dolphin. Blarney's got the rock."

"We have fish and sheep," I say flatly.

"'We'?" He chuckles. "I'm sorry. I didn't know I was talking to a native."

Eamonn comes back in, wiping his hands on a rag.

"That one's on the house," he says, pointing to the man's beer, but I don't think the stranger was planning on paying for it anyway. He was already heading back to his table.

Later, when Mr. Suit is finally gone, I ask Eamonn who he was.

"Santa Claus," he says.

I check the business card Eamonn's dropped in the basket.

JIMMY FINN
Real Estate & Investments
Cork

Every Saturday during the summer, a deejay from Dingle brings his trash disco records to Mulligan's upstairs "club," and everyone aged eighteen to twenty-five on the peninsula tries to pack into the room's four hundred square feet. If I hustle, I can usually lock up Tigh Tábhairne and arrive at Mulligan's by midnight, which gives me plenty of time since clubs can stay open until two. Mary and the lads get there early enough to get one of the few highly prized tables. Donal, Kevin, and I alternate dancing with Mary, who frequently goes all night without leaving the dance floor.

I've seen plenty of attractive girls on these disco nights, and Mary's offered to introduce me to them, but I've declined. I can't work up any interest. Donal and Kevin usually have some luck getting tourist girls to dance, and Kevin ended up spending a week as a tour guide/sleeping bag–mate of a German girl named Marta who was hitching around Ireland.

Tonight when I arrive, both guys are on the dance floor with girls I recognize as locals. Mary's sitting at a table guarding her Fanta

Orange. When she spots me, she smiles and waves me over. I muscle my way to the table, but get there just after another male claims one of the empty chairs. I do arrive, however, in time for introductions.

"Aidan," he says, shaking Mary's hand before noticing me hovering in some state of confusion.

"I'm sorry," he says to Mary. "Is this seat taken?"

She tells him he's welcome to stay, and it's easy to see why she's so inclined. Aidan has the sort of looks that would make him a lot of money in America. A walking Calvin Klein ad with a crooked smile and bangs that fall both haphazardly and perfectly down over his eyes. I take the remaining empty seat.

"Where're you from?" asks Mary.

"Dublin," he says. "I'm here for the hurling match against Kerry."

"You must be a big supporter to come all the way down," says Mary.

"Not exactly," Aidan says. "I play for Dublin."

He says it with disarming modesty and an embarrassed grin. Mary looks thunderstruck. I'm thinking of reasons to excuse myself from the table, when Darby Croker butts in and asks Mary if she wouldn't care to dance. I want to smack the toad. He does this every week. The guy won't leave her alone. Can't he tell she's not interested? Does he ever look in the mirror? He's balding at twenty and working on a third chin. Donal told me how Mary has ended up going to all these church events as his date simply because she won't tell him no. I'm thinking of taking Darby into the Gents and letting him in on a little secret, but before I can do anything, Mary's out of her seat and on the dance floor with him.

Aidan shrugs and excuses himself.

I can't stand it. I go out on the dance floor and start dancing in between Darby and Mary. Mary doesn't notice because she's dancing with her eyes closed. Darby bumps me a couple times, but I do a couple spin moves with my elbows positioned about jaw-high, and he backs off suitably. That leaves me dancing next to Mary during all of "Play That Funky Music White Boy." I like watching her get into it, still unaware that I'm in front of her. She swings her head from side to side, and the necklace she's wearing breaks. Beads rain down onto the floor. Mary opens her eyes and catches the string before the entire bunch slides off. I get down on the hardwood and start picking up beads individually. It's not easy. Lights are flashing. People are stomping. My fingers get crunched a couple times, but I'm having some luck. Mary gets down on her hands and knees with me. I have a quick fantasy about everyone following suit, thinking this is the newest American dance craze, but no one does. We must be down on the floor for three songs. It's impossible to find *all* of the beads, but we retrieve a good number. After we give up, Mary stands and sticks the dusty handful in her pocket. Then she hands me the necklace and shouts over the music, "Can you hook this for me?"

She faces away from me. I loop the strand around in front of her and, with my free hand, pull her hair away from her neck. Then I'm staring at her neck and, as I'm trying to connect the ends of the necklace, my hands are shaking. I feel just like I did as I was trying to pin a corsage onto Kate's dress in front of her parents before last

246 • ROB THOMAS

year's homecoming dance. Something inside tells me these are the only times in my life I've been in the presence of true beauty.

In what I consider a disappointing trade-off, I start seeing more of Jimmy Finn than Mary. It seems like he's everywhere: drinking in Tigh Tábhairne every other night, coming out of the house where Johanna Fitzpatrick sells books in the summer, playing pool with the younger lads at Mulligan's. Mary, on the other hand, is becoming a ghost, though she does come into the pub early one night with Donal. But she's not herself. She's fidgety, and she keeps touching her hair. There's something different about her, but it takes me a minute to figure it out.

"You're wearing lipstick," I say to her.

"And what business is it of yours, Patrick Garcia?" she says.

"St. Peter's back in town," Donal explains.

I don't get to spend much time chatting with my friends. The pub is hopping tonight. They stay just long enough for Mary to give me a present, a walking map of the peninsula that shows every road, path, shed, and sheep on it.

"This is great," I say once I've spread it out across the bar. "What's the occasion?"

"I thought a walk might be good for you," she says.

"He *is* starting to get a bit of flab on him, isn't he?" says Donal, attempting to take the piss out of me. But I know what Mary means.

After they leave, Gilly begins buying drinks for everyone he knows and some he doesn't. When he hits his third bottle of whiskey, he bursts into song. This ditty's in English, and the snatches of it I catch have something to do with arriving in Tipperary with a pocketful of coins.

"Your sheep win another contest?" I ask him when the song is complete.

"Ah, laddie, my sheeping days is behind me now," he says.

Then he tells me about the city boy from Cork who paid him outrageous money for his land.

"All that schooling, and he still has no sense." Gilly lets out an outrageous cackle before rejoining his mates.

But I've seen Gilly's land. I've picnicked there with Mary, Donal, and Kevin. His fields run from the top of a hill down to a cliff overlooking the ocean. It's possibly the most beautiful place I've ever been.

A perfect spot for condominiums.

Whatever Gilly got for his land . . . it wasn't enough.

I have a number of motivations for volunteering to take Maeve to the dentist, a friend of the family, in Cork. The first is because that's the port Grampa sailed from when he came to America. Every day I see something else that makes me remember him— the old schoolhouse Grampa attended that Veronica Call turned into a B&B; Mount Eagle Lake, where he used to swim. I swear I can feel him when I stumble on these things. Second, I don't get to spend enough time with Maeve. On top of being an effective alarm clock, she's a doll, *and*, according to her mother, she's told anyone who'll listen that I'm her boyfriend. Next, I'm out of cash, and I could use an ATM in Cork. Back home, if anyone's still paying attention, they'll know I'm either alive or I used my dying breath to giving the IRA my PIN, but they won't know where I am. They can search Cork all they want. Finally, I want to poke around Jimmy Finn's office a bit. I've got that same feeling I had about Mr. Linder and the band uniforms.

People in Kilbeg have been acting strangely for most of July, and I think there are explanations beyond what summer locals are describing as a right scorcher. ("I'll bet it reminds you of Texas, Paddy," they've been saying. *Yeah . . . in March.*) At Tigh Tábhairne, I've lost track of the number of conversations kicked off with the phrase, "Don't tell a soul, but..." before they dissolve into whispers. Two families who had been in Kilbeg for three centuries left town. But it's not just that they moved, it's the way they did it—without telling anyone first, and using professional movers—that set the town to buzzing. The collective dementia was highlighted yesterday when I caught Noel the Fisherman poring over the stock market index in a week-old Dublin paper.

The bus ride to Cork takes all morning. Maeve sleeps through most of it with her head on my shoulder. I stare out the windows.

After we arrive, I drop off Maeve at the dentist's, then find an automatic teller machine downtown. After that, I hire a cab to take me the dozen or so miles to the harbor in Cobh. I wander around wondering what was going through Grampa's mind when he made this trip for the last time. He was leaving for America. He probably knew he'd never be able to go home again. He always wanted to; he just never found a way.

When I return and pick up Maeve, I playfully show her the

wad of cash I've drawn out of my account. "I'm rich," I say. "Let me take you to lunch."

She chooses McDonald's.

"Isn't there anything you'd rather have to eat?" I ask her.

She shakes her head no. So McDonald's it is.

After polishing off a slew of McNuggets, I pull Jimmy Finn's card from my wallet. Maeve follows me outside onto what I notice is Patrick Street. Things are looking up. I put a twenty-pence coin into the slot of a pay phone.

"Jimmy Finn's office," says the female receptionist on the other end of the line.

I slip into my improving Irish accent. "I've got a delivery for Mr. Finn," I say, "but I can't read the address on the packing slip."

The woman gives me the information. Simple.

I relay the address to a taxi driver, who zips us through the traffic. On the way, I try to imagine what I might find when we get there. A bank, maybe, or a real estate office. I think I've seen a hundred movies where, in a secret office, the bad guys have a scale model of some idyllic community. After an obligatory pause for cackling and palm-rubbing, they press a button revealing what the town will look like after they've carried out their dastardly plan (generally calling for the installation of some carcinogen-belching fake vomit factory). Maybe they'll have one of those where we're going. Probably not.

The cabdriver drops us off in front of an office building, large by Irish standards. Holding Maeve's hand, I take an elevator up to the suite. It's easy enough to find, but I don't go in. The sign on the door gives me plenty of answers, just not the ones I was expecting.

Someone's rapping on the pay phone booth, but I'm on my seventeenth call and my second five-pound phone card. The booth next to me is empty. I turn with the intention of pointing that fact out to the eager beaver pounding on the door, but it's Mary. I hold up my index finger and mouth the words "one minute" to her. Then I turn my attention back to the person on the other end of the line. I've got just a couple more questions to ask. I jot down the responses in a notebook I purchased on the way back from Cork. I thank the person, then open the door to the booth.

"Hey, stranger," I say to Mary.

"Hello," she says.

The conversation continues in this soul-baring vein as we walk along the main road through and out of town. Eventually, I venture into less safe territory. "So how are things with Peter?" I ask as The Dead Man comes into view.

Mary's look of concern gives way to an unmistakable glow. "Brilliant," she says. "He's lovely."

"So what's wrong?" I ask.

Mary stops walking and takes a breath.

"Patrick," she says, "what do you know about contraception?"

When all is said and done, I've made twenty-one calls. I think even Lydia would be impressed. All the information is in this notebook. Now it's just a matter of writing it, copying it, distributing it. No commercials. No graphics. No cutaways. It's a slow night at Tigh Tábhairne. For the most part I'm able to concentrate on my notes, mentally organizing and outlining. I'll be pulling an all-nighter. The sooner the people here know what's going on, the better. Three young guys—two I recognize, one I don't—come in at about half nine. They take stools at the bar and order pints.

They've been drinking awhile when something they say catches my attention. One of the guys—one I've seen before—mentions the name Callahan. I position myself closer to the group and begin wiping down the bar. Now I can hear clearly.

"You might as well be trying to ride a nun as that one," says the guy who ordered a Smithwick's. "You'll have no luck. Better men than you have tried."

"And we failed," says the Guinness drinker.

"Better men? The local sheep putting wild thoughts in your head?" says the third, a Bud man.

"Look," says Smithwick's. "Some do. Some don't. She's plainly one who doesn't."

"Ah, now there's where you're wrong," says Bud Man. "They all do. You just have to figure out how to be one of the ones they do it with. What does it take? What do they have to hear? That you've got a cousin who's a roadie for U2? Maybe it's that you're considering becoming a priest. Sometimes all it takes is a few lines of poetry."

"Bollocks," says Smithwick's.

"It's true," says Bud Man.

"But, Peter," says Guinness, "it won't work with Mary Callahan."

The words take a moment to register in my head, but when

they do, I feel nauseous. I may have given up any claim to things pure and right, but Mary hasn't. She deserves better than St. Peter.

I join the conversation. "Work with Mary?" I say. "Sure it will."

The three friends stop drinking and look across the bar at me.

"Poetry, a few sad stories, and the girl is begging for it. And you know what else she likes?" I make sure I'm looking at St. Peter. "An American accent."

"You've—?" stammers Peter.

"Yeah," I say. Then I make the so-so hand motion.

I leave the three of them in stunned silence. I wait on Noel at the other end of the bar and wonder what I've done.

Later that night I sit at Eamonn's dining room table and type on Maria's antique Underwood typewriter. It feels good. *This* is what it's supposed to be about. Telling the truth. As I compose, I remember Lydia's advice. I let the hard and fast rules of journalistic style Mr. D. taught me become secondary to the story I'm telling. I try hard to find a voice.

Darren McCabe's family lived on the same plot of land for the better part of three hundred years. The names of every McCabe born in that time are scratched into the mortar that holds together the stones of the thatched-roof cottage's fireplace. Three weeks ago, Darren moved his family to Dublin. They're temporarily sharing an apartment with his sister while he looks for work and a house in the suburbs.

A 7-Eleven will take the place of his Kilbeg cottage.

The new owner of that land is SeaVista Inc., a ten-month-old corporation comprised of wealthy Cork investors. SeaVista is headed by James Finn, who has become a local mainstay in Kilbeg. SeaVista has already purchased at least four more properties in Kilbeg, including O'Donoghue's Pub. They plan to buy more.

"I never thought I'd sell the land," Darren said. "But what they offered—I could've held on to it forever, and it never would have been worth that much."

But it could be worth more than that purchase price soon.

Finn, in addition to his position with SeaVista, is the director of promotions for McMurtrey's Whiskey International. One of his primary duties includes supervising the annual McMurtrey's Rock Festival, which has brought thousands of rock fans from Ireland and abroad into Cork for two weeks each year. The event has pumped millions of pounds into the Cork economy for the last two decades, but that hasn't prevented city officials from banning future festivals.

"The vandalism, the public intoxication, the cleanup—it's gotten worse each year. It's just not worth it for Cork anymore," Cork magistrate Larry McDonald said.

That's where Kilbeg comes in. The town's location, less than ninety minutes from Shannon Airport and an hour from tourist hot spot Killarney, combined with its scenic beauty, cheap property, and relatively good roads, has made it the leading candidate to host future McMurtrey's Rock Festivals. Finn has put his considerable clout behind the selection of Kilbeg. If Kilbeg is chosen, as top company officials expect, current local facilities won't be able to accommodate the yearly influx of rock and rollers or the steady increase in tourism the town's new notoriety would provide.

Angela Tunney, an urban planning professor at Trinity College, in Dublin, estimated a town Kilbeg's size could expect construction of several hotels, restaurants, gas stations, grocery stores, and beachfront tourist shops offering everything from postcards to sunscreen.

"The problem is, by the end of the summer, everything has closed down. These places become ghost towns for eight months of the year."

Darren McCabe says he misses Kilbeg already, but that he doesn't regret his decision to leave.

"I don't want to be there when it changes," he says. "I want to remember it the way it was."

When I'm finished with the story, I take a pair of scissors from a kitchen drawer and cut up a week-old copy of the *Cork Exam-*

iner that Eamonn brought home from the pub. I carefully cut out letters and use them to form a headline.

INvEsTors waNT LAnd
FoR FUTuRe FeSTIvAls

The lettering makes the story look like a ransom note.

In the morning I get up before Maeve has a chance to attack me, and I hitchhike into Dingle. The car that stops for me belongs to Jimmy Finn. When I see who it is, I try to wave him off, but he rolls his eyes and throws open the passenger-side door, leaving me little choice.

For the first few minutes of the journey, neither of us speak, but as we turn away from the ocean, he breaks the silence. "Been making a lot of calls, have you?"

"Some," I say.

"Find out anything interesting?"

"Maybe," I say.

I don't know what it is, the awkwardness of the situation or something, but for some reason I want to laugh. Despite my best intentions, I smile.

"Pretty pleased with yourself, huh?" says Jimmy Finn.

"Yeah," I say. "Pretty pleased."

Those are the last words we speak to each other. He lets me out in front of the SuperValu in Dingle. They have a public photocopier there. I make fifty copies of my story. An American couple picks me up on the way back to Kilbeg. They seem tremendously excited to be talking to a fellow countryman, and they tell me about a dozen places they've seen on their two-week Irish holiday. They ask me how long I've been in the country.

"Nearly three months," I say.

"So what are your favorite places?" asks the wife. She's getting out a pen to jot down my suggestions.

"I've really been in Kilbeg the whole time," I say.

The wife doesn't jot.

"The whole time?" she says.

"Yeah."

"It must be a terrific town," says her husband.

"It's grand," I say.

"Well, maybe we should spend a night there," he says. "Is there a hotel in town?"

"Not yet," I say.

After I finish tacking copies of the story onto every telephone pole in town, I rent a bicycle from the hostel and head up into the hills. It's my newest hobby. Donal comes with me sometimes, but the beauty of the peninsula doesn't captivate him quite like it does me. He didn't grow up in West Texas. I stay out later than I usually do. It's nearly ten o'clock when I ride back into town; the sun is just setting. I coast into the Tigh Tábhairne parking lot.

It takes only a few seconds for the pub to erupt into laughter when I enter. I've been laughed at a lot since I've been in Kilbeg: when I asked Maria for a ride, not knowing that it was, in effect, asking her for sex; when I didn't put any whiskey in the Irish coffees (I thought it was just any coffee brewed on the island); when I said "but they're *all* offsides" during the replay of a World Cup match at Mulligan's. But that laughter was different from this laughter. There's a meanness in the laughter tonight.

"He's here, lads," shouts Tom. "We're saved!"

More laughing.

"Can you tell us something else we already know?" adds Sean, Gilly's sheeping partner. "Can you protect us from those big-city people?"

Ray the fiddle player hands me a full pint and wraps his arm around my shoulder. "That's for reminding us that we're a quaint folk, Patrick Sheridan."

They're enjoying this. All of them. Putting me in my place. It's the first time anyone has used my real last name since I've been here. It's an unsubtle reminder that anyone who wants to could turn me in. I set the glass down on a table and walk out. I'm just slipping my feet into the pedals when I hear my name shouted. The voice is Eamonn's. "Patrick, come back here," he says.

I roll over to him.

"Why didn't you tell me you were going to pull some stunt like that?"

Even Eamonn.

"I was trying to help. The guy's a crook. He's taking advantage of people."

Eamonn's shaking his head. "How is paying Gilly enough money that he never has to work again taking advantage of him? How is sending thousands of cars—cars that use petrol—through town taking advantage of me? You've treated us like children, Patrick. I know you thought you were doing something noble, but no one likes being told what's good for them. Besides, it seems to me that you wrote that story more for yourself than for any of us."

"What? I didn't even sign it." His accusation makes me angry.

"Fair enough, but surely you knew everyone would know who wrote it. If you were really concerned, you could have just told me, told Tom, told anyone who would listen. You didn't have to make a show of it."

"You know what Kilbeg is going to look like in a few years? Sweater shops. Authentic Irish crap stores. Fast food. Strip malls. Tour buses. It'll look like fucking America." I feel myself starting to choke up. "You'll hate that, Eamonn."

"Maybe," he says. "Maybe not. When I'm sending Yvonne and Maeve to university, I think I'll be able to live with myself."

I ride the bike over to Mary's. I know I won't be able to sleep. I knock on her door, silently praying that St. Peter won't be in attendance. Mary answers. She's dressed in a raggedy bathrobe, so I know there's no way he's here. No lipstick. She doesn't look happy to see me though.

"What do you want?" she asks coldly.

"You're mad at me too? You saw the story?"

"I couldn't care less about the story. I heard about it though. Pretty dumb, Patrick."

"Then, what's up?"

"I can't believe you're showing up here. I can't believe you've acted like a friend to me."

"What's wrong?" I say.

Mary starts crying.

"You're a bastard," she says. "You know what's wrong."

I do.

"How could you tell him those things? Were things so bad for you that you didn't want anyone else to be happy? Peter said I disgust him. Explain it to me, Patrick. Make me understand. I thought we were friends. I never thought you wanted anything more than that. Can you explain it to me? Please."

I could try. But I don't.

It's a far better thing I do than I've ever done.

It's not Maeve who wakes me the next morning; it's Eamonn.

"Bad news," he says.

Is there any other kind?

"They're coming for you."

He lets that sink in for a moment.

"Tomorrow," he adds before I ask.

The news doesn't surprise me.

I go back to sleep.

I don't get up for another five hours. It's fourteen kilometers around the tip of the peninsula, and I walk it all. By now the map Mary gave me is pretty worn, but it still comes in handy. I'm trying to burn in every last detail of my walk and save the memories for days when I'll need them. When I come across a path I haven't seen before, I check the map. That's when I notice a tiny star that's been drawn in. I've never seen it before, but Mary must have put it there. I follow the path a few hundred yards from the road. It leads me to a well at the top of a hill. From the crest, I can see the ocean and the Blasket Islands off in the distance. Way off to my left is Dingle. I can't see Kilbeg, but I know it's there behind Mount Eagle. I'm taking everything in for a few minutes before I spot the Fanta Orange bottle sitting on the edge of the well. Inside of it is Mary's necklace, the one that fell apart when she was dancing. She's repaired and shortened it.

And there's a note.

Patrick,
    What took you so long? This is yours now. You earned it.
    Friends forever,
    Mary

I stop at Pade O'Sea's pub in Ventry. By the time I make it back into Kilbeg, it's dark and I've drained an entire bottle of McMurtrey's. The first thing I see is the church. I stumble in, but the main chamber is empty. I remove the holy water fount from the brass ring that holds it, leaving the McMurtrey's bottle in its place. I wander through Kilbeg—drunk and cradling the fount—toward the sound of traditional music. O'Donoghue's Pub. Tourists singing along to "Danny Boy." I sprinkle a few drops of water on the door of the pub.

"Lord," I say, "bless this pub and make it not suck so much."

I begin blessing everything: Mulligan's satellite dish; the rows of bicycles in front of the hostel; Ranger, the stray sheepdog that dodges cars all day in front of Johanna's bookstore ("Lord, don't ever let him lose a step"). Eventually I make my way to Tigh Tábhairne's. Donal's car is parked in the lot. I sprinkle drops on the front seat through the open window. I trace the sign of the cross on the pub's one filthy window. Through the clean line I've drawn, I can see Eamonn. I can hear his laugh.

My last stop is Mary's. The lights are all out at her house. I pour what remains from the fount into the flower box outside her window.

"Lord, make everything she believes in come true."

They actually send two men to come get me. One is from the U.S. Embassy, the other works for the Irish Department of Foreign Affairs. Their job is to get me on a noon flight departing from Shannon Airport and arriving in Dallas eight hours later.

"There'll probably be a bunch of TV cameras at the airport," the American says while his comrade has a few words with Eamonn about his hiring practices.

"There probably will be," I say.

"How long were you planning on staying here?" he asks.

I shrug. I guess I had no plans to return. Hadn't thought about it much.

The American chuckles. "You could have probably stayed here forever if that girl hadn't called us."

Epilogue
LUBBOCK, TEXAS

KATE THROWS HER BACKPACK DOWN AND STRETCHES out on the lawn beside me. She takes off her shoes and makes this sound—it's the same one every day—sort of a sigh or purr, as she combs her toes through the only decent grass in West Texas. We found this spot our first week here at Texas Tech. In the afternoons, Sneed Hall provides enough shade to make the heat bearable. This knoll isn't exactly private, but it's off the lecture hall to lecture hall path. That's why we claimed it.

"You get your finance test back today?" Kate asks.

"Yeah."

"And?"

"I passed it."

"I didn't realize you were taking it pass/fail," she says, knowing full well I'm not. Kate reaches over and begins rifling through the pages of my business text, *Modern Corporations*. She doesn't comment on the cover's vintage soft drink machine–sized computers with their tape-reel eyes.

"You know you *could* wait to declare a major until after your sophomore year," she suggests.

"Commerce creates culture," I say.

Kate rolls over on her stomach and looks up at me. "You're not going to scare me until you can say those words like you believe them."

"How's Zeb doing at Stanford?" I ask, changing the subject. The two have stayed together since the prom.

Kate flops onto her back and stares up at the sky. "Great. He's playing number two singles . . . likes his classes."

She passes this info along hesitantly. She still thinks it bothers me to talk about Zeb. But it doesn't. Not much does.

"When will you get to see him again?"

"Not until Thanksgiving. He's flying home then."

I tell her that sounds great, but afterward there's a long silence. Kate and I have a lot of these lately.

"Hey, aren't you"—*If I had a dollar* . . . The figure that's moved in front of me is blocking the sun. I just see the black outline of a female—"Patrick Sheridan? From *Classroom Direct*?"

"I'll call you later," Kate says. She shakes her head as she picks up her backpack.

"Okay," I say.

The form sits down next to me and materializes into the kind of long-legged, Roper-wearing coed we're known for here at Tech. The three triangles on her visor identify her as a Tri Delt. I think I'm learning more Greek here than anything else.

"It is you. I thought it was. Somebody said you were going to school here."

"Hi," I say.

"Hi," she says. "I'm Cheryl."

"Hi."

"Wow," she says, gazing at me. She pulls her knees up to her chest and wraps her arms around them. "Do you know how freaked out we were at my school when you disappeared over there in Ireland?"

I shake my head.

"For a while everyone was talking about it. People were saying you had been kidnapped or that they were going to find you shot up in the trunk of a car. The whole thing made *Classroom Direct* look really bad."

"Why's that?" I ask.

"Well at first, they were like denying the whole thing. They kept saying not to worry—that the satellite was down."

I consider the accuracy of the reporting as I stand, brush grass off my shorts, and pull my sunglasses out of my shirt pocket. Cheryl stands at the same time. She follows me as I start making my way across campus.

"But then when all the other news shows started reporting you were missing, *Classroom Direct* tried to make it sound like they had been ordered by some mysterious authorities not to tell anyone about it for security's sake, or something lame like that. Then they turned it into a 'Get Involved!' segment, and they urged everyone to write letters to their congressmen or to the Northern Ireland government to tell them to find you. They showed all these clips of you and put them to music. It was like you were dead or something."

We pass the statue of Will Rogers in the main quad on campus. Campus lore holds that if a virgin ever makes it all the way through Tech, Will's supposed to get down off his horse and escort the girl to her graduation ceremony.

"I wrote one," she says.

"Wrote what?"

"A letter."

"Oh."

"I don't know why. I guess because you were from around here. In August, when the regular news reported they had found you, and that you were fine, I didn't know whether to be happy or pissed off."

We pass the business building, where I have most of my classes.

"I guess you had your reasons," Cheryl says.

I'm wondering: If I walk into a men's room in a residence hall we're passing, will Cheryl follow me into one of the stalls?

"Hey, we're having a party tonight over at the house. It's supposed to be a mixer with the Delta Sigs, but they're so *dull*. I know everyone would just die if you showed up. The Chi O's thought it was such a big deal when they got the guy who used to play Doogie Howser's ratty little friend to come to one of their parties."

We pass a distribution rack for the Tech student newspaper, and a headline catches my attention—"Four Die in Belfast Bombing."

Peacetime is over.

"You want to come up to my room?" I ask.

266 • ROB THOMAS

"What?"

"I'm not really into parties, but I've got an afternoon to kill. Come up. Afterward, I'll tell you all about Ireland. It'll give you a story for tonight's mixer."

Cheryl's face darkens. "Who the hell do you think you are?"

I shrug.

"Screw you," she says. Then she stomps off.

For a split second I have the urge to stop her. Apologize. But for what? I wasn't really serious about using her. I doubt she could honestly say the reverse was true.

The architecture building is the tallest structure on the Tech campus, maybe all of Texas west of San Antonio. I walk by it daily on my way back to my dorm room. It towers out over the flat West Texas landscape. From the top floor, I've heard you can see Doggett, Odessa, Muleshoe. Maybe you can even see real cowboys riding horses into the sunset. But I wouldn't know for sure, because I manage to walk by every day without climbing its stairs.